PAUL LA FARGE is the author of two novels: *The Artist of the Missing* and *Haussmann, or the Distinction*; and a book of imaginary dreams, *The Facts of Winter*. His short stories have appeared in *McSweeney's*, *Harper's Magazine*, *Fence*, *Conjunctions* and elsewhere. His nonfiction has appeared in *The Believer*, *Bookforum*, *Playboy* and *Cabinet*. He teaches at Bard College.

ALSO BY PAUL LA FARGE

The Artist of the Missing

Haussmann, or the Distinction

The Facts of Winter

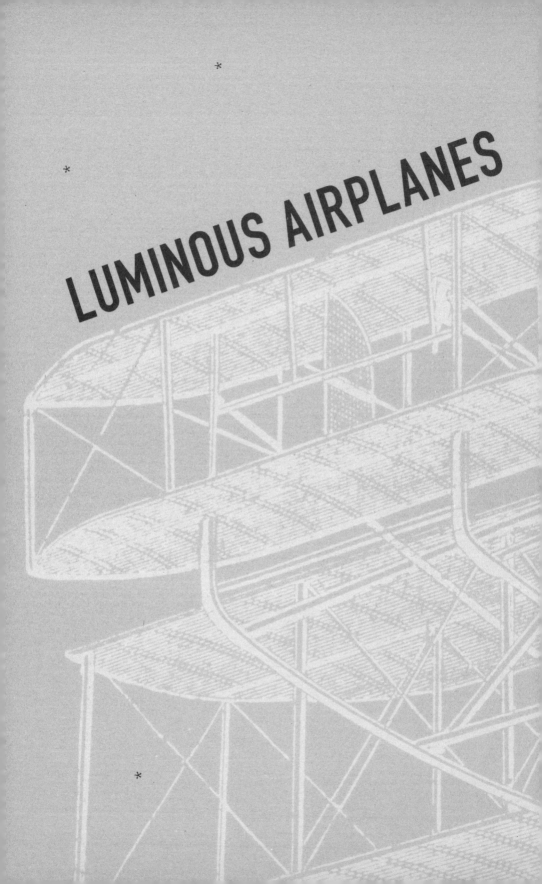

LUMINOUS AIRPLANES

*

*   *

PAUL LA FARGE

FOURTH ESTATE • London

First published in Great Britain in 2012 by
Fourth Estate
An imprint of HarperCollins*Publishers*
77–85 Fulham Palace Road
London W6 8JB
www.4thestate.co.uk

First published in the United States in 2011
by Farrar, Straus and Giroux

1

A portion of this novel originally appeared in
Conjunctions:45 as the short story "Adventure."

A catalogue record for this book is
available from the British Library

ISBN 978-0-00-745954-4

Designed by Jonathan D. Lippincott

Printed in Great Britain by Clays Ltd, St Ives plc

MIX
Paper from
responsible sources
FSC
www.fsc.org
FSC® C007454

FSC™ is a non-profit international organisation established to promote
the responsible management of the world's forests. Products carrying the
FSC label are independently certified to assure consumers that they come
from forests that are managed to meet the social, economic and
ecological needs of present or future generations,
and other controlled sources.

Find out more about HarperCollins and the environment at
www.harpercollins.co.uk/green

*

For Sarah

*

*

"Run!" —Hal Hartley

LUMINOUS AIRPLANES

ONE

CONTACT WITH OTHER WORLDS

I had just come home from a festival in Nevada, the theme of which was Contact with Other Worlds, when my mother, or, I should say, one of my mothers, called to tell me that my grandfather had died.

"I've been trying to reach you for days," she said. "Where were you?"

I told her I'd been camping. I didn't tell her I was at a pagan celebration where people danced around bonfires, a kind of dress rehearsal for the end of the world. I didn't mention the huge glowing fish or the women with wings.

Celeste told me that my grandfather had died on Thursday morning, around the time when I was leaving San Francisco in my friends' big white RV. My uncle Charles found him collapsed at his desk. He'd had a heart attack, the doctor said. His death was quick and probably not painful.

"That's good," I said, still dazed from the drugs I'd taken at the festival and the nights I'd gone without sleep. "When is the funeral?"

"It *was* this morning."

"You had it without me?"

"We couldn't wait," Celeste said in the tone of voice she

uses when eliding facts that might put her in the wrong. "Marie is closing an issue and she has to go back to work." Marie is Celeste's twin sister: by birth Marie Celeste, as Celeste was by birth Celeste Marie: another story. She works for *S*, a women's magazine.

"But," I began to protest, but Celeste wasn't finished catching me up on what I'd missed. "We're going to sell the house," she said. "Do you want any of your grandparents' things?" It would mean going back to upstate New York, she said, because the house was full from attic to basement with junk, and my mothers had no intention of sorting through it. They never got along with my grandfather, and my grandmother, with whom, to be honest, they also didn't get along, had given them the few items they wanted before she died. Celeste said that unless I wanted to clean out the house myself, they would be happy to turn it over to one of the people who specialized in estate sales. Probably the antiques dealers would take a few pieces my grandfather had inherited from *his* parents, and the rest would be thrown away or given to orphans.

"Which orphans?" I asked.

"Whichever ones they have up there," Celeste said. Then, as if she realized that she'd overplayed her frustration at not having been able to reach me, she asked, "Since when do you like camping?"

"I always liked camping."

"You did?"

"Since I was a kid."

Celeste hesitated. "Think it over," she said, "but don't take too long. The real-estate agent says our best chance of selling is before the ski season starts."

Our conversation ended awkwardly, and I stood in my kitchen, not sure what to do next. Eight hours ago, I'd been sitting in the middle of a desert, eating instant oatmeal from a plastic cup and watching the remains of a giant wooden structure called the Exosphere smolder. Now my grandfather was dead, and Celeste wanted me to return to Thebes, where I hadn't been for ten years. It was as if my life had cut abruptly from one record to another, and my thoughts were still dancing to the wrong beat: that was the image that occurred to me after three days of watching DJs perform at the festival. I tried to feel grief at my grandfather's death. I tried to imagine him dying, to see him being buried, but all I could see was Nevada, the long line of the horizon with sharp brown mountains rising up in the distance. A silver pinwheel turned slowly in the wind. I wondered if I was all right, if there was something wrong with me. It's a question I've been asking myself a lot recently, and the answer I keep coming up with is, yes, something is wrong.

SAN FRANCISCO, CITY OF GHOSTS

I had been living in San Francisco at that point for seven years, an amount of time that has always seemed to me to have magical properties. Tannhäuser lives in the Venusberg for seven years and Hans Castorp spends seven years on the magic mountain; there are the seven fat years and the seven lean years of Pharaoh's dream, not to mention the seven-year itch and the seven-year ache. As the seven-year mark approached I found myself thinking about leaving the city. I thought about going back to the East Coast, and even considered living in New York again, although the forbidding presence of my mothers on the Upper West Side acted as a repelling magnet and sent my thoughts farther afield, to Europe, where we had almost moved, once, or to Canada, where I'd heard it was possible to live well for not very much money, and where the politics weren't so frightening. In the end I made no plans to go anywhere, and the only result of all my thinking was that I ceased to do many of the things I had once enjoyed. I didn't go to the Blue Study on Thursday nights; I didn't assume the pose of a dog, a tree, a monkey or a corpse at the Yoga Tree on Valencia Street; I didn't take my bicycle and ride out to the ocean, the way I had almost every week when I first moved to the city. Overall, my life in San Francisco was so greatly reduced that it felt like an afterlife, as though I were a ghost condemned to remain in the city until I accomplished a particular task, or got someone to accomplish it for me. I wondered how long I could go on living like that. Quite long, probably. San Francisco is a good city to be a ghost in. My upstairs neighbor, Robert, had lived in his apartment for many years before I moved in. He saw no one and never went out; on Saturday nights he snorted cocaine and listened to Dylan at top volume until one of the people downstairs complained. He worked at home, proofreading legal documents that appeared on his doorstep and were taken away by messengers whom neither of us ever saw. Once a month his ex-wife brought a little girl to visit him, I think it was his daughter. Sometimes I saw the three of them in the park, the daughter holding the mother's hand and Robert walking beside her, stiff and serious, like a decrepit hippie bodyguard. The ex-wife and the girl were gone by nightfall; on those nights Dylan was always singing, and no one had the heart to ask Robert to turn the music down. I worried that I might become like him if I stayed in San Francisco too long. Or that I might be like that already. More than once, when I ran into a neighbor, I found myself cringing, as though the fact that I used to have a life was somehow visible—although if that was how ghosts really felt then they would never show themselves. They would wait in their attics, work their ghost jobs, and wait for their real afterlives to begin.

I came home from the festival on Sunday night. The next day was a holiday, and because I still didn't know what to do, I went for a walk. The air was hot, and the sky was the bright, uninterrupted blue you get in San Francisco in the late summer, a sky so blue it looks opaque, as though it were just a shell hung over the city, hiding the real weather. It was the end of Labor Day weekend and the Mission was quiet. It made me think of when I first came to the city, before the boom of the nineties, when this had been a savage neighborhood, where crazy people and heroin addicts sat at the mouths of alleys, looking up at you with flat, hurtful eyes. Then money came and swept those people away; it replaced them with stores specializing in a single brand of shoe, and restaurants named with a compound of the word *fire*. Now, in September 2000, the restaurants were in trouble. Signs in their windows offered seven-dollar lunch specials and still no one came to fill their chrome-edged tables, their cushioned nooks. I walked up to Dolores Park, which was empty, apart from some children swinging in the playground and a handful of dogs wearied by the hot weather, walking around with their heads down, like people looking for change in the grass. From the top of the park I could see downtown San Francisco, the gray towers of the Bay Bridge, the brownish line of Berkeley beyond. And beyond that was all of California, Nevada, Utah, et cetera, all the way to New York State, to Thebes. But my ambivalence about San Francisco had vanished as I climbed the hill; the city was beautiful and I wanted to live there forever. I sat on a bench, relieved that I had come home from the festival when I did—if I'd returned a day earlier I would have had to bundle myself onto a plane for the funeral. My phone buzzed in my pocket. It was Alice, my ex-girlfriend, calling to see if I was back yet.

"I'm back," I said, "but my grandfather died."

"What?"

I told her what had happened, and how my mothers had the funeral without me because of Marie's job at *S*.

"God, how vile," Alice said. "Do you want to come over?"

Alice and I had broken up months before, but we still saw each other more often than we saw anyone else, or at least, I saw her more often than I saw anyone except my coworkers.

Our conversations were frequently difficult, but Alice was the only person who made me feel solid. If we threw ourselves together at least a collision would happen.

"I'm tired," I said, "I want to stay in my neighborhood. Do you want to come here?"

"You're so far away," Alice said.

I lived twenty minutes from her by foot, or half an hour on the bus. Finally we agreed to meet at the Doghouse, a bar halfway between her apartment and mine. It looked like bikers went there, so no one else went, though in fact the bikers didn't go there either.

LOST THINGS

For a long time, from when I was very little and don't remember years or stories, until I was thirteen, I spent every summer with my grandparents in Thebes. My mothers would have preferred to send me somewhere else, but they didn't have the money for summer camp, and the free day programs in New York were frightening: this was the scary seventies, when the city was almost bankrupt and you could get attacked with a knife on the Upper West Side in the daytime. But I couldn't just stay at home, because there was nothing for me to do, and my mothers wanted a vacation from being parents, a job neither of them had ever wanted to turn into a career. The summer was their time to make art, which was what they really did: Celeste was a sculptor and Marie took photographs. So, Thebes. I looked forward to it every year as soon as the trees began to blossom in Riverside Park. They produced flowers and I produced memories: of the man-made lake with the sandy beach, of the green mountains that rose up on either side of town, the stream, or *kill*, that ran through the middle of it, the old wooden bridge that crossed the stream, and the cool hollow under the bridge. I remembered the Regenzeit children who lived next door to my grandparents, Kerem and Yesim, pronounced YAY-shum, which were Turkish names because their parents were Turkish although they, the children, had grown up in the U. S. of A. The first days of spring tortured me; the future tied my thought in knots. By the time June came around, I watched my mothers as a hungry dog watches its humans, waiting for the sign that it was time for me to go. But my mothers were proud. They ran away from Thebes when they were seventeen, and had vowed never to go back; sending me to stay with my grandparents wasn't breaking their promise, exactly, but it was close, and their way of keeping themselves aloof from this difficult fact was to pretend that it wouldn't happen.

"I hear they cleaned up the Y," Marie said one year. "It has a new swimming pool. Maybe you'd like to give it a try?" I told her the story I'd heard at school about a kid who went into that pool and didn't come out again. "Hm," Marie said, and the Y took its place again at the end of the alphabet. School ended and the real hot weather came. The windows were always open; our living room became a big, dusty receiver for the dramas broadcast from the street. The Celestes sprawled in side-by-side chairs in front of the electric fan, waiting for it to be night. They talked about the opening they'd gone to in SoHo, the artist who'd got the show by sleeping with the dealer, the writer who'd written about the show but didn't know what the word *lacuna* meant. Just when I thought they had forgotten about me completely, suddenly they turned to each other, their mirror-faces wrinkled by mirror-frowns, and one said to the other, "Don't you think it's time to send him to Thebes?"

SAN FRANCISCO, CITY OF GHOSTS

The Doghouse was crowded with Labor Day drinkers trying noisily to give substance to the illusion that San Francisco had

had a summer. There was a back patio with a phenomenal view of the underside of Highway 101; as traffic whooshed by overhead, I told Alice how my mothers wanted me to pack up my grandparents' house.

"Don't they live in New York?" Alice asked. "Let them do it."

"They don't like the house. They hate going there."

"Too bad for them."

Alice had never met my mothers, but over the years she had acquired a kind of sympathetic dislike for them, which I sometimes felt guilty about instilling in her. She would have told me to stand up to them even if she liked them better, though: Alice was in favor of standing up to people. She stood up to her professors at Berkeley, who thought that a nobody girl from the Central Valley couldn't know anything about American lit; she stood up to her college boyfriend, who was just a version, she realized afterward, of her Christ-nut father; and she stood up to me.

"Don't worry," I said, "I'm not going."

We got drinks and alit on a free table out back. "How was the festival?" Alice asked.

"Windy," I said. "There were dust storms." Alice hated dirt; she was the only person I knew in San Francisco with white wall-to-wall carpet in her apartment.

"That must have been tricky when you were tripping your brains out."

"Ha. We didn't do drugs, just some pot." I had, in fact, taken a mescaline derivative, synthesized by a friend of Star's, which made everything give off blue sparks, as if the landscape were effervescing in the cold night air, but I didn't want Alice to be jealous.

"I see." Wary of learning more than she wanted to know, she changed the subject. "Were you close to your grandfather?"

"I wouldn't say *close*. I spent the summers with him when I was a kid, but he wasn't easy to know." I told Alice about the basement workshop where my grandfather restored old tables and chairs, or rather, given that nothing he touched ever returned to anything like the life it once had, it might be more accurate to say that he reincarnated them. When confronted with an old table, unsteady on its feet, topped with warped boards that had begun to detach from one another, his ordinarily serious face would soften, and as he stroked the table's uneven surface he'd murmur, "Good grain. Good wood." I knew what was going to happen: the table would come home with us; we'd carry it into the garage, where it would linger until my grandfather tried to correct its irregularities or it fell apart of its own accord, which amounted to more or less the same thing. Even then he would save the timbers that hadn't rotted or been planed down to nothing. "Might patch something with these," he'd say. "It's good wood."

"He sounds sweet," Alice said.

"He wasn't. Kind, sure. But not sweet." Every year, he had sent me the same card on my birthday, with a picture of a Japanese fisherman in a little boat caught in the crook of an enormous wave, and each year the message inside the card was shorter. The last of the cards came just a month before he died. *Happy birthday to my great grandson*, it read, which confused me, because I was only his grandson. Finally I'd decided that he must have preferred the pun to the reality of the situation, but still, as a grandson, it made me feel less than great.

There was nothing to say about that, though, so I asked Alice how she was doing with her LSAT review class and she told me the class was for idiots, and I said yes, the point is they make an idiot out of you, and she scowled at me and said she knew some lawyers who were very intelligent. Until earlier that year, Alice had been an editor for a company in Mountain View that made Web browsers, but she'd been laid off along with half the people who worked there, so for the last three or four months she'd been freelancing, which meant spending her severance pay while she decided what to do next. She wasn't certain she'd apply to law school; other prospects beckoned with lovely phantom hands. She might become a massage therapist, or teach English to businessmen in Japan.

The wind picked up, chilling the patio, driving the summer drinkers indoors. Alice said she ought to go home, she had to get up early the next morning.

"Have dinner with me," I suggested.

"Where?"

We argued for a little while, but it really was getting cold out, and Alice agreed to a Thai place next to my apartment. I put my arm around her and we walked back to the Mission as the fog came in over our heads, white rags of mist flying past like foam in a fast stream, covering up the empty sky.

After dinner we went to my apartment and sat in the kitchen drinking whiskey. "I don't want to get drunk," Alice said, "I've got yoga in the morning."

"I don't either." I poured myself another drink and Alice motioned for me to pour her another also.

"Tell me about the music," she said. "Who was there?"

I mentioned people we'd heard at the Sno-Drop, at the Red Room. That was again an omission. Pearl Fabula had played at the festival, but I hoped Alice didn't know. We'd gone to hear Pearl too many times together before he became famous and left San Francisco.

"Ugh, Lorin," Alice said. "That guy's too ironic for me."

We talked about how it had been all the way back in 1998, when we saw Hope Sandoval dancing next to us at Liquid, and the DJ from Portishead spun a set at the Blue Study, and how we'd gone to see Pearl when he played the impossible sample from Lady Di in the car. *Dodi . . . Dodi . . .* But we couldn't stay in those memories for long. Soon we were talking about the signs that our music was in decline: the burly fraternity types we had seen dancing the pogo at an Underworld show, the long line of high school kids outside Community on Wednesday nights, the various laws that Congress was preparing to close the dance clubs down, Junior Vasquez selling CD players and Moby selling cars, the tendency of money to ruin everything.

"I feel like DJ culture is played out," Alice said. Which I thought was her way of saying, *I wish I had gone to Nevada.*

"You may be right," I said, "but what's next?"

"I don't know. There's got to be something."

Our faces touched. We kissed, we dug our fingers into each other's backs. We made love and it was just the way I remembered it, not from the last, grudging months, nor from the beginning, when our sex was wild and tentative, like a dream you don't want to write down for fear of losing track of its form, but from the middle of the relationship, however long that lasted, a year, a month. It was a solid thing, like putting two puzzle pieces together the right way, that gave us a glimpse of a larger picture, as yet unfinished. Then we fell asleep. I woke up at one-thirty in the morning with a headache. Alice's back was to me, her kinky blond hair spread out on the comforter. I thought of the foam on the crest of the wave on my grandfather's cards. For years the fisherman had been waiting for that wave to break, and it never had. I used to want it to break, not because I wanted the fisherman to drown, but so that he wouldn't have to wait any longer. I closed my eyes and imagined it breaking, a dark-blue wave with streaks of black in it, edged with white foam, crashing over the stern of the little boat, and afterward, when there was nothing to look at but blue water and wreckage, a timber, an oar. I opened my eyes. Alice was still there. The wave hadn't broken yet and maybe it never would.

LOST THINGS

Thebes was never what my memories made it. My grandmother was a good cook but she loved her garden too well, and served us vegetables that only a mother could love, worm-holed lettuces, cracked tomatoes, small starchy beans. My grandfather was frequently in a bad mood and spent whole days in his workshop, sawing and pounding some hapless antique into submission. I played with Kerem and Yesim, the children next door, but this too had its perils. There was bad blood between the Rowlands and the Regenzeits: my grandfather had sued Joe Regenzeit before I was born, and lost. Regenzeit owned the Snowbird ski resort, a couple of bald stripes shaved into the side of a mountain just past the west end of town, and the lawsuit was in some way connected to the resort, but I couldn't guess how. My grandparents didn't even own skis. It was bad enough that the Regenzeits lived next door, that my grandmother had to watch Mrs. Regenzeit gardening when she was in her garden, that my grandfather had to speak to Joe Regenzeit at town meetings, but when I went over to play with the Regenzeit children, it was too much, it was Montague cozying up to Capulet. If only there had been anyone else for me to play with, my grandparents would have forbidden me to see Kerem and Yesim, but there wasn't anyone else, apart from a few strange children who haunted the steps of the public library, children no one knew and no one wanted me to know. Although I would know them, later on.

I wasn't in love with Yesim at first—that came later—but from the very beginning I liked the ordinariness of the Regenzeits' lives. The furniture in their house was all brand-new; they had a glass-topped dinner table, which I found fascinating, and a spotless white sofa where children were not allowed to sit. Kerem and Yesim had only one mother, the formidable Mrs. Regenzeit, who was barely five feet tall, wore a pink jogging suit, and spent her days talking on the telephone. I don't know who she called, or who called her, but her remarks were merciless. "I don't give one shit about that," she said, stabbing the air with a long cigarette stained red with her lipstick. "You tell him I am fucking pissed off." She had an accent that made *shit* into *sheet* and *pissed* into *peaced*, a Turkish accent, I assumed, but later I learned that it was German. Mrs. Regenzeit wasn't fierce to me; she daubed iodine on the blood that welled up when I cut myself; she fed me plates of strange Turkish cookies. Then there was Mr. Regenzeit, an ordinary father, the only one I knew. He was a short, muscular man who spent most of his time at work. Later I'd learn that he was not ordinary—but what did I know about fathers? I thought they were all like that, compact, fussy men who reserved Friday afternoons to teach their children the customs of their native land. As a non-Turk, I was sent home, and it was only when I came to the other side of the fence that separated our houses, and saw my grandmother kneeling in the garden, and heard my grandfather sawing in his workshop, that I remembered the bad blood.

"You'd better wash up," my grandmother called to me, although our dinner would not be for a while yet. I went to the bathroom and rubbed my hands under the faucet for a long time, thinking about blood, blood and fathers.

SAN FRANCISCO, CITY OF GHOSTS

Alice left at six-thirty the next morning for yoga. Now that she was unemployed she clung even more fiercely to a schedule than she had when she was working. I got up an hour later, made coffee, and sat looking out the window at the parking lot behind my building. Norman Mailer's car was parked just beneath my window, its royal-blue roof spotted with pigeon shit. When I bought the car from Peter, the owner of the used-book store down the street, I planned to take all kinds of trips: up to Seattle, down to Los Angeles, and farther south, into Mexico, where I had never been. But in fact I had been no farther away than Point Reyes, two hours north of the city, where Alice and I camped in the state forest one foggy summer weekend. Idly, like an astronomer thinking about some distant eclipse, I wondered how hard it would be to drive to Thebes. I looked in a road atlas and discovered that, thanks to Interstate 80, driving from San Francisco to upstate New York was ridiculously easy. Once you crossed the Bay Bridge, you had to make a total of three turns before you pulled into my grandfather's driveway. I estimated that the trip would take about four and a half days, then I took a shower and left for work.

Cetacean Solutions, LLC, a provider of content-management solutions (a.k.a. laboriously customized databases) to enterprise clients (a.k.a. businesses), was in a slump. All spring we had been overrun by orders, which we worked ten, twelve, fourteen hours a day to fill, but in the fourth quarter of 2000 the orders suddenly ceased. Cetacean, which our company's logo instructed us to picture as a mighty whale diving deep into the ocean, presumably to do battle with the giant squid of unmanaged user content, now seemed less like a whale than like a whaling ship roaming an ocean from which whales had largely vanished. Dave, our captain, sent the sales team to the top of the mizzenmast to scan the water with their telescopes; meanwhile on deck the engineers mended the boats, sharpened the harpoons and polished the brass fittings. Even the maintenance work we did for our existing clients had slowed to almost nothing by August. It was like the middle of *Moby-Dick*: no whale in sight, only occasional contact with another passing ship, and nothing to fill the time except digression. Our office, a converted Victorian on the eastern flank of Potrero Hill, within sniffing distance of the Anchor Brewery, had a Fun Room in the basement: a brightly carpeted lounge where, in busy times, we rested our brains while playing ping-pong or foosball. Now that there was no work and our days could, in theory, have been all fun, the Fun Room had taken on a new, sinister purpose. Every third or fourth day we assembled there for an all-hands meeting on a different theme: Defining

Standards in Code Creation, Measuring the User Experience, Working in the Cloud. Employees with vacation days suddenly experienced a desire to go on vacation; those without them petitioned for unpaid leave. I was hoping that when I came back from the desert meaningful work would be in sight, but on Tuesday morning I found Mac, my boss, looking at boat trailers on the Internet. He didn't own a car, much less a boat, but there was something about the structure of the boat trailer that interested him, he said, something about the way it suggested absent realities. I asked if there was going to be a meeting.

"Will you look at this thing," Mac said. "This is for sure a nuclear-sub trailer."

"What happened to the sub," I asked, "that it's for sale?"

He thought about this. "Maybe there are no bridges rated for sub transport."

We fell together into silent estimation of submarine tonnage vs. bridge loads, then Mac snorted and switched to his e-mail. "All-hands meeting at eleven."

"What's the topic?"

"Hydration for Performance," he read off the screen. "Did you know that twenty percent of human fatigue is caused by improper or insufficient hydration? An optimal fluid-consumption program developed by NASA for long-duration space missions will be presented. But, aren't astronauts catheterized?"

"Does it matter?"

"Depends."

I groaned at his pun and went down to the Fun Room to get a free Coke. I twiddled the handles of the foosball machine. Something had to happen, I thought. Any minute the cry would go up from the lookouts and someone would claim the gold doubloon nailed to the mast, but nothing happened, nothing at all. Eventually I heard people coming down the stairs for the performance-hydration meeting, and slipped out the fire exit.

I took my filthy festival clothes to the laundromat, and while they washed I called Alice. The call went straight to voicemail, and I left a message, asking her whether what had happened last night meant that we were on again, whether she wanted to be on again, what being on again might mean. I went across the street and bought an iced coffee, and while I was standing outside the laundromat drinking my coffee, I saw a man in a green Army jacket crossing Seventeenth Street. From the back he looked like Swan, a homeless man who used to distribute leaflets in my neighborhood. For years I saw him every day, handing out his leaflets, or typing them, or feeding the pigeons who were his other chief occupation. He was angry, dirty, taciturn and paranoid, but at the same time he was completely extraordinary. It was as if mysterious powers had put a lighthouse in the Mission, a strange beacon left over from an era when people traveled differently and different things mattered. Like a lighthouse, Swan stood all by himself, marking a place no one else had reached—warning us off, I sometimes thought, and sometimes I thought, inviting us to follow him. Swan disappeared in the winter of 1997. My friends held a rally to protest the city's policy of driving its homeless citizens from gentrifying neighborhoods like ours, but it didn't bring Swan back. That was when my life in San Francisco began to feel ghostly. And now, I thought, here he was, as if nothing had happened! "Swan!" I cried, and I ran after him. The old man was quick; I didn't catch up with him until Church Street. And of course it was someone else. Swan was gone.

I went back to the laundromat and retrieved my clothes from the dryer. I carried the clean clothes back to my apartment, but now my apartment itself looked wrong. The living room contained only a coffee table and an ancient red futon; the dining room had an even older sofa, a TV set, and a white imitation bearskin rug that my ex-housemate Victor had inherited from an uncle in Moscow. When Alice and I were going out, she nagged me to redecorate, but I said I liked my old things. "Your things aren't old," she said, "they're just ugly." She was right, but I refused to see it. Whenever she pointed out a chair or table or sofa in the window of a store downtown and said, "Why don't you get one of those?" I objected that it wouldn't go with the furniture I already had, even though nothing would have gone with my furniture. It was a question of living with it or replacing everything. That afternoon I considered replacing everything; there was a store on Seventeenth and Valencia that catered to people like me, bohemian types who had a little money, and if I had gone there, everything might have turned out differently. The desperation of my heart, the feeling of loss that I still couldn't connect to my grandfather's death, all that emotion might have resolved itself in a sofa and loveseat, a leather armchair, a media center made from salvaged pine flooring. I might be in San Francisco now, living with Alice in my redecorated apartment; we might be happy together. But in fact I didn't have the energy or the will to buy furniture, and here I am in New York, living with a stranger.

I went out for a super vegetarian burrito, came home, opened a beer and took it into my study, which was cluttered with books and papers from the days when I had been a graduate student in history at Stanford, the pre-Cetacean era. Now I didn't use the study for anything; on the whole it depressed me. I rummaged through the drawers of my fireproof filing cabinet for Swan's leaflets, hoping that his talk of *laser wolves* and *spirit flight* and the *Coming of the Great Ghosts* would somehow cheer me up, but what I found were the notes for my dissertation. They were the opposite of what I wanted, but I was in that totally exhausted state where you don't think clearly and your goals and objectives shift around like shadows, leading you from one bad idea to the next. Soon I was leafing through xeroxed microfilms of nineteenth-century newspapers, my annotations squiggling past in the margins like flipbook animations. Was there any use for this stuff, I wondered, or was it just lost time, and not even lost time in the Proustian sense, time that comes surging back to you out of a cup of cooling tea, but time truly squandered, irrecoverable, lost to a kind of academic coma? My head hurt just thinking about it. I left the papers heaped on the desk and went to bed, and the last thing I noticed before I fell asleep was that Robert was playing "Positively 4th Street" upstairs at top volume, and that I didn't care.

THE GREAT DISAPPOINTMENT

My dissertation was, or would have been, about the "doom-minded Millerites," a group of radical Protestants who believed the world would end in 1843. They were named for William Miller, a New York State farmer who had added up the years of the prophecies in the books of Daniel and Revelation, according to a complex and not obviously correct system of his own, and fixed 1843 as the deadline for the apocalypse. Tens of thousands of people were convinced by his calculations, and as the final year approached they prayed and read and danced themselves into a frenzy of anticipated salvation. But the world did not end. Late in the year one of Miller's disciples added up the numbers again, and concluded that the world would end on October 22, 1844. On that day, somewhere between fifty thousand and half a million Millerites gathered in churches, on hilltops and in cemeteries. They sang; they prayed; they waited. Nothing happened. Eventually they returned home to sleep.

After the Great Disappointment, as the day when the world didn't end came to be known, most of the Millerites renounced their faith and went on with their lives. Some recalculated the date of the apocalypse: it was going to happen in 1846, or 1853, or, anyway, soon. And a few asserted that

Jesus had come back, and that he'd shut the doors of salvation to all unbelievers—in other words, to anyone who wasn't them. Believing that their souls were out of danger, they gave themselves over to free love and "promiscuous foot-washing," something I've always wondered about. For these "shut-door" Millerites, the world *had* ended; what they continued to experience was only a sort of appendix to history, in which a few problems that remained obscure in the body of the text would be resolved. What led these otherwise reasonable people to believe that the world was going to end, that it had ended? It was an interesting question.

SAN FRANCISCO, CITY OF GHOSTS

I woke up at dawn the next day, to the sound of a fire truck headed east on Sixteenth Street—for some reason they always went east. My body hurt with tiredness, but I dragged myself out of bed, made coffee and began mechanically to put my notes back in their filing cabinet; then with a sudden rush of resentment I carried the files downstairs and dumped them in the recycling bin. I went upstairs, put my clean laundry in the bag I'd just unpacked and wrote an e-mail to Mac, saying that an emergency had come up and I needed two weeks off. I left Alice a message, threw out the uneaten food in my refrigerator, emptied the trash and carried my bag down to Norman Mailer's car.

Four days and three turns later I was in Thebes.

TWO

LOST THINGS

Thebes is tucked away in the northeastern corner of the Catskills, more or less where Washington Irving set the story of Rip Van Winkle, and even as a child it wasn't hard for me to see why Irving chose that location. As you drive east on the only road that leads into Thebes, the mountains seem to close their gray shoulders behind you, cutting you off from the rest of the world. The valley looks older and stiller than the rest of the country, as though the land itself were asleep. There are billboards for things no one sells anymore, their photographs bleached blue by the sun, and signs for Summerland, a resort that closed a few years before I was born. It isn't a place that promises great excitement, and in fact, with the exception of my last two summers there, when marvelous and unprece-dented things happened, my memories of Thebes have a Rip Van Winkle–ish quality to them, as though I and the town and everyone in it were not so much living as dreaming.

In fact the town was bigger than I remembered, and richer. It began with a sign for the Snowbird ski resort, then the self-storage complex, the graveyard, a stand of trees, a bar called Fire and Ice, a bed-and-breakfast decked out prematurely with orange Halloween bunting, and the ski shop, which had taken over the house next door to it and become a kind of sports emporium. Across the street, the Kozy Korner gift shop and the Kountry Kitchen, then Arturo's, the Italian deli, which had a new sign with golden letters carved into a green oval of wood, then a video store and the Country Barn Antique Emporium, the crossroads, the gas station, the church, the public library, a branch of the TrustFirst Bank, which I didn't remember having been there before. Just past the bank, on the lot which used to have a drugstore, there was an organic grocery. An organic grocery! When I was little, you could barely get vegetables in Thebes unless you grew them yourself. Now there were bins of late-season tomatoes, apples and squashes, all faintly luminous in the late-afternoon sun.

I wondered what my grandfather had thought of it. When I was a child, he was always telling me about how things used to be in Thebes. He spoke of the town, which was founded by his ancestor Jean Roland in the early part of the nineteenth century, like an heirloom that had passed into the hands of strangers who were treating it badly. He knew what everything had once been: the Kountry Kitchen was the lunch counter for workers at the Rowland Mill until the mill closed in the 1940s, and Arturo's was a smithy. Sheep had grazed where the ski shop stood, and I got the impression that my grandfather would have much preferred the sheep. He reserved his greatest displeasure, however, for Snowbird, the ski resort. Not only had it disfigured a swath of Mount Espy; it brought outsiders to Thebes: not workers who would buy houses and send their children to the public school and be humbled and annealed by the long winters, but seasonal people who had no respect for the town's history or its way of doing things. It didn't help that Snowbird's owner was Joe Regenzeit, a Turk. My grandfather had never been to Turkey, and surely he exaggerated the Turkish people's fondness for winter sports, but to him the resort was un-American, maybe even un-Western. It was the intrusion of a foreign culture into the deepest, best-hidden fold of his native land. And not just any foreign culture, but the Turks, hereditary enemies of the French ever since the Battle of Roncevaux in 778 C.E., which was the historical basis of the *Song of Roland* (and here I hear my ex-housemate Victor, the medievalist, correcting me: *Those weren't Turks who slew Roland, they were Basques*—but be quiet, Victor). "The Turks don't understand what these mountains are for," my grandfather complained. "The Catskills aren't the Alps. They aren't the Rockies. These are old mountains. You can climb them, but you can't ski them. It's ridiculous."

Compared with the rest of the town, my grandparents' house was reassuringly unchanged. A white Colonial three stories tall, with flaps of black tar paper on the pitched roof, gray shutters and a gray porch with white posts, the exterior almost entirely devoid of color, as though it belonged to an era before things had been colored, or, more accurately, as if it were one of the Greek temples that had once been gaudily painted but were now worn down to a white austerity that they seemed, in retrospect, always to have possessed. The old oak tree that menaced the house was larger than ever, its leaves a dusty late-summer green. There was a pickup truck parked in front of the garage, with ROWLAND'S TOWING AND SALVAGE painted on the driver's door in yellow cursive: my uncle Charles was there. The kitchen door was open; I went in. The white linoleum floor was tracked with muddy footprints, which my grandmother would never have allowed; the radio was tuned to a call-in show. "OK, OK, I'm going to admit it," the caller said, "I really like fat women. The bigger, the better."

"Say it!" shouted the host. "Let it out!"

I called out, "Charles?"

A door shut above me, feet on the stairs. "Well, hey! It's Mr. California!"

We embraced, and I breathed in Charles's atmosphere of cigarettes and Dial soap. "Thought you'd be tan," Charles said.

I explained that San Francisco wasn't always sunny, and

besides I didn't spend that much time outside. I didn't say what I had expected him to be, the Uncle Charles I remembered from my summers in Thebes, a giant in an undershirt, with a walrus mustache and red stubble on his chin, who chewed tobacco and spat in a coffee can outside the kitchen door, to the great disgust of my grandmother, who told him that one day he'd go out to spit and wouldn't be allowed back in. He was no longer that person. There was a bend in his back that hadn't been there the last time I saw him, at my grandmother's funeral, and as he led me in he picked up an ugly black cane and leaned his weight on it. White hairs poked up north of the collar of his undershirt, in the hollow of his shrunken neck.

"So, you were out of town when Oliver died?" he asked.

"Camping," I said. "I'm sorry I missed the funeral."

"Don't hold it against yourself. Hell, I'm surprised the twins came. Not that they stayed. No. It was *whup!* Shovel of dirt on the coffin, *whup!* Off to the train. You'd think they were afraid the ground would catch fire." He laughed at his own turn of speech. "They didn't even stay for the reception, not that I blame them. You know, they don't speak the language." Charles meant this literally. The old people in Thebes have their own vocabulary, a couple dozen French phrases handed down from the original settlers. *Langue d'up*, my grandfather called it jokingly, *langue* from the French for *language*, and *up* for *upstate*. Further evidence of how tightly the Thebans cling to the past.

"Anyway," my uncle went on, "it was just a bunch of old Thebes farts talking about the nice things Oliver Rowland did for them in the long ago and far away. For example, Mo Oton made a joke about how Oliver was *generuz de son esprit*, generous with his spirit. What Mo meant was, he was a skinflint. His spirit was the only thing he ever gave away! Gabby Thule told a story about how he came to visit her in the hospital when she had her gallbladder out. And how he brought her the nicest bunch of wildflowers. Of course he did! Nothing's free like wildflowers!"

He got us each a beer from the refrigerator. "You're still living in Frisco, am I right?"

"San Francisco. No one who lives there calls it Frisco."

"Is that so?" Charles lit a cigarette and blew smoke at the ceiling. "You know, I had my heart set on going out there, back when. San Francisco, or Big Sur, more like it. One of those hippie places right on the ocean."

"You were a hippie?"

"I wasn't anything. I was just a kid."

"Why didn't you go?"

Charles coughed. "Things got in the way."

I wondered if he meant the war. Around the time I was born, Charles had enlisted in the Army, against the wishes of my grandfather, who wanted him to become a lawyer, or a banker, something commensurate with the family's status in Thebes. Instead he went to Vietnam. No one in the family was entirely clear on what he'd done there; all we knew was that he came home knowing how to fix cars. With money grudgingly loaned him by Oliver, he opened a garage in Maplecrest, the next town over. The business grew quickly; by the time I was old enough to know anything about it, Charles had four tow trucks, a half dozen drivers, and a pretty secretary named Mrs. Bunce who gave me sour-cherry sucking candies.

"You should come visit," I said. "I'll go to Big Sur with you."

Charles looked at me in a way that I didn't understand, as if, I thought, he'd known what I was going to say before I said it. "Maybe in a while," he said.

He left a few minutes later. I walked him out, and when he saw Norman Mailer's car in the driveway he stopped, transfixed by horror. "Holy Jesus," he said. "Tell me you didn't drive across the country in that."

"It runs OK. It just makes a grinding sound when it goes uphill."

"I'll bet it does. What is it, a seventy-seven?"

"Seventy-six. It used to belong to Norman Mailer, *the* Norman Mailer. My ex-girlfriend thinks I was stupid to buy it, but it turns out to be a pretty good car."

My uncle laughed. "At least you aren't gay."

I didn't know what to say to that, or even why Charles would think I was gay, until I remembered that he hadn't seen me since I moved to San Francisco. No gay man in the city would have thought for even a second of dressing like I did, but my uncle couldn't be expected to know that.

Charles said he'd come back in a couple of days to see if I was still alive. He climbed into his truck. I wanted to stop him from going, because it hurt me to think that after ten years apart we had made such poor impressions on each other, and also because I was afraid to be alone in the house, but it was too late; his truck honked and was gone, two red lights dropping into the deep blue of twilight in the country.

The radio was still on in the kitchen. "Speaking as a woman of generous proportions," a caller said, "I just want to let everybody know that I feel good."

I opened a can of chicken noodle soup and heated it on the stove. Outside, the wind whispered in the oak tree. In my hurry to leave San Francisco I'd packed only one book, Murakami's *Norwegian Wood*, which I'd been meaning to read for months; but as soon as I started it I realized that I was not in the mood. Reading a novel, especially a contemporary novel, with its small stock of characters and situations, felt like being stuffed into a sleeping bag head-first: it was warm and dark and there wasn't a lot of room to move around. I looked through my grandparents' books and eventually chose *Progress in Flying Machines*, a purplish hardback with a winged contraption stamped on the front cover in gold. My grandfather had liked reading to me from it when I was a child. Published in 1894, it was, he said, the book that inspired the Wright brothers to build their airplane. What this meant was that none of the flying machines described in *Progress in Flying Machines* had ever flown. The book was a catalog of failures: giant wooden birds with flapping wings, aerial rowboats beyond the power of any human being to propel, corkscrew-crazy helicopters which under the best of circumstances never left the ground. I often wondered why my grandfather thought this was appropriate bedtime reading for a child. Maybe he hoped the book would teach me the importance of hard work and persistence, and give me faith that what looked like failure could be transformed, by history's alchemy, into magnificent success. Perhaps he was also preparing me for the likely if not delightful possibility that the success would belong to someone else. As he didn't tire of telling me, "Remember, it isn't just the successes who matter. Even the ones who fail get us somewhere, if we learn from their mistakes."

He meant this to be reassuring, but I found it sad: even as a child I suspected that the person he was reassuring was himself. And in fact my grandfather's history, like that of many of the so-called pioneers of flight, was largely the story of his failure to get off the ground. My grandparents lived on the rent from properties they owned in Thebes, but over the years my grandfather had tried to increase this income by means of various schemes, not one of which did anything but fail. My mothers told me about them with acid glee: there was the time your grandfather bought real estate in Catskill, they said, he took a bath on that. There was the time he sold seeds from your grandmother's garden! Even Mary couldn't believe it and she loved those plants. And then of course there was the lawsuit, the great battle with Joe Regenzeit, which he lost. Oliver was not discouraged. That was what irked my mothers most of all: to see my grandfather fail, and fail again, and not give up. It wasn't just that my grandfather's hopefulness reflected badly on his common sense; it also made him unbeatable. No matter how high my mothers climbed, they could never have the satisfaction of getting above Oliver, who was always, in his sober way, hoping for something better.

My soup was ready when I came back to the kitchen. I opened a beer and sat down to read. At midnight, half drunk and far from sleep, I called Alice. Her voicemail picked up again so I read it a sentence from the book in front of me: "If one had an unlimited height to fall in, affording time to think and to act, he would probably succeed in guiding himself at will." I added: "Hi, it's me. Just wanted to let you know I got here OK. The house is a disaster, it's going to take like a hundred years to clear it out. And my uncle is dying. Miss you. Bye." I made up a bed on the sofa. The bedroom where I used to sleep was full of boxes, and I didn't want to sleep in my mothers' room, because I was haunted by the memory of what had happened there thirty years ago.

THE RICHARD ENTE PERIOD

Whenever Celeste said my father's name, she made a face; the four syllables, RICH-ard EN-tee, left her pursed lips like the taste of something rotten. Richard Empty, she called him, but when I asked what she meant, whether my father had really been empty, she only shook her head, as though to say that actually she had meant the opposite, and I was not supposed to understand. Despite my mothers, and *to* spite them, I was endlessly curious about Richard Ente. I collected facts about him the way other children collect stamps or baseball cards, and I assembled them into a story that I reviewed from time to time, solemnly, just as I went over the deposits and withdrawals in my savings account, checking and double-checking the total even though it was never more than a hundred dollars.

This is my father's story: once upon a time there was a

lawyer named Richard Ente. Six foot two, eyes of blue, none-theless a New York Jew, Richard came to Thebes in 1969 to sue Joe Regenzeit on my grandfather's behalf. Richard was handsome, and my mothers didn't meet many strangers. They couldn't get enough of him and—to their surprise, probably—he didn't find them silly, or provincial, or young. Richard must have been fifty at the time, my grandfather's age; my mothers were sixteen. I don't know how Richard chose between them, but in the end, the one he fell in love with was Marie, and their love was, what, I don't know, lovely, but brief. Oliver caught his lawyer romancing his daughter; Richard fled in my grandfather's sports car, and my grandfather chased him in my grandmother's station wagon. For some reason the two cars collided, and it was a miracle neither Richard nor my grandfather was hurt. The love-suit was over but the lawsuit went on, until, on the morning of the day when the jury was to announce the verdict in *Oliver Rowland et al. v. Snowbird Resort, Inc.*, Richard Ente ran away from Thebes. He died of a heart attack in Denver that summer, three months before I was born.

I tried to supplement this little collection of facts with information from my grandparents, but they had less to offer than I hoped. "Richard was a genius," my grandfather said, but when I asked him *how* my father was a genius he declined to give concrete examples. The most he would say was, "It was impossible to beat him in an argument, although I certainly tried."

My further questions got no answer so I turned to my grandmother. "What was my father like?"

"He was very intelligent," she said judiciously. "He worked very hard." I had the feeling she was sugarcoating the truth, in the hope that she could create a better father in my mind than the one who was already working mischief in my blood.

"Was he a good arguer?"

"I suppose he must have been. He was a lawyer, after all."

"Why did he run away?"

My grandmother shrugged.

"Did he know he was going to lose the lawsuit?"

"I have no idea. Now stop grilling me, and get some peas from the garden. They're just big enough to eat."

That was the sum of the information I had about the Richard Ente Period, which lasted from the summer of 1969 until the spring of 1970, from Woodstock until about Kent State. Over the years I added to it scraps of less relevant or less assimilable information which my mothers let slip in careless moments. When I said I didn't want to go to school, because I was smarter than everyone there, Celeste said I sounded just like my father. When I wouldn't go to bed before my mothers, when I protested that if there were rules, then they ought to apply to everyone, adult and child, equally, Marie told me to stop lawyering, for Christ's sake, it made me sound like a little Richard Ente. From these and other reproaches I learned that my father was a selfish person who didn't do homework and hardly ever slept, who didn't say *thank you* when he received a gift, who forgot to call when he was going to be late, who watched television during the day, who made up stories about places he had not been and people he had not met and told them as if they were the truth. All of which made me think he must have been very interesting, and made me regret not having known him.

Years later, when I was in college, I learned that Richard hadn't died of a heart attack. My grandmother was very ill; she had a rare blood disease that carried her off to a teaching hospital in Syracuse. I went to see her there, and came in as a medical student was drawing her blood. "Does this hurt, Mrs., uh, Rowland?" he asked, as though he had been thinking about her disease so intently he'd forgotten that she was a person also.

"Of course it hurts," she said.

The medical student left, and we talked about her illness, which was causing quite a sensation in the hospital. Specialists from several departments had been in to see her; she showed me the bruises on her forearms where they'd drawn vial after vial of blood. On the whole, she seemed pleased to be the object of so much attention. "If I'm lucky," she said dryly, "they'll publish me. I asked if there's any chance they can use my real name." My grandmother told me about the people who had been to visit: an aunt I hadn't seen in years, cousins I barely knew. Charles had come several times to re-supply her with the mystery novels she loved. My mothers came once. "For an hour," my grandmother said. "It takes four hours to get here."

"They should have stayed longer," I said.

"I worry about them," my grandmother said. "They want to live like they came out of a clamshell." It took me a long moment to understand that she was referring to Botticelli's *Birth of Venus*. "But everyone has a family, even in New York City." She looked at me with alarming lucidity. "Do they ever talk to you about what happened?"

"In New York?"

"With Richard," my grandmother said impatiently. She took my hand. She must have known that her own life would soon be over, and that whatever secrets she kept would then be known by no one at all. Her time to tell was limited. And she was selfish, as I imagine many people are at the end of their lives; my feelings mattered less to her than they had when she was well. "You poor boy," she said, "do you even know Richard shot himself?"

So it came out. One night in the summer of 1970, a police detective called from Denver and told Oliver that Richard Ente was dead of a gunshot wound, in all likelihood self-inflicted. The detective wanted to know if Richard had any next of kin. The only reason he called Oliver was because he'd found a check from him in Richard's wallet. "We couldn't help the gentleman," my grandmother said. "Richard never talked about his family."

"They didn't tell me," I said numbly.

"Exactly," my grandmother said.

This story flattened me, and it weakened my grandmother also: maybe she had come without knowing it to the age when her last few secrets were what kept her alive. She leaned back against the pillows of her hospital bed. Her eyes closed and her lips trembled, as though she wanted to say more, but when she did speak, finally, what she said was, "Ring for the nurse." I did, and a minute later the nurse came in and chided my grandmother because she hadn't eaten her vegetables. "These aren't vegetables," my grandmother said, "they're," and she shrugged, her face lit up with disgust.

I called my mothers that night from my motel room in Syracuse and had a bad conversation. Why hadn't they told me? Why had Richard shot himself in Denver? The first question was easier to answer than the second. My mothers had been trying to protect me from having to feel what they still felt, a kind of baffled sadness, which made Richard Ente impossible either to dismiss or to forgive. They wanted me to have two parents and not be haunted by the ghost of a third. But *why* did he do it? My mothers didn't know. Celeste believed Richard's suicide had to do with things that had happened a long time ago, before he came to Thebes. "Any fifty-year-old man who falls in love with a sixteen-year-old girl has serious problems," she said.

Marie sobbed into the phone; she didn't know either.

"Let him go," Celeste said. "Suicide is a mystery with no solution."

"I'm so sorry," Marie said. "I wish I could have done something to stop him." She *could* have done something, but I wouldn't know that until much later. Finally I got off the phone with my mothers, wiped my eyes and tried to take Celeste's advice and put Richard out of my mind. Dead was dead. The fact that Richard had killed himself didn't make him any more lost to me than he had been already. How could it matter if he died of a bullet or a heart attack? But I couldn't let go of the question *why?*

When I came back from Syracuse, I looked for my father in the Bleak College (not its real name, but that's another story) library, but nothing I found cast any light on his death. The membership directories of the New York State Bar Association told me that Richard Ente practiced law in New York from 1949 until 1970. He worked for Silberman & Mischeaux, a personal-injury firm, then in 1961 he went into private practice. His office was a few blocks from Times Square, in a building that has since been demolished. Lexis, which was just becoming available at the time, and which I got access to with the help of a friend in the law school, confirmed that my father was of counsel in *Oliver Rowland et al. v. Snowbird Resort, Inc.* The lawsuit, which my family had talked about only in vague terms, turned out to be stranger and more significant than I'd expected. According to Lexis, my grandfather sued for an injunction to prevent Joe Regenzeit from "interfering with the clouds and the natural condition of the air, sky, atmosphere and air space over plaintiffs' lands and in the area of plaintiffs' lands to in any manner, degree or way affect, control or modify the weather conditions on or about said lands," which, reading farther down in the document, seems to have been a response to Joe Regenzeit's "cloud-seeding devices and equipment generally used in a weather modification program," the purpose of which was, in short, to make it snow. As if it didn't snow enough in Thebes! Beginning sometime in the autumn of 1968, Joe Regenzeit was sprinkling the clouds with silver iodide, bringing further gloom to the gloomy mountain town, with the intention of turning it into a winter paradise. My grandfather objected. He, or rather his counsel, Richard Ente, Esq., argued that Regenzeit's snow had encumbered the land, choked the roads, and clouded the minds of Thebes's inhabitants, who were already unhappy enough come winter. He did not prevail. Having failed to demonstrate, in the first place, that Joe Regenzeit's weather modification program was responsible for any particular snowfall, and, in the second, that the plaintiffs' hardships were brought on by snow, specifically, as distinguished from cold, darkness, old age, excessive consumption of alcohol, rheumatoid arthritis, poor eyesight, poor diet, unusual devotion to their domestic animals, acts of God, or any other cause, the injunction was not granted, and *Rowland v. Snowbird* assumed its place in the history of weather-modification law, an important precedent, but one with few successors. According to an articled titled "Who Owns the Clouds Now?" 73 Mich. L. Rev. 129, *Rowland v. Snowbird* established, tacitly, a doctrine of "modified natural rights," which is to say that if Regenzeit could make money off the clouds, and my grandfather didn't lose any money thereby, then the clouds belonged to Regenzeit, which would have made him, my law-school friend said, the first person in American history ever to own a cloud. I took copious notes, and even thought of writing a science-fiction story that would take the case as its starting point, and project from it a world where not only the clouds but all natural phenomena, rain, wind, sunlight, fog, and even such intangibles as "clear skies" and "autumn chill," were privately owned, so that the experience of the outdoors would involve an endless series of payments, and become in all likelihood a pastime for the rich.

Lexis had nothing to say on the subject of Richard Ente's character. Since childhood, I had pictured my father as a handsome man, a distinguished lawyer in a dark suit and a blue-and-gold Bleak College necktie, because yes, he went to Bleak, just the same as my grandfather, the same as me, and I wonder if I didn't go there in part because I hoped I'd find some trace of him. I imagined Richard Ente sitting at dinner with my grandfather, twirling a glass of wine between his fingers, like an old version of the young Sean Connery, if you see what I mean. Richard Ente offering his considered opinion on legal matters, then turning and catching Marie's eye. Richard Ente pressing my mother's hand as they said goodbye, and murmuring something in her ear. Richard Ente under cover of darkness climbing the roof of the garage, still in his dark suit, and slipping through my mothers' open window. My love! said his love. Ssh, Richard Ente murmured, a cross now between James Bond and Humbert Humbert, although I suppose Humbert Humbert is already that. We don't want to wake them, do we? Marie's hands at the knot of his tie. Richard's hairy fingers—with a ring, perhaps, on the third left one?—undoing the top of Marie's dress. Then an unclarity, willful, on my part. Then Richard Ente murmured, You mustn't tell your father. —Damn my father, Marie said, rolling away from him and snugging her back to his chest. He's a good man, Richard said softly. Not as good as you, Marie said. Hm, said Richard. He got up and dressed in the moonlight. Is my tie straight? —You look dashing, Marie said. —Then adieu. —No! But Richard Ente was gone; he had climbed out the window and down to the ground, and now he walked to where his car idled silently among the trees. None of this explained him taking his own life. I invented other scenes in which Richard Ente's suicidal tendency would be manifest: Richard draining a flask before he gets into his car. Richard growling, I can't go on with this charade! Richard speeding around a curve and closing his eyes. No. The story I'd made up about my father had petrified in my memory; adding the story of his death in Denver didn't change him any more than the addition of paint to a rock would make it not a rock. My story was beyond contradiction, to the point where even now I think of it as being about my real father, even though I know for a fact that it is wrong in almost every particular.

Finally I stopped looking for the truth about Richard Ente. I was left with a mystery, a love of library research and a desire to get as far away from my family as I could: these last two came in handy when I went to Stanford to study American history.

The sun was already high over the mountains when I woke up, my neck and back frozen at bad angles from sleeping on the sofa. I washed my face and drank sulfurous water from the tap. By day, the house didn't seem haunted, only cluttered. Four generations of Rowlands had lived there and as far as I could tell not one of them had ever thrown anything out. Cigar boxes and tobacco tins from the early twentieth century were heaped on a table in the hall, teapots, hatracks, mugs, pens, bowls full of buttons and pins, vases, stacks of old magazines, china statuettes of shepherds and milkmaids, candlesticks, bundles of letters, books, albums, records, telephone directories, ashtrays, bottle openers and pens given away by businesses that no longer existed, framed photographs of long-dead cousins, sewing kits, skeins of wool, coasters, place mats, watercolors of the Catskills that my grandmother had painted in her youth, road maps, paperweights, letter openers, seashells, lamps. Every horizontal surface in the house was heaped with stuff; every cabinet was full. There was no separation between the priceless things and the worthless ones: in the parlor, the silver inkwell which supposedly came over from France with Jean Roland was full of paper clips.

I went upstairs to my mothers' bedroom, which looked just as it had when they ran away from Thebes in the spring of 1970. Embroidered bedspreads covered the twin beds; the trunks where Celeste kept her art things stood against the wall. There were two windows and two desks, and a poster tacked to the wall between them: Russian Folk Music, University Performing Arts Center, December 19, 1969. Their closet was a museum of fashion from the late sixties. Their bookshelf was the *summum* of thought from the same era: *The Bell Jar*, *Being and Nothingness*, *Steppenwolf*, *The Stranger*. The room had always seemed strange to me, and it was strange that my grandparents hadn't done anything with it, the way they'd changed my uncle's room into a study. It was as if they were still hoping my mothers would come back. But the room was creepy, and I could understand why the Celestes hadn't wanted to come back. I felt like an idiot for agreeing to come in their place. I should have let them hire someone to get rid of everything. Without looking at my grandparents' room, or the study, or the attic, my god, the attic, I got dressed and drove into town.

I parked in back of the Kountry Kitchen, took a booth by the window and looked blankly at the big sign outside the ski shop, which said

GOD BLESS AMERICA

WINTERS COMING

GET UR GEAR

There was almost no one in the restaurant, a couple of teenage girls in purple parkas smoking at the counter and a large party at the other end of the room, it looked like a business lunch, three men and a woman in suits, their jackets hung on the backs of their chairs, their cuff links gleaming. As I ate, I thought one of the men was trying to get my attention. He looked at me and raised his eyebrows inquisitively, and I wondered if it was because of my San Francisco clothes, my burgundy leather jacket and thrift-store shirt with the monkey Curious George depicted performing various activities against a yellow background. I nodded in what I hoped was a friendly, masculine way, as if to say *yup*, and went back to my lunch. Each time I looked up, he was watching me. I wondered if he was trying to pick me up, if he had come to the same conclusion about me that Charles had. A middle-aged businessman with curly gray hair and gold-rimmed eyeglasses, a dark-green suit a shade nattier than the suits around him, it was possible. My *yup* might have sent him the wrong signal; I didn't know how grown-ups communicated in this part of the world. It was too bad, the woman sitting beside him was attractive. I would have liked to look at her wide mouth, her thick red lips and narrow chin. Even the faintly perceptible shadow of hairs on her upper lip was enticing. She would probably have fine brown hairs all down her back and arms. Instead I had to look at my lunch special, a breaded pork chop snuggled against the flank of a mountain of mashed potatoes and bathed in brown gravy. Then, suddenly, the man was standing in front of me, leaning toward me, eager, worried, saying my name. "Kerem," he said, and held out his hand. "Do you remember me?" It was Joe Regenzeit's son, grown and changed, thick where he used to be thin, shorter than me now. We embraced and his chin hit my shoulder.

"What are you doing here?" I asked. The last time I saw Kerem, he was fifteen years old, and bound, I thought, for fame in the world of professional soccer or notoriety in the underworld of punk rock.

"Running the family business," Kerem said, grinning. He put his hand on my back. "Come say hello to my sister."

He guided me to their table, where the woman, who had looked mysterious and attractive before I knew who she was, transformed herself into Yesim, Kerem's younger sister, the way a certain shape beloved of psychologists changes from a rabbit into a duck. The hairs on her lip multiplied; her eyebrows grew closer to each other; her thick black hair became unruly. She stood up and shook my hand.

"We heard about your grandfather," she said. "I'm sorry."

Meanwhile Kerem was introducing me to the other men, who were up from New York, "to give me a shot in the arm," he said. They shook my hand and offered me truncated, almost furtive smiles, as though they could tell I was a negligible person, and regulations forbade them from associating with negligible persons while on duty. Still Kerem insisted on telling them who I was.

"We used to party together," Kerem said, which wasn't entirely true: we'd only gone to one party together. I kissed his girlfriend, but I don't think he ever found out. Yesim looked at her brother anxiously.

"Are you in town long?" Kerem asked.

"A few days," I said. "I've got to clean out my grandparents' house."

"Well, come have dinner with us. Come tonight!"

The city people glanced at each other. I wanted to warn Kerem that by talking to me he was reducing his importance in their eyes, but there was no way to do it and he wouldn't have listened. Kerem had always been like that, generous when it would have been better to be selfish. I thanked him and paid my check. I looked back at Yesim, but she was talking to the city people, explaining that in a small town you were always running into people from the past.

REGENZEIT

That afternoon, instead of getting to work on the house, I picked up *Progress in Flying Machines* and read about M. Hureau de Villeneuve, the permanent secretary of the French Aeronautical Society, who built more than three hundred model flying machines, all of them with flapping wings. His experiments culminated with the construction of a giant steam-powered bat, which was connected by a hose to a boiler on the ground. When M. de Villeneuve turned the machine on, it flapped its wings violently and did, in fact, rise into the air—at which point M. de Villeneuve became afraid that it would pull free of the hose, and switched it off. The bat fell to the ground and smashed one of its wings, and the story ended with M. de Villeneuve waiting for someone to invent a lighter motor so he could resume his experiments. I wondered what, if anything, the early-aviation community had learned from his failure.

Don't make any more giant bats? Hose-tethered flying machines not a good idea? The hard fact of it was that ornithopters, machines with flapping wings, were a digression from the path that led to the airplane. No matter what motor you used, none of them would ever really work. M. de Villeneuve had devoted his life to *something*, but I couldn't think of exactly what it was: flight's penumbra, maybe, the weird shadow of hopeless invention against which the Wrights' brightness defined itself.

After a few pages of *Progress in Flying Machines*, my attention wandered, and I found myself thinking again about my grandfather. I remembered how he used to entertain me and my grandmother with stories from the *Catskill Eagle*: a police station was opening in Jewett, there was an art fair in Woodstock, the new pizzeria in Hunter was a big success. "Run by actual Italians, that's their secret," my grandfather said, as though we were the owners of a rival pizzeria wondering at our own sluggish business. "Apparently they import their flour from Italy." My grandfather reflected on what he had just said, and frowned. "Not that there's anything wrong with American flour. Mary, don't you bake with American flour?" My grandmother affirmed that she did. "Perfectly good flour," my grandfather said. He considered how much more he should say about it, or whether he ought to praise my grandmother's baking. Instead he said, "It must be a question of technique. The Italians have been making pizza for a long time, you know."

My grandmother rolled her eyes. "Do tell. Did the ancient Romans have pizza?"

But my grandfather was immune to her teasing. "I don't believe so," he said, "at least, not the kind we have today." And he was off, explaining to us that the tomato, a relative of the deadly nightshade, was thought to be poisonous until the eighteenth century, and as for our modern pasteurized cheeses, the Romans had never known anything like them. I wondered when my grandfather had developed his taste for puns. I thought about how life turns people into the opposite of what you would expect them to be, as it had with Charles, and now with Kerem. I wondered if I seemed as strange to Kerem as he did to me, and, if so, what I was the opposite of.

It took me a long time to decide what to wear to dinner. All my clothes were wrong, and in the end I put on a white button-down shirt and one of my grandfather's jackets, which was tight across the stomach but all right if I left it unbuttoned. I looked like my adviser at Stanford, a portly ex-Jesuit named Schönhoff. What was worse, the jacket smelled like my grandfather's closet, like naphtha and wool and ever so faintly of aftershave. At various points in the evening I would catch myself sniffing my own shoulder, wondering if it still smelled, and whether Kerem and Yesim could smell it too.

Kerem greeted me at the door. He was wearing a black sweatsuit that made him look even older than the business suit had, and at the same time recalled his athletic youth. He hugged me and I pulled back, trying to protect him from the jacket. "You're looking great," he said. "Come in, hey, you didn't have to get dressed up."

The house had changed, but my memories of it were too old to say how, exactly. The black leather sofa and the enormous television were certainly new, as was the tiny silver stereo playing almost inaudible jazz. But the rugs were the same, and the smells, too, of cumin and cloves, onions and meat.

"My sister's cooking," Kerem said, "but don't think it's like this every night. We're a take-out family, most nights we eat the most amazing junk. Do you drink martinis?" He came back with two of them, big ones, in highball glasses. "Sit."

Kerem lowered himself into a black leather recliner that tried to open up its footrest. "I'm a lazy bastard," he said. "What can I do?" He kicked the footrest back. "Welcome to Thebes!"

We drank. Kerem explained how they had come back to

the old house: after he flunked out of Cornell, he'd scraped through SUNY Purchase and got a law degree from Villanova. He'd married a lawyer named Kathy and they had a son, Max, who looked down on us from a brass-framed photograph on the windowsill, a small fair boy with an overbite. Two years ago Kerem's father was diagnosed with a cancer of the pancreas that was fatal in about 95 percent of all cases, but not Joe Regenzeit's. It was a miracle he lived, and when the cancer went into remission he had a, "What could you call it? A mid-death crisis," and decided that he was through with America. He and his wife returned to the village where his ancestors had come from, "a place in Anatolia with about three goats and a well," and he lived there to this day. Yesim had already moved back to Thebes to take care of her father, and when he went off to this village, which was called Akbez, and really was so small you couldn't find it on most maps, she stayed on and took care of the ski resort. At first Kerem had helped her only a little; then he became interested in the business, and then: "I had this idea, I want to take what we're doing here in a new direction. I can't talk about it yet. You understand, right? You can't show anyone until it's finished?" He moved back up to Thebes; Kathy stayed in Philadelphia; they agreed to separate. "I have to tell you, I miss the hell out of Max, but I'm happy here. And it wasn't good for my sister to be alone. Now," he concluded quickly, as if he regretted having told me so much, "what about you?"

I told Kerem how I'd gone to Stanford for history, dropped out of the program and gone to work at Cetacean, then Yesim called to us that dinner was ready. I followed Kerem into the dining room, pursued by the jazz, which could be piped, he explained, into every room of the house, including the bathrooms. The dining-room table was covered with dishes. Yesim was still wearing her business clothes, but she'd exchanged her contact lenses for large eyeglasses with square red frames. Her hair was restrained by a flock of bobby pins. Kerem maneuvered me into a chair to his right, and his sister sat facing me. "Did you know he's an Internet entrepreneur?" Kerem asked.

"How would I know that?" Yesim said. "He hasn't told me anything."

"I'm not an entrepreneur," I said.

"I should have known you'd end up in the computer business," Kerem went on. "Do you remember when I had that computer? You made it do the most amazing stuff."

"Not really," I said. "I just copied some programs from a manual."

"You wrote that game, didn't you? We played it for days. We played it all summer." Actually Kerem hadn't played it at all. I was amused at what his memory was doing to the past, how he was making me grander than I had ever been. One look at Yesim and I decided to let his misrepresentations stand.

We finished the bottle of wine, and Kerem remembered another, a gift from the Karmans last Christmas. Soon I was telling Kerem and Yesim that *content management* was a misnomer, actually what I had managed was *dis*content, my own, mostly. Every project was the same, every client was looking for a way to turn the Internet into one of those ads you see on late-night television, for the carrot peeler that also makes soup. The only difference among them was that some clients wanted to give you the peeler for free and charge for the carrots, whereas others wanted you to pay for the peeler up front. Yesim's lips and teeth were stained purple. She wiped her mouth with her napkin, and our eyes met. She seemed to be asking me, what do you want? A question to which I had no answer.

Finally the meal was over. Kerem said, "How about some coffee, sis?" and Yesim carried our plates into the kitchen. "We have this great Chilean coffee," Kerem told me. "Can you believe it, great coffee in Thebes? We get it from the new grocery, they have everything." He grinned. "You know who owns that place?" I couldn't imagine why he thought I would care, but before he could tell me, Yesim came in with the coffee. I asked what she had been doing since I saw her last.

"Oh, me," she said. "Actually, there isn't much to tell. I was living in Albany, then my father got sick, and I came back up here. Now I'm a ski-resort administrator." She looked at Kerem, as if, oddly, she were judging *him*.

I asked what she had been doing in Albany, but Yesim didn't answer, and it fell to Kerem to wave his hand vaguely over his glass. "Yesim is a born manager. She's the one who keeps things going. I like to think of myself as an idea guy, but the truth is, without Yesim, I'd be nowhere. Snowbird would be nowhere. Even my father admits it."

"My brother is a little drunk," Yesim said.

Kerem lifted his glass. "Drunk enough to tell the truth. To my sister!" But the glass was empty. "Yesim, there's a bottle of Scotch in the cabinet over the refrigerator . . ."

"You can get it. I'm going upstairs." Yesim touched my shoulder as she went past and said I shouldn't leave without saying goodbye.

Kerem got the bottle of Scotch and two glasses and I followed him into the living room, where he poured us about half a glass each. He used to hate the stuff, he said, but there was some kind of rule that lawyers had to drink Scotch. He stuck his hands into the tangles of his hair. "Holy shit, I'm a lawyer," he said, and collapsed into his recliner. This time the footrest came up.

I slumped on the sofa, and we drank what he told me was a very good Scotch, from an island where they fertilized the soil with goat shit, could I believe that, goat shit? No, it wasn't goat shit, really, you can't trust what lawyers say, lawyers are always making up the most fantastic crap. The conversation slipped away from me. Kerem was talking about how his wife had been freaking out ever since someone broke into her Lincoln Navigator, and wanted to bring Max to live with Kerem in the mountains, *the mountains*, she said, as though these were real mountains, as though this was fucking Colorado, and of course it wasn't going to happen, in a couple of weeks she'd calm down and tease him again for being a survivalist, which, in fact, she'd already called him, as though his move to Thebes had been part of some plan, Kerem said, as though he had planned any of this.

Then he was telling me about his sister, who was, he said, a poet, and had been in trouble. "What she needs," Kerem said, "is encouragement." He made me promise that I would encourage her. "We're going to get through this," he said, and he told me that, if I stayed around, I would see, the glory days were coming back to Thebes, but by this point the conversation had escaped from me entirely, and all I remember are images: rosy clouds against a pale-blue sky, trumpets, people dancing in a tent, things Kerem can't have said. I had to go to the bathroom, so I stood up and hit my shin against the coffee table. The pain was unbearable. I hopped around the living room, and when I stopped I was sober again, but exhausted, as though I'd just sat through a very long film. Yesim had already gone to bed. I said goodbye to her brother and staggered across the little gulf that separated the Regenzeits from the Rowlands. I lay on the sofa, got up, took off my clothes and lay down again. I thought of Yesim, and what it would have been like if I had followed her into the kitchen, reached around from behind and cupped her breasts, and if I had just, and if I had only.

REGENZEIT

Kerem was four years older than I was; in the beginning he was my champion, my protector. In the stories I told myself, which were largely plagiarized from J.R.R. Tolkien and Lloyd Alexander, Kerem was the prince and I was the squire. I trudged across the wilderness in his footsteps, because even my most fantastic daydreams involved a fair amount of trudging, and when the imaginary wind froze me, Kerem loaned me his cloak and I was warm. This went on until puberty stripped Kerem of his princely qualities. One summer he went away to a soccer camp and returned with formidable legs, a slouch and a new way of talking, or, more precisely, of not talking. I had no claim on his attention; the most I could get from him was "Unh," as he noodled past on his way to some incomprehensible teenage activity. That summer I was friends only with Yesim, who was just my age. She was willing to try my games, but with her for a companion all our quests got muddled. We trudged across the landscape, but I didn't know what we were trudging toward or what we'd do when we got there. Then it became clear that we were headed toward Yesim's bedroom.

"You are Prince Charming," she said, "and I am Sleeping Beauty."

She threw herself onto her twin bed and closed her eyes. For a long time neither of us moved. Then Yesim looked at me and said, "What are you waiting for?"

"I don't know. What happens now?"

"You kiss me, and I wake up."

She returned to her slumber. I leaned forward and kissed her forehead. Yesim burst out laughing. "That's not how you do it."

"You're awake," I pointed out.

"If you can't do better than that," she said, "I'm going to make you a dwarf."

I didn't have anything against dwarves, who were, in Tolkien's work at least, noble and tough, dwarves who had their own runic alphabet and their kingdom underground, but I didn't want Yesim to be unhappy. "OK," I said. I leaned toward her.

Yesim recoiled. "What are you doing? You have to wait for me to go to sleep."

We tried the whole thing again. I leaned in and kissed her lips. Yesim opened her eyes. "Finally," she said. "Now, go out, and come back in."

"Why?"

"Narcolepsy," Yesim hissed, a word I didn't understand.

I knew we were playing a strange game, but I didn't know what was strange about it until Mrs. Regenzeit caught me coming down the stairs and said, "You are a leetle beet in love with my daughter. That is all right. Just you do not try to marry her."

"I'm not in love with her," I said. "Besides, I'm too young to be married."

"This is true, fortunately for us all."

I asked if Yesim was engaged, which sent Mrs. Regenzeit into a coughing fit of malicious amusement. "No," she said. "She is too young, also. But when the time comes, she will marry a Turkish boy."

I accepted her proclamation dutifully. Besides, I knew for a fact that there were no Turkish boys in Thebes but her brother. I had time. So I played along with Yesim's stories, which only got stranger as the summer went on. I sat for an afternoon at the foot of the forbidden tower (or bed), listening to the princess read aloud from *Nancy Drew's Dos and Don'ts for Girls*; I stumbled around in the enchanted forest (Yesim's bedroom, with the lights off) and was thwacked with cushions by spiteful forest creatures. Yesim and I drank "poison," actually grape soda with a St. Joseph's baby aspirin crumbled into it, and lay side by side on her bed, feigning eternal sleep. Even then I knew that something was wrong with Yesim's imagination: it stored its kisses too close to its tears. But I had no idea how to tell her so, and would not have spoken if I could. I loved Yesim a leetle beet too much for that.

Earlier that year, I had stolen a book called *Man and*

Woman from my mothers' shelves, at least, I thought I'd stolen it. In retrospect I think they must have left it out for me, as no book like that existed during the era when my mothers could have learned anything from it. *Man and Woman* was written in simple, direct language, and illustrated with pencil line drawings, carefully shaded, of men and women who were supposed to look ordinary, but in fact, because of the changes of hairstyle that had taken place since the book was published, seemed to have come straight out of the 1960s. For the first time, I saw clearly the difference between the sexes: the woman's arms were crossed over her stomach, while the man rested a confident hand on his buttock. Late that summer I shared this information with Yesim. I told her solemnly that she had a uterus, as though I were a scout returning from a mission to a forbidden city.

Yesim nodded regally. "Let's see," she said, and we did. Our bodies looked nothing like the illustrations in *Man and Woman*, so I put my hand on my buttock and told Yesim to cross her arms over her stomach. The likeness wasn't even approximate; I thought it would be better if Yesim wore her hair in a braid, but it was cut too short. Still we touched, and retreated, neither of us certain what had happened. Yesim pulled her pants up and we sat on the floor, not talking, because *Man and Woman* didn't say what we were supposed to do in that moment, although it had a certain amount of information about what would come later, not all of it incorrect, as it turned out. And that was all. We didn't take off our clothes again. The game of men and women ended and another began, I don't remember which, maybe it was the game of Life, which Yesim liked, or Uno, which she also liked, but which I liked less than Life because it had no finely molded pieces.

For years afterward Yesim came to see me at night. She touched my imaginary hair, and in time she learned to do other things as well, but by then she wasn't Yesim anymore, or not only Yesim; she had put on other faces and become general, a warm weight by my hip, a hand on my chest, she could have been anybody. I didn't even remember what she looked like with her clothes off, I thought. But apparently I was wrong. As I lay on my grandparents' sofa, drunk, my knuckles rubbing against the waistband of my underwear, I thought of Yesim again, not the woman but the girl, standing with her arms crossed over her stomach. I imagined myself placing my hands on her shoulders, kissing her, moving her arms out of the way, pressing myself to her flat chest. Was I grown up in this scene, or was I a child? We were both soft, I know.

SAN FRANCISCO, CITY OF GHOSTS

The phone rang just as I was falling asleep. It was Alice. She wanted to know if I was all right.

"I'm dead drunk," I said.

"Your message was scary," Alice said. "Are you losing your mind?"

"I don't think so."

"It sounded like you were going through some kind of *Shining* thing."

"Ha. I'm not even alone up here. My childhood friends live next door."

"But you're drinking. You're going to start seeing the twins."

"Jesus Christ, I'm trying to go to sleep."

"Redrum, redrum."

Alice was coming home from a party too, it turned out. Her friend Raoul . . .

"Raoul? Who's Raoul?"

"You met him, he came to the salon a couple of times." No hair parlor this but a group of writers who met in a bar in the Tenderloin. When the salon started, a year earlier, there had been a lot of them, but as people found work or left the city their number shrank, until the salon became a group of bar friends like any other, who played pool and gossiped and argued about who owed whom a drink. I didn't remember anyone named Raoul. "He works for Petopia, the pet-supply people," Alice said. "He wants me to write copy for them."

"How glamorous," I said.

There was a beat of silence. "I just called to see if you were all right," Alice said. "Not so you could cut me down."

"I'm sorry." Beat. "Was it a good party?"

"It wasn't bad. There weren't enough people and there was too much to drink."

"And this Raoul, he's a nice guy?"

"Will you be jealous if I say *yes*?"

"Not at all," I lied. "I want you to be happy."

"I don't know," Alice said. "I feel like I'm floating. You know? It's like I'm floating in the dark, in a sensory-deprivation tank, and nothing I see is really happening."

"Maybe it's just that we're drunk."

"Maybe. But," beat, "I just feel like that's what we're all doing now. Like we're all just, like, floating."

Beat. "Maybe we are."

"What does that mean?"

"I don't know."

"I wish you were here."

"I'll be back," I said.

"And what's going to happen then?" Alice asked.

"I guess we'll find out then."

"I'm sorry," Alice said. "It's the middle of the night there, isn't it? Make sure you drink some water before you go to bed."

"OK."

"OK."

"I'll talk to you soon."

"OK."

"OK."

Beat. Beat.

My uncle was back early the next morning, making things move in the kitchen like an angry ghost. I groaned and wrapped the quilt around my head. He asked what had happened to me, and I said I'd been hit by a car.

Charles laughed. "I know that car."

He made coffee, and when it was ready he shook my shoulder. Instant. Charles pointed at me with his mug. "So, you were just drinking by yourself, or what?"

"I was at the Regenzeits'."

"Ah, our enemies," my uncle said.

I felt dull and sick to my stomach. I wished Charles would leave so I could go back to sleep, and in fact I didn't know what he was doing, coming over when the sky was still green with presunrise light. Did he think that the world was full of people like him, angry men who drank bad coffee at dawn?

"Why are they our enemies?" I asked.

"Because they're Turks, that's why. The Turks are an Oriental people. They've hated us ever since the beginning."

"Turkey is a Westernized democracy. It's even a member of NATO."

"Believe what you like, the history speaks for itself. Think about the Ottoman Empire."

"The Ottoman Empire ended just after the First World War. Anyway, Kerem and Yesim were born in America."

"But they remember," Charles said, "they all remember that we won. The Americans and the Western Europeans."

"That's not true, the Ottoman Empire collapsed under the weight of its own bureaucracy. That, and the rebellion of the so-called assimilated peoples." I couldn't believe I was discussing the fall of the Ottoman Empire at dawn in Thebes with a bad hangover.

"Assimilated peoples, my ass, it was us. We won, on account of our superior military technology."

"You must be thinking of the Cold War, although even there—"

"You don't get it," Charles interrupted. "Snowbird is their revenge."

"That's ridiculous," I said. "Snowbird is a ski resort, and this is the late twentieth century. You aren't going to convince me that Joe Regenzeit and his family have been holding a grudge ever since Mustafa Pasha's defeat at the gates of Vienna, or, even if they did, that they would take their revenge here, in Thebes."

Charles growled at me that I didn't understand a damn thing about Thebes, and I said I understood enough, Thebes was just a small town in the mountains that no one cared about, and there were more important things happening in the big world, and wasn't it time to think about something else, and he said, what something else did I mean, which something else did I want him to think about, when every day they ruined Thebes a little more, and the old families were dying out, and people were tearing the old houses down and building Swiss chalets, and a barn sold for two hundred thousand dollars, a *barn*, and I said, you wanted to move to California anyway, don't tell me that you love Thebes, and he said, I wanted to leave, but I didn't want this place to die, and I said, it wasn't dying, and he said, you don't know what dying is, then he started coughing in a way that left little doubt that on this subject at least his knowledge was vastly greater than mine.

"Do you want some water?" I asked.

He waved me away, stood up and went into the kitchen. I heard him washing his coffee cup. "What are you doing here, anyway?" he shouted.

"Packing up the house," I said.

"Then pack up the house, and don't get mixed up with people who hate us."

The screen door banged shut. I sat in the living room, hurt

by my uncle's words. Was he really so confused, I wondered, that he thought the Regenzeits were out to get us? It was ridiculous. People like Charles were the problem, I thought, intolerant people who can't let go of the past.

After a while, I went up to my mothers' room and opened one of Celeste's trunks. It was full of magazines and newspapers heaped up roughly according to size, the raw materials of her work. What the Rowlands had accumulated, Celeste cut up: worn back numbers of *Scribner's Magazine*, *McClure's*, *Harper's*, *Frank Leslie's Illustrated Newspaper*, mixed in with issues of *Life* and *Vogue* and *Look*. I used to look in the trunks when I came to visit in the summer, each time stealthily, as though I were breaking a rule; in fact no one said anything to me about the trunks and I don't think my grandparents would have minded if they'd known. I liked the way the holes Celeste had cut in the pages of the old magazines acted as windows onto the pages behind, so that where the head of, say, a Bohemian fortune-teller was supposed to be, you'd see words or parts of words:

> little known epis
> the remarkable discover
> ich it directly and indirectly
> properly be regarded as m
> the progress of thought
> . The central figur
> young woman
> ome scoundrel
> oor of her cot

Now that I was looking at them again, the effect was completely different. The magazines seemed to me typical of Celeste's angry way of dealing with the world: she took what she needed with no regard for anyone else.

I opened the second trunk, where she kept her collages.

Each white sheet was kept safe in a big black sheet of paper folded in half. I unfolded the top sheet and picked up the collage beneath. It had a woodcut of a feather, angled as if drifting toward the bottom of the page; above it a slender hand in a lace cuff reached down, either to let it go or to pick it up again. Below the feather, at the center of the page, set between quotation marks that had been pasted down separately, was part of a typewritten phrase: "ollow me." *Follow me*, it must have been, or, just possibly, *hollow me*. The date was penciled in the bottom right corner, in neat, small letters, July 1970. I was about to be born. I had seen the collage before, but something passed through me as I sat on the floor, looking at the paper, a cool dark something like the shadow of a cloud. It was as if Celeste were about to tell me something. I opened the second folder. This collage was from April of the same year; it showed a pair of hands on the keys of an enormous typewriter, and, emerging from the top of the machine, the prow of an airship. Cherubs beckoned to the airship from above, while from the bottom of the page a Chinese dragon rolled its eyes angrily. The references to birth, to my birth, were easier to spot than in the other: the cherubs, the round head of the zeppelin poking out of the typewriter's slot. The dragon might have been my grandfather. Still, I was disappointed. *Ollow me*, the first picture said, and I wanted to ollow, to follow, but how could I follow when I didn't know where it went? The collages led backward, further into the past, away from me and my time. Celeste's style devolved, words and blocks of text appeared, floral borders, dancers, neckties and the heads of famous people. The collages retained their formal elegance but became, unmistakably, the work of a young person. Ollow me, ollow me. If only there had been another collage to show me where to go, but there was nothing, because, in July 1970, probably no more than a few days after she made this collage, Celeste and her sister left Thebes. They were seventeen and a half years old, and they took with them nothing, or almost nothing: a warm protrusion that would in a few months become a child.

LOW-FLYING STARS

It was for my sake that my mothers ran away from Thebes. They didn't want to have their child in a little town in the Catskills where things happened so slowly that people were still speaking French six generations after the first settlers arrived. By Thebes standards, my mothers were more like weather than like people: they changed fast, and they moved on. They took me to New York, where they were going to be famous artists, only they had no idea about money and knew how to do nothing, nothing. For a few scary years in the 1970s my mothers barely scraped by, she, waitressing, and she, clerking in a photo lab; she, selling ladies' clothes, and she, waitressing; she, answering telephones for a Senegalese clairvoyant, and she, answering telephones for an Israeli dentist. The three of us, she, she, and me, lived in an apartment on West Ninety-eighth Street, with two tiny bedrooms and a view, if you leaned dangerously far out the living-room window, of a blue-gray shard that was alleged to be the Hudson River.

Later, when they had real jobs and even health insurance, my mothers liked to tell stories about those years, to prove how tough we had all been and how close we'd come to not making it. There was the time, Celeste said, when she lit a fire in the ornamental fireplace, because the heat in the apartment was broken, and how was she supposed to know the chimney had been sealed since the nineteenth century? The apartment filled with smoke and the three of us were nearly evicted and if you lifted the living-room rug you could still see the burned boards where the fire had spread before the super put it out, using a blanket from my mothers' bed, which was a technique for fire prevention that Celeste had never seen before. And the worst of it was, she said, that afterward the blanket was ruined, and she and her sister had to sleep in their coats.

"You slept in *my* coat," Marie said, if she was present. "Your coat had those big horn buttons, remember? You said they dug into you?"

Celeste pretended to be perplexed. "But if I slept in your coat, what did you sleep in?"

"Sweaters, I guess."

"Those were difficult times."

There was something in Celeste's voice, though, that made me think she missed those years, that in retrospect they seemed less difficult than the ones that came later. My mothers went to Hunter College; after they graduated Celeste got a job teaching art to middle-school students in the Bronx. Marie worked in the offices of semilegitimate publications with names like *California Lifestyle* and *Platonic Caves,* typing, making copies, answering the telephone, always in a short skirt, which Celeste didn't approve of, but Marie rebutted that she couldn't type to save her life, and without the skirts she'd be back to working for the clairvoyant, who could, presumably, see up her skirt no matter how long it was.

In the evenings my mothers sat at their worktables in the living room, making their art. They knitted sweaters for monsters with wrong arms and extra heads; they stamped papier-mâché medallions of modern saints of their own invention; they mixed brightly colored fluids in the sink and bottled them in glass phials on which they pasted labels, Potion of Temporary Resistance to Temptation, Elixir of Getting That Opportunity Back, Low-Flying Potion, Potion for Those Afraid to Drink the Other Potions in This Collection. Celeste painted miniature landscapes in the manner of Hieronymus Bosch, in which the Upper West Side revealed its true, hellish character; Marie applied a Ouija board to a subway map and took photographs of the places the spirits told her to go. I loved the things they made, which was fortunate, because our apartment was becoming a museum of their work. The potions took up residence in the medicine cabinet; the demons capered over the nonworking fireplace. I found a three-armed sweater in my dresser, a joke, I think, but maybe not; the apartment wasn't big and my mothers were always making.

They weren't famous yet, but they had friends, and those friends had friends who had taken steps in that direction. My mothers talked about them all the time, enthusiastically but not uncritically, as though they, my mothers, were commenting on a sport from which they themselves had retired some years before. From their conversation I got the impression that it wasn't hard to become famous. One day a gallery owner came to visit, and the next you had a show; the critic from the *Times* praised your work even if he didn't understand what it was about. Then collectors sought you out, and you had to be careful; it was important to turn away from the collectors and their vulgar need, to encapsulate yourself in solitude and silence, so that you could emerge a few years later with your mature work, which was extremely difficult and cut no deals with anybody. That's when the museums took you on, and afterward things happened without you, international exhibitions, retrospectives, scholarly monographs; the secret nominators spoke your name in secret and you got the MacArthur genius grant and as to what happened after that, why, you could imagine it yourself. With a mixture of excitement and dread—I wanted them to get their wish, but I didn't know what would happen to me when they did—I pictured my mothers rising into the sky like two unwinking stars, possessed, finally, of all the solitude and silence they could ask for. Mostly it was a matter of not making mistakes along the way. Not like Leonora Kurtz, who worked with Marie, and had talent but *listened to her boyfriend too much*; not like Donatello DelAmbrosio, Celeste's friend of the wonderful name, *who needed to get out of the shadow of Fluxus.* Not like Katy Gladwin, whose paintings were *too theoretical,* or Hugh Heap, whose string sculptures were *cute but not really about anything,* or Guy Anstine, whose white boxes were *just white boxes, you've seen one you've seen a thousand.* Not like Javier Provo, whose murals were in a Warhol movie and who was becoming actually famous, but was nonetheless *completely preoccupied with his own body image.* My mothers would not make these mistakes. They were ready to go up; they were waiting in our apartment, waiting and making.

Maybe their potions weren't strong enough, maybe the demons they compacted with turned out not to have the powers they, the demons, had promised, maybe their saints were spurious; the ascension my mothers were waiting for did not arrive. Of course we were still waiting for it. We would always be waiting for it, but by the time I was nine or ten years old, my mothers had begun to glance backward to those first years in New York when food was scarce and success certain.

"You remember the time we saw that rat?" Celeste asked Marie wistfully. "It was about four feet long, sitting on the kitchen windowsill?"

"*I* saw the rat," Marie said. "I told you about it. You wouldn't come and look."

"There were a lot of rats on the Upper West Side back then. Do you remember?" she asked me.

"No," I said. "I remember bugs, but no rats."

"Ah, bugs," said Celeste. "Those enormous roaches. I remember when I was taking a bath, and this roach fell into the tub. I'd never seen such an enormous cockroach."

"I remember your scream," Marie said. "I'd never heard such an enormous scream."

"Those were difficult times," Celeste said.

Celeste Marie, Marie Celeste. My low-flying stars.

I spent the rest of the day on the sofa, reading *Progress in Flying Machines*. When it got dark I thought about going over to the Regenzeits'. I had promised Kerem I would visit soon, that I would consider myself a part of the family, just like I had been in the old days, but no one was home. They must be working late, I thought, getting Snowbird ready for the winter. I imagined Yesim at her desk, a pencil stuck in her hair. I imagined a brilliant blue day, the ground crackling with golden leaves, Yesim and me sitting on the Regenzeits' porch, wearing bulky sweaters, holding mugs of hot cider. Then, in my imagination, one of my hands unpeeled itself from the side of the cup and settled on Yesim's shoulder. In no time my tongue was in her mouth, my hands were in her black hair. In my imagination.

It was raining in gray sheets when I woke up the next morning, and with the rain came the autumn cold. I didn't know how to turn on the heat; finally I went to the basement and looked at the furnace. It had gone out, and I couldn't get it to start. I called the furnace company; they said they'd send someone as soon as they could. Looking out the kitchen window, I determined that Yesim drove a Subaru Outback, and Kerem a Ford Explorer. I went up to the attic bedroom and discovered that the boxes that filled the room were full of questionnaires left over from my grandfather's lawsuit. Put a check next to every statement you agree with: 1. Morning is the time when I feel best. 2. My weight stays the same all year round. 3. I rarely cry for no reason. 4. I consider myself a "social person." I sat on the bed and spent a long time thinking about I don't know what. At five o'clock I called the furnace people again. A woman explained to me that they were waiting for a shipment of heating oil, which had not arrived because of a late-season hurricane in the Gulf of Mexico. You want heat, talk to

ExxonMobil, she said. I told her that I didn't think Exxon-Mobil would take my call. Maybe not, she said, her voice weary and stiff.

Around six-thirty, I drove to town and bought a six-pack of Genesee Cream Ale and a box of chocolate donuts. Two teenage girls stood outside the gas station, in the shelter by the pumps, wearing more makeup than I would have expected girls at a gas station to wear.

"Hey, mister," one of them said as I passed, "will you get us some beer?" She was prettier than she looked at first; I wanted to tell her not to wear so much makeup. I said I'd give each of them a beer if they wanted, but I didn't feel comfortable buying them more than that.

The girl said they needed it for a party, it wasn't like they were going to drink it all. I said no, really, I couldn't, and the girl sighed and said, "OK, give us each a beer."

I wondered whose daughter she was, where she lived, whether she had grown up in Thebes. For a moment I thought of asking if I could go to the party, if only so that I would have something to do on Saturday night. But the thought of being at a party, any party, was unpleasant, and in any case I doubted the girls would agree to take me. I pulled two beers out of the six-pack and handed them to the girls, with a warning not to drink in public. They rolled their eyes and made complicated hand gestures, as if communicating how uptight I was to a deaf observer.

When I got home, the Outback was alone in the Regenzeits' driveway. I watched a martial-arts film on television. "You will be punished," said the hero, or the hero's dubber. "All of you. Punished!" I wanted to correct his use of the passive voice, I wanted there to be heat, I wanted to be done with the packing, which I hadn't even begun. Instead I showered, washed my hair and shaved under the hot water, which, thankfully, still worked. I put on a clean shirt, found a bottle of wine in my grandparents' pantry and went across to the Regenzeits' house.

Yesim was wearing a big shapeless sweater; her hair was tied back in a squiggly ponytail. I held up my bottle of wine and said I was afraid we'd drunk their entire supply the other night.

"Oh, no," Yesim said, "Kerem always has more hiding somewhere."

I thought that would be the end of our conversation, but Yesim, after hesitating for a moment, asked if I wanted to come in. I said I didn't want to interrupt her, it was late, I was sure she had things to do.

"You wouldn't say that if you knew me," Yesim said.

We sat in the kitchen, which hadn't changed much since I was a child. The olive-green tin canisters that said FLOUR and COFFEE and SUGAR in orange faux-woodblock lettering still stood on their rack; the same red-and-white-checked tablecloth still covered the round kitchen table. The old white curtains printed with blue game birds hung before the window; the same clock counted off COCA-COLA TIME over the massive olive-green refrigerator. Now that Mrs. Regenzeit had returned with her husband to Turkey, I wondered whether she missed the Populuxe splendor of her kitchen, the streamlined mixer, the color-coded fondue forks she sometimes used to twist her long black hair into a bun. Yesim made us tea. I asked whether her parents liked living in Akbez, and Yesim said she didn't know, she hardly spoke to them anymore. "The truth is," she said, "I can't talk to my father now that he's found religion."

"He's found religion?" I remembered Joe Regenzeit as having been religious already. Hadn't he thanked the god whose name I misheard as *Olaf* for nearly everything?

"Yes, he's become a fanatic. It's his way of saying *fuck you* to secular America." The Yesim I remembered would not have said something like this. She did not curse; in fact, despite her sexual curiosity, she had always seemed to me somehow innocent. She told me that Joe Regenzeit had joined a *medrese*, that every third word out of his mouth was *obscene* or *whore.* Referring to America sometimes, and sometimes to Yesim.

"It sounds like he's gone off the deep end."

"Yes," Yesim said, "and the really strange thing is, he wants me to come live with him. It's the only thing that will save me, he says."

"Save you from what?"

"Myself, I think he means, but probably America, too."

"It doesn't sound like a hard decision. Don't go."

"What if he's right?" Yesim asked.

I wanted to ask what he might be right about, but Yesim didn't look as if she wanted to be questioned. Instead I asked how Snowbird was doing, and Yesim told me they were building a terrain park for snowboarders, basically a place for them to break their arms and legs. "It's all right with me as long as they don't sue," she said.

Some Coca-Cola time passed silently.

"I'm glad we're still friends," I said.

Yesim smiled. "Were we friends? I thought you were friends with my brother."

"What about the summer when Kerem went to soccer camp? What about *Man and Woman*?"

"What?"

"You don't remember?"

"Oh, that," Yesim said finally. "I'd forgotten what it was called."

"I used to think about it all the time."

"Is that so?"

"Never mind," I said, blushing. "I'm babbling. My grandfather's house doesn't have heat, and the cold must have affected my brain. I'm used to San Francisco weather, although it gets cold there too . . ."

"If you don't have any heat, you should stay here," Yesim said. It was as though she were telling me that if I touched the stove I would burn myself.

She offered to make up a bed for me in the study. I protested, I'd be in Kerem's way, and anyway there were plenty of blankets at my grandparents' house. Yesim said Kerem was visiting Kathy and Max in Philadelphia and it was really no trouble. "Just stay there. I'll get things ready." I studied my reflection in the toaster: I was elongated, bent beyond all recognition. My hands were enormous and unusable. Yesim came back. She didn't know where Kerem kept his pajamas, would I be all right?

I would give a lot to know what Yesim was thinking as she led me upstairs to Kerem's study, where she'd made up a bed on her brother's black leather sofa. Did she feel sorry for me? Did what I told her set some idea in motion, some desire? All I know is that she smiled, or seemed to be smiling.

ADVENTURE

All through the winter that followed the summer of *Man and Woman*, I dreamed of seeing Yesim naked again, and when spring came I was in an erotic frenzy. I was a year closer to manhood, and I imagined Yesim as having made even more progress toward maturity. What wouldn't we be able to do, once I had woken her from her enchanted sleep? I'd discovered masturbation that year, and if that was what *that* felt like, I imagined that lying with Yesim would be something completely unearthly. With strange courage I asked my mothers to send me to Thebes the day after school ended, and to my surprise, they agreed.

"If you want to see your grandparents so badly, of course we'll send you," Celeste said, as though it had been my diffidence, and not theirs, which kept me in New York, some years, until the beginning of July.

I got on the Trailways bus triumphantly, and when my grandmother picked me up in Maplecrest (the bus didn't stop in Thebes), I was so excited that I couldn't speak. This worried my grandmother, and when we got home she called my mothers. "You sent him too soon!" she said. "He doesn't want to be here!" I can only imagine what my mothers replied. I wasn't there: I'd already dropped my bag and run across to the Regenzeits'.

Mrs. Regenzeit was on the phone, but she motioned for me to sit down, opened the refrigerator, took out a bowl of twilight-purple eggplant and set it on the table. "I don't give one sheet about that," she said, opened a drawer and handed me a fork. "He should know better than to listen to such stupid things. Yes, goodbye." She hung up the phone forcefully.

"Is Yesim home?" I asked, my mouth still full.

"Yesim? Yes, she is here. But I don't think she is alone."

I climbed the stairs, my stomach light with nervousness, and knocked on Yesim's door.

"Come in," Yesim said, and I went in, and found her sitting cross-legged on a pillow, and across from her, seated on a pillow also, a girl with long brown hair which fell across her face as she leaned forward to play an Uno card. "Oh, it's you," Yesim said. "I didn't know you were coming back." The other girl sat up and parted her hair just a little, revealing a skinny nose and a gleaming brown eye. "This is Matilda," Yesim said. "She's my best friend." Both of them giggled, as though to suggest that they had become best friends by virtue of a long and humorous adventure, over the course of which their other, non-best friends had one by one been killed off.

"Who's winning?" I asked.

"She is," Yesim said, as I could have seen for myself from the few cards that remained in Matilda's hand.

"Can I play?"

Matilda looked at me with horror, as though I were a biology experiment from which she had been excused for ethical reasons.

"Not now," Yesim said, and with a grunt of satisfaction, played the Wild Draw 4 card.

"You bitch!" Matilda shrieked. "I hate you, I hate you, I hate you, I hate you."

I backed out of the room and pulled the door closed quietly, no longer a prince, only a palace eunuch, dismissed and fearful for his head.

Downstairs, Mrs. Regenzeit beamed at me with full consciousness of what I might be feeling and asked, "You like that?" Meaning the eggplant. I nodded. "Good. Now listen, I need your help."

Kerem was in trouble, she told me. Soccer had made him popular and popularity had turned him into a hoodlum. "He used to have good friends, people like you who make good marks in school and read books, but now his friends put safety pins into their pants. One of them has shaved part of his head, not the whole thing, and now Kerem is talking about doing that too." Mrs. Regenzeit did not know what would be next, whether it would be drugs or crime or what people did when they had hair like that. "We try to talk to him," she said, "but in his head there is only the terrible music he listens to."

"Do you want me to talk to him?" I asked.

"No," Mrs. Regenzeit said. "What could you tell him that we did not say?" She stabbed the air. "I want you to work with him on the computer."

This, Mrs. Regenzeit explained, was their latest and maybe their last hope for Kerem, a computer they had ordered from a catalog, which might get him interested in science and mathematics. The computer came in a kit, the whole family had labored long to assemble it, Mr. Regenzeit had given up many hours of work, and finally they'd hired an engineering student from Rensselaer Polytechnic to finish the job. Now it was working, but would it work?

"You're a good boy," Mrs. Regenzeit said. "Help him to take an interest in this computer."

Kerem came downstairs, rubbing his eyes and scowling. In the last nine months he had become skinny and pointed and his curly black hair stood on end with the support of some glistening goo. He looked like Spencer Bartnik, a social pariah in my class at the Nederland School for Boys who was renowned for his frequent and disruptive midclass nosebleeds.

"Good morning, Kerem," Mrs. Regenzeit said sweetly.

I wanted to ask him a thousand questions. Finally, timidly, I asked if he was going to soccer camp again this summer?

"Football," Kerem said. "The name of it is football. It's only Americans who call it soccer." Unbidden, he explained to me that last August he'd met an English assistant coach named Billy, who had demonstrated to him the superiority of all things English, and, incidentally, turned him on to punk rock. "He got me started on the Pistols, right."

"If you say so."

"That wasn't a real question," Kerem said. "You just say *right* at the end of a sentence, right."

I didn't say anything.

"Right," Kerem said. "Let's go upstairs."

England had invaded Kerem's bedroom, and brought with it disorder and the smell of feet. A big Union Jack hung over his bed, and opposite it a poster of Sid Vicious, who also looked like Spencer Bartnik, and who was, according to the poster, dead. Then full-color photographs of soccer players, or *footballers*, as I was supposed to call them now, razor-cut from imported magazines, ruddy men who seemed to be all tendon, caught in midleap, grimacing, as though they were keeping themselves aloft by force of will. The bed was covered with clothes and the remnants of more than one meal. I asked Kerem if that was where he slept. "Naw." He pointed to a sleeping bag that lay unrolled by the window. "I'm squatting." He steered me to the desk, where a gray box waited inertly: this was the computer, the last hope for his salvation.

Computers belonged, at that point, more to my imaginary world than to the world I shared with other people. Computers were *2001* and *Forbidden Planet*; they were big, blinking cabinets, sinister friends who did what you wanted to but couldn't, like causing the New York subway to trap your enemies in perpetual darkness, or could but didn't want to, like math homework. They looked nothing like the Heathkit H88 on Kerem's desk, a gray box like a bulbous TV set, devoid of lights and switches, an appliance that was no more exciting in appearance than my grandmother's microwave oven, and considerably less exciting than her electric toothbrush, which, with its rocket-ship styling and brightly colored interchangeable heads, its three speeds and warm rechargeable battery, seemed truly to announce the beginning of a new era. But this computer was real.

"Check it out," Kerem said. He switched the machine on, and on the gray screen, underneath a pennant for Manchester United, green words appeared and vanished, leaving only a prompt,

>

the beginning of the beginning. The Heathkit H88 was intended more for serious hobbyists than for recreational users, and came with no software other than a BASIC interpreter and a game, intended to demonstrate the computer's capabilities, where letters and numbers appeared near the top of the screen and fell slowly downward; you had to type each one on the keyboard before it reached the bottom, or you lost. Kerem played a game, then I played. It was too easy at first, then, as the letters speeded up, it became too hard. Only a machine could have kept up after the third or fourth round.

"It's stupid," Kerem admitted, "but look at this." He typed,

```
>10 PRINT "FUCK YOU!"
>20 GOTO 10
>RUN
```

and an unstoppable column of insult flickered up the screen.
That was power. It didn't matter that it was a tiny, ineffectual
kind of power that would strike no fear into the hearts of my
enemies nor save me from any trouble; all that mattered was
that the gray box was in our camp. It did what we wanted
without questioning; our power was, in the first instance, power
over it. We taught the box new obscenities, and had it shout
them over and over at the top of its lungs, until Kerem's mother
called him down to dinner.

I wanted more. By the end of that first day Kerem and
I reached an understanding that seemed brilliant to us at the
time, although it had disastrous consequences for me later on:
I would teach myself to program the computer, and Kerem
would take the credit. I wouldn't have known where to start,
but the Heathkit came with a book of programs you could
type in to play games, perform calculations, or sort a list of
names in alphabetical order. Even the shortest program was
many dozens of lines long, and stayed in the computer's memory only until you switched the power off. If you wanted to
run it again after that, you had to retype the whole thing. The
work was excruciating, endless, monastic, exalting. If I typed
a line wrong, the only way to correct my mistake was to type
the entire line again; if I didn't catch it right away, the Heathkit would bide its time, then ambush me with a syntax error
when I tried to run the program. The screen was tall enough
to display only twenty lines at a time, which meant that I had
to check my work in tiny increments, looking for a typo-
graphical error that was sometimes to be found in the book
itself.

I worked in Kerem's room while he slept, twisted up in a
torn t-shirt, on a sleeping bag by the window. After a couple of

hours he woke up. He looked around the room and sighed, as though the people who were supposed to take care of the décor had once again let him down.

"I fucking hate America," he said.

"Too bad you live here," I said, nettled.

"It *is* too bad, mate. I'm getting out as soon as I can. America is full of racist hicks."

"Where are you going?"

"London."

"They don't have racists in London?"

"You'd better believe they don't." Then, reconsidering, Kerem said, "Or if they do, they get their asses kicked by red-lace skinheads."

I didn't believe him, but I couldn't refute him either. Kerem stalked to the bathroom; I heard him pee, then water in the sink. When he came out, he pulled on the jeans he'd worn the night before and we went downstairs.

"Morning, Mum," Kerem mumbled, forgetting that he was supposed to have been awake for hours.

"You have a good lesson?" Mrs. Regenzeit asked.

"Really good," I said.

Kerem agreed that I was making progress. He jogged down the hill, kicking at rocks, dodging the invisible members of the opposing team. I went home. At dinner I listened impatiently as my grandfather read us the news from the *Catskill Eagle*. Eastern Gas was laying a new main in Ashland; police had chased a group of suspicious youths out of the cemetery; meanwhile the library was selling unwanted books to raise money for its new reading room. I helped my grandmother clear the table and wash up, then I went to the Regenzeits'. Kerem was listening to a tape he'd made off the radio, Dave Stein's show from WCDB. He paced around his room, looking for something, a sock, a leather wristband.

"Where are you going?" I asked.

"None of your business."

"Did you ever go to the cemetery?"

Kerem glared at me. "Mate," he muttered, "stick to the box."

He found what he was looking for and climbed out the window; the rubber cleats of his *football boots* shushed down the garage roof.

I was afraid that Mrs. Regenzeit would discover our trick, but she never did. She must have wanted badly to believe that the computer was working, that Kerem was working. How she believed! Sometimes, when I came over in the morning, I'd hear her talking on the phone about her son, the whiz kid. All of the signs that she'd read formerly as meaning that Kerem was in trouble now meant that he was a genius. He had messy hair, he wore the same clothes day after day, he didn't speak much, but on the computer he was something! I think Mrs. Regenzeit believed he was the equal of the young Bobby Fischer, or the boy in Florida who could solve any Rubik's Cube in a minute flat. I didn't mind that Kerem's genius was all my doing, because I got to listen to his music: Minor Threat and Murphy's Law, the Dead Kennedys, the Circle Jerks, a live Sex Pistols recording that had been copied and recopied until Johnny Rotten's call to the faithless was practically lost under the hiss of tape. I shared his secret. What was better, what was even better, Kerem passed on to me a portion of the adoration he was getting from his parents. He was the *whiz kid*, but I was the Wiz. One night he took me with him, down to the steps of the public library, which were broad, deep and secluded. I met his friends, a boy named Eric with a shock of red hair and protruding ears; a girl named Shelley who had made her skirt by cutting up a sweatshirt and sewing it back together. Kerem introduced me as his mate from New York City, and Shelley and Eric drew long hollow breaths.

"I really want to go there," Shelley said. "I've just got to check out the scene in New York."

"Lower East Side," Eric said. "CBGB, right?"

I thought he meant the SeaBees, the Navy engineers. I wondered if there was a naval training center in lower Manhattan.

"When we come to New York," Shelley said, "can we stay with you?"

"I can ask," I said, "but my apartment is pretty small."

We walked to the Texaco station and stood by the pumps, watching people go in and out of the convenience store. Now and then one of the group would point to a customer and murmur to the others: Known fag. Definite fag. Total fag. Once Shelley approached a couple of men in a low-slung Camaro and persuaded them to buy her cigarettes. She offered me one; I said no but this didn't change Shelley's mistaken idea of my status.

"I shouldn't be smoking either," she said. "My mom's really on me to quit."

We talked about what we would do if the world ended. "Like if there was a nuclear war," Eric said, "but all the people up in the mountains were OK."

"We'd still have democracy," Shelley said. "You can bet the people up here would keep it going."

"Not bloody likely," said Kerem. "You wouldn't have television, so there couldn't be democracy. You can't have democracy without television."

"You could still vote on stuff, though," Eric said.

"Television and the central bank," said Kerem, who had ordered some tracts from an ad in the back of one of his *football* magazines. "Without that, you have anarchy."

"Anarchy!" My friends knocked their beer cans together.

"What I think is, we would still be together," Shelley said. "No matter what other people were doing, you know?"

We agreed that we would be anarchists together. Shelley would make our clothes, and Eric would provide our food, because his family had a farm farther down the valley, with cows and shit. Kerem would be the leader, because he knew the most about how anarchy was supposed to go. And I, "You'd be, like, my adviser," Kerem said. "You'd help me plan our takeover." Because we wouldn't be content to be isolated anarchists. We'd get other people to join; we'd spread anarchy up and down the valley, and on the far side of the mountains. The apocalypse held no more fear for me that night. I leaned back against the convenience store's wall and closed my eyes, warm with the knowledge that I wouldn't ever have to be alone.

"My adviser is falling asleep," Kerem said. "I better take him home."

My magnum opus that summer was a game called Adventure. It was at the back of the book of programs that came with the computer, and I avoided it for weeks because it was much, much longer than any of the other programs, a thousand lines or more, an epic of code. It was written more densely than the other programs, also, so that it was hard to figure out what the game was supposed to do. I tried to make sense of the long DATA statements, the multidimensional arrays, the variables marked with unfamiliar signs, the complex string functions, the subroutines, but I kept getting lost; I hoped the Heathkit would understand it better than I did.

For a long time, Adventure did nothing at all. With each line I fixed, a new error manifested itself, more cunning than the last one had been, better at hiding its true nature, or appearing to be in one part of the program while in fact it was in an entirely different part. I was haunted by the thought that someone would turn the computer off before I was finished, or that there would be an accident, Kerem would trip over the power cord, a storm would blow down the lines that led to his house, a generator would fail, Russian missiles would arc over the horizon, civilization would collapse with Adventure still unfinished. I had stomach pains, dark circles under my eyes, and the beginnings of an irreversible stoop. My grandparents worried about me.

"What's that Turk teaching you now?" my grandfather asked.

"He's tutoring me in science," I said.

"So Kerem's good at science?" asked my grandmother.

"Yeah. He's a whiz kid."

"I'm glad to hear it," my grandmother said. "I heard he was in trouble."

She let the subject drop, but, and this was my grandmother's usual strategy, she returned to it days later, hoping to catch me off guard. "*You'd* know," she said, looking up from the Sunday newspaper. "How does oxygen become ozone?" Or, as she trimmed bushes in the backyard, "Maybe you can tell me, are these little critters going to turn into butterflies?"

But I had learned something from Kerem. "Unh," I said, studying the green squiggles that scurried across the underside of a leaf.

My grandmother shook her head. "Go eat something. You look as gray as a grub yourself."

It must have been late July when I finished Adventure. Something gave, something moved, something opened. Run, I could say, and it would run. Nothing flashed across the screen, no dancing letters, no space invaders, no canary cries or ping-pong pings. Only words.

Entrance to Cave

You are standing outside a dark and gloomy cave.
There is a gold key here.

>

I had made a world. Not a large world, not even, from any reasonable point of view, an interesting world, but a world nonetheless. Compared with the work of getting the program to run, the adventure of Adventure was absurdly simple. You typed,

>take key

and took the key; you went into the gloomy cave and crossed the subterranean river at the ford, you found the sword, surprised the troll and navigated the maze where all the rooms looked exactly alike. You entered the castle, you read the note, you opened the secret door and found the locked treasure chest. Did you have the gold key? You did, you did! The castle, the maze, the troll, the river and the cave were the whole of my kingdom, but they were, to my mind, like one of the holograms pressed into a tiny button or pin, where, as you turn it in your hands, a three-dimensional pattern seems to repeat itself in infinite space. I saw not what was there but what could be there, if only I had written it, a world of rooms where I would be free to wander as I pleased. It was as though the gray box had been working in secret to fulfill my oldest dream about its powers, although, like many dreams, the coming true bore only a metaphorical or tangential relation to the dream itself. Yes, I could know all, do all, create and destroy at my whim, I could make subways and strand my enemies within them, yes, everything, yes, only I would have to do it in the gray box. It was enough.

It was too much to take in. After I had unlocked the treasure chest and won the game twice, I needed to tell someone what I had done. I found Kerem with Shelley and Eric at the gas station.

"My game works!" I said.

"Oh?" Kerem frowned at me, as though he'd expected me to say something completely different. "Yeah, OK, that's great. Good work."

"We have to play," I said, "before the power goes out."

"Play what?" Shelley asked.

"This game I wrote on the computer," I said.

"You wrote a computer game? Wow!" Shelley put her head very close to mine and whispered, "We're a little stoned."

I nodded gravely, as though Shelley had told me that the three of them had contracted an incurable disease. Their lives had become more serious, suddenly, and also more exciting. They would probably die. But secretly, if their being stoned meant that I got to have Shelley's breath in my ear, I was all for it. Eric was hopping in tiny circles around the air pump.

"Are you ready?" Shelley asked Kerem.

"Shelley's brother is having a party," Kerem said. He must have felt bad that he hadn't appreciated my game, because he added, "Want to come?"

"We're going to have a great time," Shelley said.

"OK," I said. Consequences were whirling around me in a cloud of great seriousness. If, and if, else if, else. Then. Then. Then.

ADVENTURE

You are standing at the entrance to a dark and gloomy cave. Ahead of you, in the darkness, there is music.

"You're OK?" Kerem asks. "Just be cool, and if anything happens that you don't like, come find me. OK?"

Say OK.

"Let's go-oo," Shelley moans.

You follow Kerem and Shelley and Eric into the cave.

You're in Shelley's brother's apartment, on the second floor of an apartment complex at the far end of Thebes, by the storage facility and the graveyard. There are many people here, and you don't know any of them, although some of their faces are familiar from town. There's the guy who works at the grocery store, and there's one of the guys from the ski shop. You associate them so closely with those places that seeing them here is like being in a dream, where heads are pasted on new bodies and one city borrows the name of another. What's more, everyone in the room is twice your size. Shelley has gone off to talk to her brother, and Eric is talking to the grocery-store guy. Only Kerem stays with you, and only because he doesn't know anyone here, any more than you do.

"Let's get some beers," he says.

Follow Kerem. You follow him into the kitchen, which is, if anything, even more crowded than the living room. You are pressed by waists, hips. Girls in tall vinyl boots are laughing. Men are looking at you, they want to know what you are doing here. Kerem opens the refrigerator and gets a can of beer for himself and one for you. It tastes awful, but you hope that if you are seen drinking, people may mistake you for a midget, or a late-blooming fifteen-year-old. Kerem says something to you, but everyone is talking at once and you can't understand him. He waves, he is leaving you, he is gone. You are alone in the forest of giants.

"Hi," says a girl with vast blond hair. "What's your name?"

Say your name.

"How old are you?"

Lie.

"Do you live in Thebes?"

"In New York," you say.

"Oh, wow, that's really great!"

You tell the tall girl about New York. She screams, "Mike!" and one of the giants turns around. "I want you to meet my new friend."

"Hey." Mike tips his beer toward you.

"Hey," you say, and tip your beer toward Mike.

"He's from New York," the tall girl says.

This is good, Mike no longer looks at you as if you were a pituitary oddity. For all he knows, everyone in New York looks like this. It might be something in the drinking water. Keep people small to make the housing more efficient.

"The big city," Mike says. "I love it! Wish I got there more often."

"It's not very far away," you say, emboldened. "There's a bus from Maplecrest. It's like two and a half hours, and it goes straight to the Port Authority."

Mike grimaces. You didn't need to tell him about the bus. You turn to the tall girl, hoping for reassurance. "Do you ever go to the city?" She shrugs as though now she doesn't know what city you're talking about. "Or do you mostly stay up here in Thebes?"

You have come to a dead end.

Find Kerem? You look for him in the living room, but there are too many big people; if you go into that crowd you may never come out. You end up perched on the back of a sofa next to a kid with stripes shaved in his hair, who is willing to talk to you about the Dead Kennedys. "I kind of like the lyrics," you say. "Like, you know, too drunk to fuck? That's funny."

The kid looks at you. "Have you ever fucked?"

"No," you admit. There is a lull in your conversation. "Have you?"

The kid shrugs. "I think so."

Much later, you'll understand that this is what Mrs. Regenzeit meant by *only part of his head*, and you will laugh, and wish you could tell her that there is nothing to fear from the partially shaved. You excuse yourself, you have to pee. You wait on line for the bathroom.

Shelley is here. "Oh, my god," she says, "it's you!" She takes your hand. "I am so happy to see you." Her eyes are red. "I just don't feel like I ever got a chance to know you, and I think you're probably a really great person." She tells you how few great people there are in the world, and how her ambition is to own a big farmhouse somewhere in the mountains, and to get them all together, the great people, in a big sleeping loft in the barn, and, like, talk. The bathroom door opens.

"Don't go away," Shelley says.

She goes in, she comes out, you go in. You have never peed so quickly in your life. But she's gone when you come out, and you can't find her again. The apartment is crowded with strangers, and not one of them wants anything from you at all. What is this game you're playing? Who wrote the code for it? You wish you were back in Kerem's room, seated in front of the Heathkit H88, but you aren't. You go back into the kitchen. Three boys are sitting at the table, taking turns throwing a quarter into a glass of beer. If the quarter goes in, they drink; if it doesn't go in, they drink. One of them is dangerously overweight and appears to have been dipped in oil. He takes the quarter out of the glass and licks it on both sides.

"You want to play?" he asks.

You understand now that this is a game with no victory conditions. The rooms lead only to other rooms, and there is no treasure in any of them, and no way out of the cave once you have gone in. You aren't afraid anymore, but you can't remember ever having been as sad as you are now.

Leave world.

You can't leave that.

Go.

Where do you want to go? The kitchen is full of smoke, and there's no place for you to sit, and you suspect that people are looking at you again, thinking midget thoughts. You find a door that leads out to a balcony. From here you can see the graveyard, the upslope of the ski hill, the stars. A few people Mike's size are leaning on the railing and talking. They pay no attention to you. You sit on the ground with your back to the wall. You are suddenly very tired. You fall asleep.

Time passes . . .

Lightning wakes you up. A storm has crossed into the valley; the wind hisses through the trees across the road. Beyond the roof's overhang, rain falls in sheets. The big people have gone inside, sensibly. The thunder breaks over you, then the lightning, then the thunder again. You would be happy to stay here all night, watching the weather.

Shelley finds you. "Thank God," she says. "I thought you might have left." She sits next to you and takes your hand. "I'm so glad Kerem brought you. He's sweet. Do you think he likes me?"

"Definitely."

Shelley rests her head on your shoulder. "It's just so hard, you know?" She complains that Kerem has been avoiding her; she's afraid that he drinks too much and smokes too much pot. You aren't sure you should hear these things, but you're so grateful that someone, anyone, Shelley! has found you that you will listen to anything.

"You know what I think the problem is, really?" says Shelley. "Thebes is so small. Kerem needs to be somewhere big, like New York City." She gives you an unreadable look.

Read it? You can't. It's unreadable.

"Do you want to kiss me?" Shelley asks. You would like to, but you don't know how. Shelley presses her hands to your cheeks, immobilizing your head. Suddenly her tongue is in your mouth. Her eyes are closed; you stare at the smudges where her eye shadow used to be.

"Mmm," Shelley says, and lets go of your head. "You're a good kisser." Compared with what, you wonder. Robots? "Don't tell Kerem," she says.

Shelley goes inside. A few minutes later, you go in too. The shiny boy still sits in the kitchen, resting his chins on his hands, staring at a half-full glass of beer.

"Your turn," he says.

The living room is ruined, human beings will never live here again. Kerem and Shelley are holding hands in the middle of the room.

"Where did you go?" you ask Kerem reproachfully.

"Where did *you* go?" Kerem asks. "I spent half the night

looking for you. I thought one of Mike's friends had stuffed you in a closet."

"I think we should sleep here," Shelley says. "If we go out, we're going to get soaked."

"Do you think Mike will let us?" Kerem asks.

You imagine the two of them lying together on the sofa, or on one of the coat-covered beds. You want to prevent them from doing this. Here's the prompt: act promptly.

"I'm going home," you shout. "Come on!"

Run.

The wind takes you like a downed leaf, it pushes you down the street, and when you look back, you see that Kerem is running after you. "Punk lives!" he shouts, and he kicks over a newspaper box. Copies of the *Catskill Eagle* tumble out and are blown away. You run up the hill as fast as you can, the wind very strong at your back, so that it seems as though you're flying.

When you're almost home, doubled over and out of breath, Kerem grabs your shoulder and presses you against a soaking tree. "Promise me you won't tell anyone what you did to-night," he says.

You promise, you never will.

The next morning you learn that the storm knocked down a power line, and Adventure is gone. It doesn't matter. You have already won. Did you kiss Shelley? You did, you did!

REGENZEIT

At some time in the night I woke up, and Yesim was sitting on the edge of the sofa. She was wearing a white t-shirt and flan-nel pajama bottoms. I pressed her hand to my face. It smelled of soap; the skin along the side of her index finger was dry. I opened my mouth and Yesim put her finger between my lips. I sucked on her finger; it had no taste beyond the smell of soap. Yesim made a small happy noise. I squeezed her flannel thigh just above the knee and let my hand travel upward. Yesim wasn't wearing a bra; I put my hand under her shirt and confirmed my suspicion: almost imperceptible hairs covered her back. Yesim leaned toward me. The tips of her breasts brushed my chest. My hand moved farther up her back, to the space between her shoulder blades, and then down to the waistband of her pajamas. "Don't," Yesim sighed, after a while. "Sleep."

REGENZEIT

When I woke up again, Yesim was in the living room, drinking coffee and watching the news. "I'm engaged," she said. "Did you know that? I'm supposed to get married next June."

"Congratulations," I mumbled.

She told me that her fiancé was someone she had worked with in Albany, at an employment agency that staffed construction jobs. They had gone out for years, on and off, and had just become engaged when her father got sick and she returned to Thebes. Since then they had put off the wedding twice. Her fiancé, Mark, was very patient.

"Yesim," I began.

"I know. It's a little late to be telling you this, but Mark isn't the most important thing about me. He's not always the first thing I talk about. But I owe him a lot. I can't tell you what a mess I was when I met him."

"You can tell me. I complained to you last night, didn't I?"

"This is worse," Yesim said. She told me that she had gone through a hard time after she graduated from college, a very hard time. It began when she moved to Cambridge to work as the personal assistant to a famous poet whom she'd call Professor X. Yesim herself was writing poems, which was something she'd always done, though it was only in college, when she won a prize offered by a real literary journal with nationwide distribution, that she began to think of writing as something she might do instead of other things, rather than along with them. Anyway, she was living in Cambridge, and spending most of her time in the car, because Professor X suffered from chronic weakness in her legs, which was almost certainly psychosomatic, but nonetheless prevented her from driving or walking any distance, so that the work of being her assistant turned out mostly to involve driving Professor X around and waiting for her to emerge from buildings that Yesim wasn't invited to enter. After a few months of this vehicle-bound life, Yesim abruptly and stormily left Professor X. She got a job waiting tables at a restaurant called Casablanca, where her Middle Eastern looks compensated for her lack of experience, and sat up late in her studio apartment on Mt. Auburn Street, writing poems that came slowly and turned out to be ill formed. One night, while she was writing, she had the sensation that a hand was closing on her throat. The feeling went away, then returned; it got so bad that black stars with green coronas appeared in her field of vision, as though she were asphyxiating.

Yesim thought it might be strep throat, or asthma, or maybe the city air had found some latent flaw in her lungs. She went to a doctor; the doctor found nothing. She thought that if only she knew whose hand was grabbing her by the throat, she might be able to do something about it, which was, she admitted, a ridiculous way of thinking, but at the time it really was as though someone had cast a spell on her, as though someone's hand were seizing the throat of a doll as someone's voice muttered a spell. Whose hand was it, whose voice? Yesim suspected the jilted Professor X, who was witchy, if not literally a witch. Her condition worsened. She quit her job, and she wanted to leave Cambridge but couldn't think of anywhere she wanted to go, or what she would do once she got there. It was as though the crooked streets, the plan of which she had never been able to master, were keeping her in, like the walls of a maze. She left her apartment on Mt. Auburn Street less and less often, only to get food, then not even to get food. If her father hadn't come for her, she didn't know what would have happened, but he did come. She weighed ninety-eight pounds. Her father, not a large man, carried her downstairs and drove her out of Cambridge, although, she noted with satisfaction, he got lost on his way to the Mass Pike. The city's evil influence affected everyone.

Joe Regenzeit took her to the Pines, a clinic near Albany. She wouldn't say too much about it, except that it wasn't a malign place, just quiet. It was so quiet, sometimes she imagined that she had died and no sound that came from the world could reach her any longer, as though the hand had let go of her throat too late; now she could speak but there was no one left to listen. Eventually, Yesim moved to an apartment that she shared with other women who had graduated from the Pines, and in time she took a job at the staffing agency. The work was not demanding and she enjoyed the compactness of the lives that passed through her hands, file-sized lives, on their way to file-sized jobs. They were almost like poems, but with the advantage that they never had to be revised or read aloud. She met Mark, a large, competent person, who had been a construction worker in an earlier life. He was a decade older than she was; his first question, after they kissed for the first time, was whether she wanted children, and her answer was yes, of course. If only her father hadn't got sick, they would have gone ahead with all the plans they'd made with natural, heartening quickness: to marry, to buy a house that Mark would fix up, to have a child, children. Yesim really did want children, she'd always wanted them. She could have been happy forever after. Only Joe Regenzeit did get sick, and because he had saved Yesim's life—seriously, she was certain she would have died on Mt. Auburn Street, that Cambridge would have let her die—she owed him the effort to save his life in return. There wasn't much more to tell, Yesim said. Her father got better and left for Akbez, while she stayed on in Thebes.

As I listened to her story, I thought about how much Yesim and I had in common. We had both fucked up, or maybe we *were* both fucked up, and we'd both come to Thebes to start over. What if we could start over together? Of course I didn't say anything about that. I nodded and tried to look grave. But inside, I was thinking about the future.

Meanwhile, Yesim was talking about Mark again. "He used to come up here," she said, "but the visits went so badly, he said he'd wait in Albany until I'm through figuring out what I need to figure out."

"What's that?"

"Whether I'm going back."

Yesim said she had to go; as she climbed into the Outback I took her hand. She left her hand in mine for just a second, then took it back. She attached no importance to the gesture; it was as though she were about to leave her hand behind then remembered that she would need it after all.

LOST THINGS

Charles came over that afternoon to help with the packing. "Goddamn, this place is an icebox," he said. "Don't you want to turn on the heat?" I explained about the hurricane in the Gulf of Mexico. Charles snorted. He took his cane and limped down to the basement. He studied the furnace, sniffed, lit a match and stuck it into a hole near the base of the big cylinder. With an explosive *whumph* the heat came on, grumbling and grinding its way back into the house. I said we didn't have central heating in San Francisco, I'd never needed to know how it worked before. "OK, Mr. California." Charles laughed. "Let it go." I wanted to tell him not to call me that, but I was afraid we'd start to fight again. We went upstairs and sat in the kitchen, looking awkwardly past each other. For days I'd been thinking of how to apologize to Charles, but now he was here the words wouldn't come, and it was my uncle who spoke first.

"I've been thinking about you. How it must have been hard for you to grow up without a father. And with the twins, jeezus."

"I don't know," I said. "I never grew up any other way."

"Still, I guess you have the right to be angry."

"I'm not angry."

"Come on," Charles said. "Even I'm angry at him."

"At my father?"

"Sure. At what he did."

"Because he killed himself, you mean?"

My uncle shook his head. "I'm talking about when he was alive. Richard Ente was the biggest hippie bastard that ever lived."

"A hippie?" Goodbye, Sean Connery, I thought. "But he was my grandfather's age."

"He was. He was an old hippie. Or maybe just an old man who wanted to be young again. I don't pretend I ever understood him. I'm just telling you, he did things that no one should ever have done, definitely not someone his age. I'm not offending you, am I?"

"Go on."

As Charles spoke, the father I'd built from a few sentences, a word here and there, a shrug, a frown, was drowned under the mass of his words—it was, to change metaphors, as though the currency *father* was devalued, and my savings were worth nothing. If that was all the father I had, I might as well have had none at all. And here, striding up out of nowhere, came the new, high-denomination Richard Ente, a fifty-year-old hippie who smoked pot and inclined his head to get a better view every time one of the Celestes bent forward.

"He didn't even try to hide what he was doing," Charles said. "Oliver, he said, you have two lovely daughters, I'll buy them from you for a dozen camels. Like he was some tribal Jew in the desert, which is really what he should have been. I bet he would have done all right in the desert." Richard Ente told bad jokes at the dinner table and got food in his salt-and-pepper beard. He came to Thebes by bus because he barely knew how to drive a car. He didn't wear deodorant, he didn't cut his nails, he didn't wear socks. He ended sentences with the word *dig*. And from the first he was after the Celestes. "You know how he got away with it? I'll tell you. Richard was very shrewd, and one of his talents was to guess what you were dreaming, not like in your sleep, but what you *wanted*, and then he'd say that thing out loud, and be, like, that is certainly going to happen. And since you heard it coming from another person, who didn't know you'd been dreaming of it, you thought maybe that meant it would happen. He got us all that way."

Richard Ente made promises to everyone. To Oliver he promised victory, and not just that: he said that if the lawsuit went the way he thought it would, Joe Regenzeit would pack up and leave. To Mary, my grandmother, he promised the world. "She'd always wanted to travel," Charles said, "but she'd never been able to, on account of Oliver not having enough money, and being generally tied to Thebes." To the Celestes he promised fame. "He was, like, you girls are geniuses, and you aren't getting what you deserve here, and I know some people in New York who would really be into what you're doing. Why don't you let me introduce you? He told them he was friends with Andy Warhol!" There was, apparently, no lie of which my father was not capable. And the Celestes, who were smart, and should have known better, believed him. "He said he'd get them a loft in New York. He told them they could model. Like, part-time, for good money, right? You tell me if *that* happened."

It didn't, I said, but I was still thinking about what my uncle had said earlier. "He smoked pot?"

"All the time."

"And he had long hair?"

"A ponytail."

"What kind of music did he like?"

"Joan Buy-yez, that kind of thing. He even had a bead necklace. Can you imagine that, a fifty-year-old man in a bead necklace? He was ridiculous!"

"Wow." I felt giddy: the child who had been saving all his life was suddenly rich. I had more *father* than I knew what to do with. And yet the new Richard Ente that I had received from my uncle didn't fit either with the story I had told myself as a child or with the fact of his suicide. My uncle and my mothers and I were like witnesses identifying different people in a lineup; and like a stubborn eyewitness I continued to believe that the Richard *I* saw (even if I had never seen him) was the one who had done it. Charles must have got him wrong. Maybe he had misinterpreted Richard's behavior, although what he could have misinterpreted to come up with *his* Richard Ente, I had no idea.

"Anyway," my uncle said, "I'm here if there's anything you want to get off your chest."

We spent the rest of the day cleaning out the basement. I didn't get anything off my chest, other than dozens of heavy boxes, the contents of my grandfather's woodworking shop. If anything, it seemed to me that Charles was the one who still had something on his chest; now and then he looked at me as though he was about to say something, but he didn't. I didn't press him. It was only after he left, when I was in the kitchen, drinking the last of the beers I'd bought the day before, that I remembered something he had told me a long time ago that fit with his description of Richard Ente, something that made me wonder if my uncle had not, after all, been right.

After the storm wiped Adventure from Kerem's computer, I lived in a state of excited inaction, as though, like the Heathkit, I lacked instructions about what to do next. I avoided Kerem and didn't go to town to look for his friends. It didn't even occur to me to find Shelley again. I was consumed by the feeling that something was going to happen, something wonderful, but because I knew it was going to happen I wanted to put it off just a little longer.

"Aren't you getting behind in your studies?" my grandmother asked.

"We're taking a break," I said.

"Oh, a break," she repeated, as though this were even less plausible than my studies had been in the first place. "Well, a few days away from the Regenzeit boy won't do you any harm."

Then it turned out that I had waited too long, and the glorious something I'd been waiting for was no longer mine to enjoy. Mrs. Regenzeit telephoned my grandfather to inform him that Kerem had been arrested for smoking marijuana in the cemetery, that I might be involved too, because I'd been spending so much time with her son, and that she was *peaced* as hell. "All right," my grandfather said stiffly, and hung up the phone while Mrs. Regenzeit was still talking. His dislike for the Regenzeits, his outrage at the implication that I could have been responsible for corrupting one of them, and his astonishment at Mrs. Regenzeit's indelicacy in breaking a ten years' silence just to tell him so, all together convinced my grandfather that the whole business was the fault of the perfidious Turks. He warned me about falling in with bad company, and told me how important it was to find out what people were really like before you put your trust in them. It was like choosing antiques, he said, some people looked good on the outside but when you opened them up you saw there was just nothing you could do, whereas other people, who didn't look so good, could be fixed up, and would, with a little work, become solid, usable friends. He patted the arm of the chair on which he sat. It gave a solid, usable thump. It was all I could do not to remind him that he hadn't fixed the chair; it had come into the house via my grandmother's sister, who had donated it because there wasn't a decent place in the whole house to sit. He forbade me to see Kerem again and that was all.

My grandmother was less convinced of my innocence, and her reproaches were harder to endure. When I said something in her presence, even if it was the most innocent and matter-of-fact statement, for example, that I wasn't going to the lake because the radio said it would rain, she seemed to break what I had said into its component parts to determine whether the statement was worthy of her trust. If the clouds overhead convinced her that I was justified in staying indoors, or if she happened to have heard the same weather report, she would nod hesitantly, as though she were taking a chance on me despite her better judgment. If, on the other hand, the weather looked fair from where she stood, my grandmother would only shrug, as though to say, who knows what you will do, you, who doesn't tell us the truth?

I began to understand certain things my mothers had said about my grandmother. Sometimes, at the end of their frequent though brief conversations, Celeste would grind the telephone receiver back into its cradle and cry out, "That unforgiving so-and-so!" Then it would be Marie's job to tease from her an account of what had gone wrong, an account that always began the same way, "This time she's really lost her mind!" I used to think this was just Celeste being her angry self, but that summer I wondered what it would have been like to have my grandmother for a mother, to be the object, again and again, of her shrug. It was no wonder my mothers ran away from Thebes, I realized, and in fact, my mothers' hardness, their self-containedness, their unwillingness to give out information, especially with respect to Richard Ente, all made more sense to me now that I knew what doubt my grand-mother was capable of. Her shrug explained my mothers, and it taught me everything I had left to learn about heredity. And heredity, naturally, made me think of Richard Ente. Was it possible that traces of him remained in the people—me—who he had left behind?

One day, when the forecast was fair, and I had no reason in the world not to go to the lake with my uncle, I turned to Charles and asked, "Why did my father run away from Thebes?"

Charles sighed as though he had been expecting the question for a long time. He rolled onto his stomach, baring the tattoo on his right shoulder, *Je te frapperai sans colère.* "I'll tell you," he said, "but you have to keep it to yourself. Promise?"

"Yes."

"Just between you and me, then, your father told me he was going to discover America."

"America," I repeated, amazed. We had studied the discovery of America in our history class the year before, and I knew that Christopher Columbus was an Italian, and that he had named the continent for another Italian, Amerigo Vespucci, which, I thought, meant that really it should be called Vespuccia. I said so in class and got laughed at, and afterward Ronald Kaplan taunted me, *Ve-spooge-ia,* the land of spooge, and I'd been embarrassed. Then something about Leif Eriksson and the Vikings who had perhaps discovered another part of it. My father didn't fit into either of these stories, so I guessed that Charles meant some other kind of discovery, or maybe some other America, a continent with the same name as ours that nobody had discovered yet, which was a thrilling idea but not probable, given the size of continents and the advanced state of geographical knowledge.

"Did he discover it?" I asked.

"Maybe," Charles said. "Maybe he did."

My father had gone to discover America. It's just the kind

of thing an aging hippie might have said before hitting the road, circa 1970, but to me it had a different force: not that of truth, but that of myth. I stood up, brushed the sand from my legs and dove into the lake, down as far as I could go, beneath the children whose legs hung down like dark branches from the silver overhead.

Charles's secret was about to get me into a lot of trouble, but I didn't know it and in fact I had other things on my mind. A few days after our trip to the lake, I went home to New York and found my mothers changed. Celeste wore a cardigan and pants, like an old man; she'd pulled her hair back into a bun, uncovering the whole of a face that looked more and more like my grandfather's, big, waxy and serious. Marie, meanwhile, had permed her hair into loose curls, and, what I found even more shocking, wore dark-red lipstick that made her look like a film star from the 1940s.

"What happened to your lips?" I asked.

Celeste laughed.

Marie was working for *S* now, as an assistant to the Quick Styles editor, and already something of the magazine's glamour had been transferred to her, in the form of narrow black skirts that she bought from the designers at a discount, and little jars of beauty products which she got for free and arranged on the bathroom sink, where the potions of imaginary powers had once stood guard. In the medicine cabinet, there was a small, round beige plastic case, whose purpose I wouldn't have been able to guess, except that next to it lay a tube of contraceptive jelly, crinkled at the bottom. A new kind of potion for a new kind of life. Celeste, meanwhile, had given up talking.

"Did you have a good summer?" I asked her, but it was Marie who answered, "Comme ci, comme ça, you know? Up and down. Celeste hasn't been working." Celeste, not work? But she was always working. Something tremendous must have happened while I was away, a reversal of my mothers' polarity, so that Marie was now leading the way, and Celeste trailed behind.

I was so puzzled by my mothers that it didn't occur to me that their perspective on me might have changed also, and I was surprised when Marie asked me at dinner, "What happened to you?"

"To me?" I squeaked.

"It looks like you did a lot of growing up this summer."

"Not really," I mumbled. "I was just hanging around." I was afraid the Celestes would mention the lies I'd told my grandparents, but they never did. Either they didn't know about them, or they'd dismissed them as nonsense from my grandmother, the unforgiving so-and-so.

"Hanging around with a girl, I bet," said Marie.

"No," I lied, "just with Kerem."

"The Regenzeit boy?" Celeste said. "Hm."

"Anyway, you look older," Marie said. "I like the way you're doing your hair." I'd experimented with gel, in imitation of Kerem.

"Thanks," I said. "I like your hair, too."

"Ha!" said Celeste.

Marie blushed and touched her curls. "The magazine did it for free."

As soon as the meal was over I fled to my room and put on one of the cassettes I'd dubbed from Kerem. After a few minutes Celeste opened my door and stuck her head in.

"What's that music?" she asked.

"Dead Kennedys."

"Hm," said Celeste, and closed my door again.

It was as though my mothers no longer had any idea what to do with me, as though they were a childless couple taking in an orphan, a child who belonged only to a mystery. I was a mystery, I had been kissed, my father had discovered America, and in this exalted state I began my seventh and final year at—or as I sometimes thought, in—Nederland.

The Nederland School for Boys was founded by the Dutch a long time ago. How long ago, exactly, was a subject for perpetual inquiry by the school librarian, an enormous shiny man who looked very much like Thomas Nast's caricatures of Boss Tweed, and who discovered, once or twice a decade, a document that proved the school had been founded at an earlier date than anyone had dared to guess. With due ceremony the year on the school's coat of arms was changed and the Board of Trustees ordered new letterhead for the staff. Occasionally this led to incongruities, as when Nederland celebrated its 350th and 375th anniversaries only two years apart. My mothers were invited to both galas, and the school's pretensions became, for a while, one of their favorite jokes. In a few years Nederland would be older than New York, older than the New World, older, probably, than the rock it was built on. I laughed with the Celestes, but with the consciousness of being wronged: they were the ones who had chosen the school for me in the first place. I think they sent me to Nederland because it was close to our apartment, twenty blocks down West End Avenue; also, and more to the point, I started first grade at a happy moment in the seventies when Nederland's trustees, moved by the protests of some upperclassmen and recent alumni, raised scholarship money for underprivileged students. My mothers were poor but not unsavory, I did well on the entrance exam and the end of the story was that I went to school practically for free, provided that I kept my grades up and posed yearly for a special group photograph.

My last year there began as every year did, with an assembly in the Great Hall, which was what Nederland called its auditorium, where our principal, Mr. Van Horn, a grim homunculus who might for all we knew have been as old as the school itself, amplified for us on the motto, *Recht Maakt Maakt,* or Justice Is Our Strength, and on the importance of correct behavior generally. We, clean, chilly and newly awed by the gloom of the Great Hall and the red banners that hung from the ceiling, celebrating NEDERLAND AT 375, behaved correctly for about as long as the assembly lasted, then we were released to our homerooms and began the important business of sizing one another up. Who posed a new threat? Who had something new to offer? The truth was that most of us had been at Nederland since the first grade, and we already knew more or less everything we could expect from one another. We were like characters on a long-running soap opera, who are required to display the same personalities for so long that they stop being personalities at all, and become mere functions, guidelines for the production of dialogue in the style of X or Y. August Waxman, who had been the fastest runner in the third grade, fished for something in his nose; next to him Andrew Ames, honor student, drew insane rabbits in the margins of a blank notebook. David Metzger had finally convinced his parents to let him grow his hair long, like the singer of Def Leppard, whose name I forget but who has certainly not been forgotten by David Metzger, wherever he is now. Ronald Kaplan and Gideon Peel, indistinct, indistinguishable, had spent the summer in the Hamptons and said they'd both got laid. "Right," sneered John De Luca, who had curly black hairs on the backs of his knuckles, "more like you fucked each other up the ass." There it was, *ass* and *fuck* in the same sentence, a sign that the gloves were once again off. The rituals had all been observed; Mr. Fitch could yell at us to be silent and the year could begin.

Actually two things marked the year as different from the ones that had come before: we had American history with Mr. Savage, and I discovered Nederland's computer room. The two strands which, twined each around the other, would occupy the next twenty years of my life, presented themselves almost simultaneously, maybe even on the same day, but at first I understood the importance of only one of them. The computer room was housed in the basement of the New Building, formerly a residential hotel, which the school had purchased in the sixties and renovated in a fantasia of Formica panels and fluorescent lights. The computer room was down there because no one knew, yet, how important computers would be, whether they would spread, like coeducation, or dwindle, like civics and home ec. Still, the trustees had approved the purchase of a magnificent machine, an Alpha Micro with ten terminals and eighty megabytes of storage, which seemed like enough room for all the information in the world, although now you could emulate five hundred such machines at once on a cheap laptop. There was a dot-matrix printer and a staggering stack of manuals, thousands of pages of instructions, all written in a language that presupposed that you already knew how to do the thing you were trying to learn. As soon as I found my way to that low, stuffy basement, I knew that I wanted to re-create Adventure on a vastly larger scale, a world of words without end. But it was beyond my ability to make even the smallest part of my world appear on the other side of the terminal's dull glass. I had typed Adventure in from a book, and although I figured out many things about how the program worked in the course of getting it to run, the ideas behind it remained completely mysterious to me. I was like a caveman who had, by dint of banging, repaired an automobile, and now set out to build himself a new car. With a great deal of effort I could make nonworking replicas of some features of the original, a seat, a wheel, a grinding sound, but no matter how well I made these things they wouldn't add up to a vehicle, or take me anywhere.

One day I came home late and Celeste, who was home already, told me that I was looking serious, which was the highest compliment she ever paid anyone. "What are you doing?" she asked.

"Working on the computer."

"Hm," said Celeste. She mistrusted computers herself and had very little idea how they worked. "Well, it looks like you're doing it seriously."

I threw myself on my bed. I didn't feel serious, only consumed, exhausted, permanently puzzled. At dinner Celeste asked me questions about programming, which even someone who knew more about it than I did might have found difficult to answer. "How does the computer know what you want?" I tried to explain that it wasn't about what you wanted, you had to say things just so. "But what if you mean one thing, and the computer means another?" Impossible; all the words in computer language had fixed meanings. "The words, all right, but what about the sentences?" I dodged, I ducked, I grunted Keremishly. I was a caveman, but Celeste refused to believe it. No matter what I said, she nodded gravely and asked another question.

By the time we came to dessert, even Marie could see that I'd run out of answers, and she tried, out of pity, I think, to change the subject. "You won't ever guess what happened at the magazine today," she began, but Celeste interrupted, "Hold on. This computer thing is serious, and I think we should take it seriously."

Celeste's faith in me was steep and sharp. She gave me a book called *Algorithmic Programming in Structured BASIC*. "For every logical function *f*," the preface began, and that was as far as I got. In retrospect it seems clear that Celeste was using me to leapfrog over her sister, who was, she feared, getting ahead of her, her sister whose new clothes she mocked because they were only a *fashion uniform*, her sister who was making money, her sister who was invited to *media events* where she made friends with *media people*, with *sheep*, with *those Ivy League bitches* who ran New York. At the time, I knew only that Celeste's confidence was hard to take, almost as hard as her doubt had been. I wanted to be the person she believed in, but I was constantly afraid she would figure out that I was not that person, I was no kind of programmer, I was a caveman, banging stones together and grunting in something that wasn't a language yet, not even to me.

THE DISCOVERY OF AMERICA

In class I sat by the window, looked at the sky and thought about my invented world. My teachers were happy to let me go. I was quiet and as long as I did well on their tests and showed no signs of abusing alcohol or drugs, unlike August Waxman, who came to school one day with pupils the width of pencil leads and his shirt buttoned askew, and said, *Say what?* to every question, no matter how many times you asked it, Mr. Fitch didn't mind if I slumped forward in my chair, and Mrs. Booth let my unrolled French *r* pass without comment. Only Mr. Savage, who taught American history, still wanted something from me. "You asleep?" he shouted when I rested my head against the wall. "Wake up, we're making history here!" He called on me to answer questions, and embarrassed me when I didn't know the answers, oblivious to the rolling eyes of my classmates, who had seen me embarrassed so many times that they could take only a moderate pleasure from it. Mr. Savage didn't know this. He was a new teacher who had come to Nederland the year before from a public school in Detroit. He was short and dark, with menacing eyebrows and a five-o'clock shadow that was in full bloom by one-fifteen, and he dressed like a plumber at a funeral. Mr. Savage had made the mistake of telling last year's American history class that he had a black belt in jujitsu, and could flip someone twice his weight. Now, when he bored us, Ronald Kaplan would raise his hand and ask, "Um, is it hard to learn jujitsu?" And when one of us misbehaved, the others would shout, "Flip him! Flip him!" Mr. Savage was not amused. "Violence is serious," he said, the first week of American history. "If you learn only one thing this year, it should be that violence is serious." *Violence is serious*, I wrote in my notebook; then I stopped listening again.

"Hey! How's the weather?" Mr. Savage called to me.

I opened my eyes. "Partly cloudy."

"You think it's going to rain?"

I looked at the sky. Low lumpy clouds grazed the spire of the chapel, the black weathervane with a figure of a Dutchman atop it, the school's emblem. "It might."

"No chance," said Mr. Savage. "Those are stratocumulus clouds. You never get rain from stratocumulus."

He continued the lesson as if this checking of the weather were an ordinary event. Gideon Peel looked at me and rolled his eyes. I couldn't tell if he meant that I was an asshole for not knowing that stratocumulus clouds were not rain-bearing, or that Mr. Savage was crazy for telling me so. I rolled my eyes back and returned to the window.

Mr. Savage stopped me as I was leaving class. "Why don't you come with me?" he said. He led me to one of the small rooms, furnished with a coffee warmer, some vinyl chairs and a strong sour smell, where the teachers lived. He asked if I wanted coffee, I said no. "You aren't paying attention," said Mr. Savage. "You don't notice anything. It's like you're living on another planet." How close you are to the truth, I thought. "Are you like this in all your classes?"

"Yes." It was the truth, and besides he was a decent person and I didn't want him to think I found his class any less interesting than the others.

"What is it? What do you think about?" I wanted to tell him about the game, but it would have been too humiliating to confess that I was consumed by a project I didn't have any idea how to do and would probably never figure out. The secret of it was all I had; if I told him I would have nothing. "Are you thinking about girls? I could understand that," Mr. Savage said.

"I think it's terrible that you don't have girls here. You're like"—he waved his hand again—"you're like astronauts, on some space station up in orbit." He shifted his jacket, which was, I saw, too small for him; in another life he could have been an athlete, or a bouncer. I was afraid that he would pick me up by the lapels of my jacket, lean his stubbled face to mine and whisper threats featuring the word *youse*, even though there was only one of me. I giggled. "Astronauts, it's funny, right? But you have to learn how to live on earth." Mr. Savage struck his knee with his fist. "Help me," he said. "If there was one thing you wanted to learn, something you really wanted to know, what would it be?"

"I don't know."

"Anything," said Mr. Savage. "Just one thing you want to know."

I looked at the coffeepot. "Maybe the discovery of America." It came into my mind because of what Charles had told me.

"Really?" said Mr. Savage. "Who discovered America?"

"Columbus or Leif Eriksson," I said. "We had it in world history last year."

"But you're not convinced, is that right?"

"I guess."

"Good." Mr. Savage tapped my breastbone with a thick finger. "That's a good place to begin."

The next day, Mr. Savage asked how many of us had read Plato's *Timaeus*. Not a hand went up. "In that dialogue," Mr. Savage said, "Critias tells Socrates a story that comes from the priests at Thebes, which is where? Andrew, yes. Egypt. Thebes is the oldest city in Egypt, which is quite possibly the oldest nation in the world. The priests at Thebes told a story which was already thousands of years old, about a land to the west of the western ocean, which they called Atlantis." He wrote ATLANTIS on the blackboard. "Anyone heard of it?" So we embarked on the discovery of America, the discovery of the discovery of America. Strange facts were coming to light in Mr. Savage's sixth-period class, stories about seafarers and prevailing winds, about the climate in Greenland and the Gulf Stream, about carved stones and burial mounds. For a week, it couldn't have been more than a week, we studied the people who might have discovered America, not only the Vikings, but the Phoenicians, the Basques, the Chinese; there was a story that Welshmen had been the first Europeans to arrive in North America, so we learned about that. Mr. Savage spared us nothing, not even the story that the Indians were one of the Lost Tribes of Israel, the proof of which was that the Jews, like the Indians, once lived in tents, that both races had been known to anoint themselves with oil and that the Indians did not eat pork, or at least some of them didn't.

Our textbook had nothing to say on these subjects, so Mr. Savage photocopied the maps drawn by people who had seen much, a little or none of the New World, the fantastic maps that show California as a peninsula the size of all the rest of North America, the maps that stocked the interior with lions, serpents, dragons and gold. "Why gold? Matt, yes. Good, yes, so that people would keep exploring." We kept exploring. Mr. Savage talked about cannibals, about how each tribe the Europeans met reported that there was another tribe, over there, who ate human flesh. "Anyone want to draw any conclusions? Andrew, yes."

Reactions to the unit, which put us a week behind the other section of American history, taught by Mr. Rye, a very tall man with yellow teeth, were mixed.

"Man is crazy," said Gideon Peel after the first class. "He smoke too much weed."

"He is a disciple of the pipe," Ronald Kaplan said. "His thoughts are unsound."

David Metzger liked the idea that the Indians were from Israel. "Jews, yo!" He pumped his fist in the air. "You honkies can all get off our land!"

"Dude, even if the Indians were Jews, that doesn't make us honkies," said Gideon Peel.

"You are so a honky," said Ronald Kaplan, whose father was Jewish.

"And besides, we did this last year. History is repeating itself, man."

I kept quiet. There was no way I could have explained what I felt when I looked at the maps, how, running my finger over the big whiteness between the coasts, I went queasy with excitement, as though what Charles had told me was literally true, and my father was hidden somewhere on the map, a tiny black dot, not reproduced at this scale, but there all the same. As though, when I looked at the map, I was also, in some obscure, magical way, looking for him.

At the end of the week Mr. Savage divided us into groups, each of which had to make the case that a different people had discovered America. The group that made the most convincing argument would receive a pizza lunch. I was, with David Metzger, Andrew Ames and Matt Bark, the Chinese, not a good assignment. We met in the school library, where we found no books on the subject of the Chinese discovery of America, no mention of it, even.

"Well, so we make it up," said Matt Bark.

"We can't make it up, that's plagiarism," said David Metzger.

We argued about whether it was plagiarism if you were just lying, and concluded that it might be all right. But I held out for facts.

"There are no facts," said Matt Bark.

"Just rock and roll," said David Metzger.

"It's not fair," Andrew Ames said. "We should have got the Vikings."

I said that I could probably find some facts, and that afternoon I took the Broadway bus to the public library on Fifth Avenue and Forty-second Street. It was the first time I'd ever gone there, and of course I wasn't allowed in; only adults could enter the Reading Room. My first encounter with the library was an anticlimax; I was shunted to the Mid-Manhattan Library two blocks south, where men in smelly coats coughed in the fluorescent light. I leafed through a book on the Chinese navy, and another on ancient seafarers, and learned about the Polynesian islanders who navigated by means of knotted strings, an interesting subject but not one that convinced Matt Bark to change his plan.

"String, fuck, this isn't a report on string."

"But imagine, if the Chinese had these string maps . . ."

Matt put up his hand. "Shut up, weather boy."

"Weather boy." David Metzger laughed.

"You shut up," I said.

No one acknowledged me. I slumped in my chair and closed my eyes. There was no use in fighting them; the facts were all on their side. How could I argue when I didn't know what kind of clouds rained and what kinds didn't?

On the appointed day, Gideon Peel reported to our class that archaeologists had found Norse houses in northern Newfoundland, dating from around the year 1000. If the Vikings hadn't discovered America, he concluded, prudently, at least they'd been here before Columbus. John De Luca stumped for the Phoenicians, the first masters of the ocean; he described the Phoenician inscriptions found on rocks in Brazil, and also certain man-sized slabs of stone found in a cave in New Hampshire, which, he said, smiling, were probably sacrificial altars left behind by the Phoenician priests. John explained that the Phoenicians sacrificed human beings to the great god Baal, whose wrath could be appeased only by blood, so probably virgins had been tied to these New Hampshire slabs, and stabbed, and stabbed, with bronze daggers, which by the way people had also found in New England. When the harvest was bad, or the wind blew the wrong way, or someone was angry, whoa, human sacrifice! The blood of the virgins steamed on the cold stone, and John's smile grew wider and wider, and the great god Baal too was pleased, because he was a god of war and destruction and he could drink *gallons* of blood . . .

"OK, John, thanks," Mr. Savage said.

John sat down heavily. Wayne Echeverria spoke briefly for the Basques, then Matt Bark gave our group's report on a certain Admiral Ho, who was blown across the Pacific by a storm, and founded a Chinese colony on the California coast. The proof of it was that there was more Chinese food on the West Coast of America than there was on the East, not to mention the dish that was actually called Admiral Ho's shrimp, which Matt Bark had eaten in Los Angeles and which was, he assured us, very tasty. And then there were the Chinese place names in America, for instance, San Francisc . . . ho! and San Dieg . . . ho! and even, even the legendary El Dorad . . . Ronald Kaplan began making strangled laughter noises halfway through, and before Matt Bark could finish he put his head on his desk and moaned, "Oh, my god, oh, my god," and he wouldn't look up, even when Mr. Savage yelled at him to stop, and that was it, everyone was laughing, and when Mr. Savage tried to raise Ronald back to a sitting position, Gideon Peel thought we were finally going to get the jujitsu demonstration, and howled, "Flip!"

Mr. Savage took Ronald and Gideon out and stood them in the hall; he came back and told the rest of us, quietly, without anger, that it was good to laugh sometimes, and that it was true, sometimes the things you studied as history were just stories that someone had made up, but the important thing, in this case, was to make up a good story, he didn't expect us to understand, but he would tell us anyway, that this effort was in some ways the most important thing, more important than memorizing dates or the amendments to the Constitution, and that if we learned anything from him that year, it was that we should try as hard as we could to tell a good story, if we tried hard enough we would get to the truth somehow. No one reminded him that if we learned one thing, it was supposed to be that violence was serious, but we must all have been thinking it.

"The Vikings win," Mr. Savage said.

I tried to catch his eye, to communicate that it hadn't been my fault, but he wouldn't look at me. The Vikings went out to pizza and American history picked up where it had left off. The Puritans were making treaties with the Indians, the French were up to no good in the woods, the Dutch founded schools, among them Nederland, glory, glory be. The story about Admiral Ho got back to Mr. Rye, who was the head of the History Department, and Mr. Rye talked to Mr. Savage, and that was it, there were no more deviations from the textbook. Oh, but I got my revenge: with the help of something the middle-school principal let slip, I figured out how to log in to the school's accounting system, where I gave Matt Bark and David Metzger each a five-thousand-dollar charge for athletic equipment.

Soon afterward we had Christmas vacation. I spent most of it in my room, avoiding my mothers, who were embroiled in a series of small but bitter arguments about the holiday parties to which Marie was invited and Celeste was not. On New Year's Eve, I went with Celeste to a party in a SoHo loft that belonged to a famous art critic in her sixties. When we arrived, the critic was sitting on a black leather sofa, her legs folded under her, like the stone image of a primitive god.

"You're early!" she shouted at Celeste. "Why did you come so early?"

"The invitation said ten o'clock," said Celeste hesitantly. I'd never heard her hesitate before.

"How stupid of you," said the critic. "Now you've interrupted my meditation."

"I'm sorry. We can go."

"Too late! I've already come out of it. You'll have to sit down and endure my displeasure. Well, sit!" The critic lit a cigarillo and poured herself a glass of bourbon; the bottle stood on the table in front of her, an aid to meditation, I supposed. "What are you working on?" she asked.

This was the era when Celeste was working with fabric: she made costumes for bodies that could never be, gowns for women with no heads or arms. At home, she talked about the costumes as *explorations*, but now, fixed by the critic's stare, Celeste froze. "Clothes," she said finally in a schoolgirl's voice.

"Clothes!" boomed the critic. "You're letting your sister's job rub off on you. Celeste, my darling, when are you going to understand, it's not an advantage to be a twin?"

Celeste blushed, but the critic's attention had already turned elsewhere. "Is this your son? He looks interesting. What does he do?"

"Tell her," murmured Celeste.

"I write computer games," I said.

"Yes," said the art critic. "And you like music?"

"I guess so."

"Who?"

"Sex Pistols?"

"Ha!" said the critic. "You're just at the beginning." For two hours she talked about the musicians she'd known in the East Village in the seventies: Johnny and Lizzy, Debbie and Patti, Richard, Lou, and David who wore a dress everywhere. The names didn't matter, although years later I would learn who they were, some of them.

"David in a dress?" Alex would shake his head sadly. "You are an ignorant motherfucker."

"Why, who was that, David Byrne?"

"Haven't you ever heard of the New York Dolls? Oh, you child."

When I *was* a child, what mattered to me was the critic's face. Her eyes were partway closed and her head turned to the door, as though one of the people she was talking about might walk in at any moment. Time didn't work for her the way it did for me; she had her finger on the crossfader and she could slide it back and forth. Present, past, present, past. She was mixing. Of course I didn't think of it in those terms; at most I had a dim awareness that in the notion that goes by the name of *history*, there might be room for more stories than even Mr. Savage had told me about. Now and then the critic interrupted herself to pull a record from a sagging shelf of records and play a song or part of a song. As she lifted the needle from the record, she poked at me with her cigar, and said, "That's the real stuff, isn't it?" I hadn't ever heard anything like it, and if it had been played for me in another context, I wouldn't have been sure that it was music at all. It was the sound of cavemen figuring out how to make cars, and I liked it immensely. Celeste was on the point of asking a question, then she turned toward the window and shrugged impatiently. In vain. The critic was lost in her own memories; she no longer saw either of us, or the apartment, or herself, as she talked on and on about basement clubs and the dead. When I came into her view again, she closed one eye, opened it and said, "You should get a Mohawk."

Then it was midnight. We drank champagne from plastic cups and watched the fireworks rise into a bank of low cloud. At twelve-thirty the other guests began to arrive, some of them people I knew: there was Celeste's friend Donatello DelAmbrosio, and Hugh Heap with his wife, who looked like an ornamental pillow, and Javier Provo in mirrored sunglasses and a leather vest, leaping in the air, crying out. As the guests arrived, Celeste looked more and more disappointed, as though she had been expecting something that became less likely with every body that entered the room. At one o'clock, when it was no longer possible to move from one side of the apartment to the other, she put her hand on my back and said it was time to go. I'd been drinking champagne unobserved for some time, and on the subway home I told Celeste about Kerem,

the authentic punk rocker, and how I used to go to parties with
him in Thebes, and met a boy whose head was partially shaved,
and maybe I would get a Mohawk the way the famous critic
had suggested, did Celeste think that was a good idea? "Sure,"
she said, then went back to staring at her reflection in the window of the subway car. Just before we reached our stop, she
did something I'd never seen her do before, she stuck her fingers in her hair and combed it forward, so that it covered her
forehead and hung down over her eyes.

A couple of days later, Nederland resumed with another
assembly in the Great Hall. I found myself sitting next to David Metzger, who had turned a deep orange-brown in the in-
terval. We sang our school song,

> From the shore of Noten Eylandt
> To the Zuyd River's strand,
> We ne'er will forget thee,
> Our old Nieuw Nederland,

et cetera, and as we filed out of the Hall, David Metzger
hissed, "You're dead."

I went through the day waiting for someone to beat me up,
and in the afternoon, puzzled but no longer frightened, I found
Spencer Bartnik, he of the spiked hair and nosebleeds, in the
courtyard, talking to a sophomore named John Littlejohn,
who had very pale blue eyes and was reputed to have given
himself a blowjob. I had just mentioned certain bands, whose
names I'd learned from the famous art critic, when Mr. Geist,
the middle-school principal, appeared between me and the
low winter sun, looming like a rock formation with a human-
shaped profile. He pointed at me and said, "Get up."

Together we climbed the grand staircase, which was not
ordinarily used by students, because it led only to the offices of
the school administration, and walked down a corridor, which,

I swear, if I did not remember better, I would say was lit by torches, to a heavy barred door, or rather to an ordinary door, behind which Mr. Van Horn waited. Around his office hung portraits of the former principals of Nederland, beginning with the recent ones, who wore coats and ties, like Mr. Van Horn himself, but adopting, as you looked around the room, stranger and stranger forms of dress, until, at the back of the office, behind Mr. Van Horn's desk, they wore lace cravats and white wigs; these portraits, however, were the most recent of the lot, they had been done as a result of the head librarian's research, which pushed the date of the school's foundation further into the past. From what models they were painted I do not know.

"Come here," said Mr. Van Horn.

Mr. Geist put his hand on my shoulder and guided me forward.

"We know what you've done," Mr. Van Horn said. "I under-stand that it began with a certain"—Mr. Van Horn licked his lips—"with a certain Admiral Ho." He told me the whole story, how I had come up with this preposterous tale about Ho, and how, when it didn't work out the way I'd planned, I had taken revenge on my partners, who were, in fact, opposed to the Ho business from the start; how I had used my formidable com-puter skills to alter their financial records, alarming Mr. Metzger, who was, did I know? on the Board of Trustees, and creating an embarrassing situation for the school.

"But . . ."

Mr. Van Horn held up his hand. "There isn't anything for you to say. Every step of your catastrophic career has been witnessed."

"But . . ."

"It may surprise you to learn that men are more intelli-gent than machines," Mr. Van Horn said. "You may fool ma-chines, but men, never." He licked his lips again. "This is my question for you. Do you understand that what you did was wrong?"

"Yes," I said.

"Do you feel that it was wrong?"

I looked around at Mr. Geist. He nodded, but I didn't know what that meant. I didn't feel anything. I did what I did because I had figured out how to do it, which, it seems to me, is the main reason why things like that happen, because angry, slighted people have figured out they're possible. They open the door, they go into the next room. Who knows whether what they will find there is good or bad.

Mr. Van Horn sat up in his chair. "Let me offer you a metaphor that you will understand. In this world, there are ones and there are zeroes, just like in your computer. Only they are not perhaps in equal numbers. This is a school for the ones. What are you?"

I didn't answer.

"I expect you will have a great deal of time to ask yourself that question," Mr. Van Horn said. He left it to Mr. Geist to take me back to his office and explain that I had been expelled.

LOST THINGS

What I found in the next room was a semester of danger at Intermediate School 44, where I relearned a number of subjects that I had mastered in the fifth grade and became dodgy about physical violence. My grandfather, when he heard that I'd ended up in public school after all, told the Celestes that I ought to learn a trade, and for a brief but frightful moment it seemed as though I might spend the summer studying woodworking in his basement. It's odd that the prospect of going to Thebes should have been frightful. I had cried when my grandmother put me on the bus to New York, only a few months before, and after the bus pulled out of the station I took a pocketknife from my bag and scratched SHELLEY on the plastic window. I don't remember when or how I lost the desire to go back to Thebes. Probably I didn't lose it all at once; Thebes faded in me as a season fades; it dropped its leaves and a new kind of weather moved in. When, in March or April, Celeste asked me if I would be interested in learning carpentry, because my grandfather was willing to take me on as his apprentice, what came into my mind was not the Thebes where I had kissed Shelley, or even the Thebes where I was in love with Yesim, but a hot, stuffy Thebes that was made from my grandfather's workshop and visits to antiques shops and long dinners listening to the news from the *Catskill Eagle.*

"Can't I go to camp?" I asked.

Celeste raised her eyebrows in surprise. "I thought you liked spending the summers in Thebes."

For years I'd wanted her to acknowledge that fact; now that she had, I contradicted her without hesitation. "Thebes is stupid," I said. "There's nothing to *do* there."

I couldn't really have forgotten about Kerem and Shelley and Yesim; rather, I think Thebes was always a picture done on both sides of the page, and I was able to keep only one side in my mind at a time. Now I had turned the page over. If I *had* gone to Thebes that summer, I would probably have been surprised at how interesting it was, and surprised that I hadn't remembered. But I went to Camp Hockomock, in Maine, where I became friends with Spencer Bartnik. It was a happy coincidence, a little thread of continuity, like a drumbeat carried by a DJ from one song to the next. We spent the summer smoking cigarettes that Spencer's brother sent him in the mail, and listening to the heavy heavy monster sound of Madness. I didn't think of Thebes once, or if I did, it was as a place I had been a long time ago, or maybe a place I had read about, where everything was smaller than in real life and very close together, like the figures in a diorama, who represent different aspects of native life, say, washing clothes and hunting, faithfully, but not the distance that would have kept those activities apart. That's how my summers in Thebes are in my memory, and even now, as I try to return them to their actual size, I notice that the interesting events cluster together, as though all that was good or decisive in that part of my life happened all at once, to relieve me of the burden of having such a long past. Was the summer Kerem got his computer really the summer after I was in love with Yesim? Was the summer I was in love with her even the same summer as *Man and Woman*? I don't know. It might just be that I've run the tracks together at the point where their beats match, to keep things going, to keep there from being a long moment when no one dances. If so, I'm sorry, and I hope you will understand. I've been wanting to dance, myself, and maybe to have others do a little dancing.

In any case, my grandfather was wrong. There was still some hope for me in school, thanks to the recent discovery of attention deficit/hyperactivity disorder, which, according to the people who had discovered it, was responsible for all sorts of misbehavior. I went to see a Dr. Jeremy Ott, who asked me if I had trouble following what people were saying, if I experienced periods of intense anxiety, if I thought about violent acts, if I had ever felt the desire to set persons or objects aflame, if I took drugs, what kind of music I liked to listen to, and why, and whether I ever had trouble following what people were saying. Yes, yes, yes, yes, no, punk rock, because it was so fuckin' loud, what did you say? I was saved. My mothers enrolled me in St. Hubert's Prep, which took a charitable view of misbehavior, offered financial aid to half the student body and admitted girls, some of them refugees from Nederland's sister school, the Anglesey School for Girls. SHP had a computer room, but I hardly ever went there. Another current had me in its pull, American history, who knew? It was as though

I wanted to prove to Mr. Savage that he hadn't been wasting his time. Or maybe—thank you, Dr. Ott!—maybe it was just that I couldn't pay attention to any one thing for too long.

A GALAXY OF CHICKENS

Much later I found a story that the Chinese *had* discovered America. It was in a book on the history of Santería in Central and South America, don't ask me why I was reading about that. There was a chapter on the nature and purpose of chicken sacrifice, in which the author, one George F. Carter, discussed the difference between the European and the American chicken: the former has white feathers and white flesh, whereas the flesh and feathers of the latter are black. In this the American chicken resembles the chickens of, yes, China. "Since the Asiatic chickens are very different from the Mediterranean chickens and most of the traits that reappear in the flocks of the Amerindians are found in Asia, the obvious conclusion would be that the Amerind chickens were first introduced from Asia and not from the Mediterranean . . ." You can hear Mr. Carter growing excited here. "When one considers the total data available on the chicken in America, a conclusion for a Spanish or Portuguese first introduction of chickens into America is simply counter to all evidence. The Mediterraneans, as late as 1600, did not have, and did not even know of, the galaxy of chickens present in Amerind hands . . ." A galaxy of chickens spun through my imagination; white European hens shone against a black mass of Asian wing- and tail-feathers. Mr. Carter went on to observe that in China, too, the chicken was thought to have magical properties; the Chinese used to read the future by dripping chicken blood on parchment. I watched the blood spatter on the page, and what it showed me was not the future but the past: I was back at Nederland, telling Matt Bark that I'd found something really good. *I* gave the report on the Chinese; *I* had irrefutable, un-suspected proof that Eriksson and Columbus were latecom-ers; Mr. Savage nodded his approval, and when I sat down he declared that if we learned only one thing from American history, it should be that if you trusted yourself you would get there in the end. I won; I went out for pizza; I was not ex-pelled. Of course none of this would ever have come to pass. Even if I had somehow stumbled on the Asian-chicken hy-pothesis back then, Matt Bark would have laughed it off. Chickens? Dumbfuck, who cares about chickens? —But . . . —You think chickens discovered America? —No, they were carried on ships . . . —What, to start a chicken farm? Chicken-shit! Chicken boy!

Even in my daydreams I lost the argument. But the chick-ens remain, all over Central and South America, black, silky-feathered Asiatic chickens that lay blue-shelled eggs. So, Matt, what do you make of those chickens?

THREE

On Monday morning it occurred to me that I hadn't visited my grandfather's grave. The cemetery was at the other end of Thebes, on a gentle slope that steepened farther ahead and became the flank of the ski hill. An iron fence surrounded it, though the railing was falling down in places and lengths of baling wire had been strung across the gaps. The Rowlands were buried at the back of the graveyard, in the shadow of a pair of maples that were slowly pushing up the earth with their roots, so that, if they continued, the oldest skeletons would eventually be exhumed. Jean Roland lay beside his wife, Anne, who had outlived him by a decade. Small gray stones, their heads flush with the earth, remembered children who had not survived. Their son Oliver and his wife Claudine, born a Gerer, kept a respectful distance. Not all the Rowlands come back to Thebes in the end—my great-great-uncle Othniel, for example, is buried at the foot of a cliff in New Mexico—but I used to wonder, if my mothers came back, what distance they would keep from my grandparents. I passed the white column erected by the citizens of Thebes to John Rowland, who had turned the failing Rowland Mill into the profitable Thebes Furniture Company, manufacturer of the three-legged "Thebes stool," of which my grandfather had a few examples, and found the rough gray stone my grandfather had picked out when my grandmother died. Its shape was suggestive of a naturally occurring rock, as though the Rowlands, having reached the zenith of their humanity with John, were sinking back into the natural world. Mary Rowland, born Ashland, 1924–1990, and the inscription, *Beloved Wife*, which enraged my mothers. It was just like my grandfather, they said, to turn my grandmother into another of his possessions.

Oliver lay between Mary and his father, John. There was no stone for him yet, only a wooden marker, to which a sheet of paper in a plastic envelope had been stapled. Oliver Rowland, it said, 1922–2000, and the words, *May He Be Remembered*, which, as they were printed in twenty-four-point Helvetica on a piece of paper that had been warped by the rain, undermined the sincerity of this wish, even though there were fresh flowers on the grave, indicating that people still remembered him. Here he was. I put my hand on the bare earth. I tried to imagine my grandfather lying beneath my hand. *Body*, I told myself, *this is a body*. But all I could think was that I should have brought flowers, and that my knees were cold. I stood up and brushed dirt from my pants. I walked past the graves of people who had died fifty or sixty years ago, mill workers, probably, covered by last year's leaves. Their children were not buried here, no one wanted to be buried in Thebes anymore, except the Rowlands and the other old families. The town must have shrunk almost to nothing, I thought, when the last of the mill people died and their children moved away. What a grim place it must have been when no one came to the lunch counter, when the meeting hall stood empty and the musicians stopped playing at Summerland. Left on its own, Thebes would have died too. It would have become a place like the ones you pass on Route 23B, settlements so small they no longer merit their own post offices or general stores, Main Streets with nothing on them but a garage or the offices of a Bible study association. Who would want to live in a gloomy town hemmed in by mountains, cut off from the rest of the world? It was only when Joe Regenzeit arrived, when he opened Snowbird and made the snow fall, that life flowed back toward Thebes in the form of weekend visitors from New York City, who liked what they saw and rented houses, caused antiques stores to open, demanded Chilean coffee, created, out of mud and rock and poverty, a branch of the TrustFirst Bank, the Kozy Korner and Kountry Kitchen, the organic grocery with its bins of glistening fall apples. Regenzeit had rescued Thebes; he fixed what my grandfather could not fix. No wonder Oliver hated him.

I drove to the grocery and picked out a bouquet of white flowers, lilies, I hoped, from their small, expensive floral department. I took them to the cashier, who turned out to be the pretty girl I'd supplied with beer two days earlier. I asked if she'd had fun at the party.

"It was OK," she said, mistrustfully.

I told her not to worry, I wasn't going to report her. In fact, my friends had stood outside the same gas station when I was younger than she was, trying to get college students to buy us beer.

"I didn't know you were from here," she said. I could see from the change in her expression that she'd admitted me into her human race: I was no longer an anonymous beer-donating adult. I thanked her for the flowers and went out, whistling. A Subaru Outback pulled up as I was getting into my car, and Yesim got out. She was wearing a black parka and a pair of night-black sunglasses that hid half her face. She looked like a secret agent, or rather, like a person dressed in a secret agent costume, someone who was making no secret of her secretiveness. I sat in my car with the door open and my legs stuck out.

I wanted Yesim to see me, but she came out of the store holding a cup of coffee in its brown paper sleeve and got into her car. I decided to follow her. She took Route 56 out of town, past the main entrance to Snowbird, and turned onto a service road. I turned too, wondering what I was doing, but not really wondering. The road climbed steeply, and Norman Mailer's car began to rumble and thump, as though Mailer himself were in the engine compartment, duking it out with the forces of inertia and rust. The temperature gauge crept toward Hot and I had to slow down: fifteen miles an hour, ten. I came around a curve and saw the Outback ahead at a fork in the road. For a moment I imagined that Yesim had stopped for me to catch up, then she took the left branch and I thought she'd been moving all along. The road switchbacked through a pine forest, climbing what was, from the Theban point of view, the far side of Mount Espy, the side that looked north to the next ridge of the Catskills. A break in the trees offered a momentary panorama: the flatlands through which the Hudson ran, an almost invisible silver strand. There were people down there sitting on their porches, mowing their lawns, walking their dogs. They had never seemed so far away, and also, curiously, they had never seemed so happy, those invisible people in the valley, but I wouldn't have changed places with any of them. I coaxed Norman Mailer's car up the hill, toward Yesim, who was out of sight.

I found her at the summit of Mount Espy, standing near the shed that housed the machinery for one of Snowbird's chair-lifts, her hair blowing in the chilly wind. We could see the whole valley from there, with Thebes tucked away at the end of it like a cluster of pale cells stuck to the wall of a dark-green womb.

"I wondered if it was you," Yesim said. I couldn't tell from her tone of voice whether or not she was pleased.

"I hope I didn't frighten you," I said.

"No," Yesim said. "Don't take this the wrong way, but you're not very frightening."

"Oh, yeah? I frighten plenty of people. My neighbors in San Francisco think I'm a ghost."

"Really?"

"At least, I think they do." San Francisco wasn't what I wanted to talk about, and I regretted having mentioned it.

Yesim turned away from me, and walked toward the shed.

"What happened on Saturday night?" I asked.

"It's complicated. I tried to explain."

"About Mark? It sounds like you're having second thoughts about him."

"Mark is only part of it." Yesim took off her sunglasses, which were, in any case, unnecessary: purplish cumulus clouds were coming over the mountains from the east, their bottoms dark and unpromising. She touched her eyes with her fingertips. "Did I tell you I was in love with Professor X?" she said. "Not platonic love, not love from a distance. I washed her when she couldn't move. I washed her stomach, between her legs. I fucked her with my hand." She watched me to see what reaction this new word, *fucked*, would provoke.

"OK," I said, "but you don't love her now." I had never formed a mental image of Professor X, so Yesim's words had little power to disturb me.

"No," she said, "not anymore. But then there was my therapist, Dr. Y. Nice man, he showed me pictures of his grandchildren. We fucked everywhere but on the couch, he said he didn't want to look at one of his other patients and think of me lying there." She said *fucked* as if it were a technical term borrowed from another language, like *cogito* or *Geist*. It was a pretension, a word that didn't belong to her, although it might have belonged to Professor X or Dr. Y. "Then there was Miss Z, who lived with me after the Pines," she said, "and her friend, Mr. . . . shit, I should have started earlier in the alphabet, now I have to call him Mr. AA. I couldn't say no. Do you understand?"

"I understand that you had sex with a lot of people, but so what? Does that mean I can't like you?"

"Mr. AA liked me," Yesim said. "He was very nice. He had a daughter in Wisconsin, and he sent her a postcard every day. He played classical guitar. He gave great massages."

"So what was wrong with him?"

"He wasn't the most stable person," Yesim said, "although he was better than Mr., what should I call him? AB? BB?" Yesim looked up at me. "Now you know."

Just then, as if to prove some idiotic hypothesis about the world, it started raining. There was almost no warning: the clouds were just on top of us, and a fat cold rain was falling. "Fuck," Yesim said. She fiddled with the padlock on the shed. By the time she got it open we were both wet. "What are you waiting for? Come in."

The shed was cold and dim. A few chairs, or benches, dangled from the curved track that would send them back down the mountainside, their safety bars open as if they'd been waiting for passengers since the end of the last winter. The air smelled of dirt. Yesim said she had to check to make sure the power was working, that was why she'd come up here. She tugged at the cover of the fuse box but it wouldn't open. "Fucking stupid thing," Yesim said. I pointed out that there was a catch; Yesim released it and the cover opened. She peered into the fuse box and flipped a switch and the lights came on.

We sat for a while on one of the chairs, not talking, just swaying back and forth, our feet dangling in the air, listening to the enormous sound of the rain. Yesim said she was sorry, she hadn't meant to burden me with her tale of woe. I said I didn't mind. She smiled. Was that the turnaround point? The place where we stopped struggling against gravity and let ourselves be carried downhill, toward whatever there was at the bottom, the lodge, home, life together? No. All we'd done was to turn on the power. We sat in the shed until the worst of the storm had passed, then we went out. The sun was shining again, lighting up the edge of the clouds like a curtain; red and yellow trees on the northern mountains stood out and seemed almost to sparkle.

Yesim said she had to go to the office, Kerem was probably wondering what had happened to her, and we walked to our respective cars. The flowers I'd bought were still lying on Norman Mailer's passenger seat. I took them back to my grandfather's house and rinsed out a vase; I set the vase full of flowers on the kitchen table, but it was too wobbly so I moved the flowers to the windowsill. They looked good there, their white petals taking on subtle color in the daylight. They made the house look as if someone lived in it.

REGENZEIT

The next day I ran into Kerem at the Kountry Kitchen. He was waiting in line to pay as I came in, and he embraced me. He had a black eye, which he'd tried to cover with makeup, but it didn't work. The puffy blue flesh around his eye stood out like a burial mound seen from the air. I asked what had happened to him, and he told me he'd been in Philadelphia over the weekend. "Man," he said, "there are some assholes in Philly!" He told me how this *homeless*—he used the word as a noun—had called him a *sand nigger*. "You should have seen what I did to the guy, though. I think I busted his collarbone." Then: "Hey, you talked to my sister." I nodded. Kerem asked if she had shown me her poems and for some reason I said yes, she had.

"Did she show you 'Uyum'?"

"Sure," I lied.

"'Uyum' is incredible," Kerem said. "You have to admit I'm right. People are going to be reading it a hundred years from now."

"They might."

"She's a genius!" Kerem said. "What I need you to do is hook her up. Do you know anyone in publishing?"

I thought of the people at Marina's salon: Holly the graphic designer who wrote a zine called *Hollylujah!*, sullen Ted who kept an online diary about the girls he hadn't slept with. "I don't know if my friends will be much help," I said, but Kerem wasn't listening. He leaned close to me, and for a second I had the strange feeling that he and Yesim were two parts of the same person.

"I don't believe in fate or anything like that," he said, "but I do think you showed up just when you were needed." He hit my arm. "You should stick around until winter! I'll hook you up with free passes to Snowbird." He patted my shoulder one more time and left. I ate my lunch, a bowl of chicken soup and what the menu referred to as *Yankee pot roast*, though I doubted it had seen the inside of a pot, or an oven, or anything the old Yankees used to prepare food.

I went home and called Yesim and told her about my conversation with Kerem. I said I wanted to read her poems, and Yesim said that was very flattering, but she didn't know how she felt about the part of her life that had ended in Cambridge years ago. I said of course I understood, but I still wanted to read the poems.

"You have to be patient with me," Yesim said. "I have good parts and bad parts."

"Everyone is like that," I said.

"That may be true, but I'm a little more so."

"Anyway," I said, "I want to see you again."

Yesim said I could come over anytime. After all, I knew where she lived. But I said I meant just her, alone. There was a longish silence, then she said she would stop by on her way home, but just for a minute.

I spent the afternoon on the sofa, reading in *Progress in Flying Machines* about Screws That Lift and Propel. Outside, the sky got darker and darker. Just when it seemed like Yesim wouldn't come, the Outback arrived in my grandfather's driveway, and there she was, a brown paper bag in her arms. She'd brought food, she hoped I didn't mind, she hadn't eaten all day.

Yesim paused on the doorstep. "You know I've never been here?" It hadn't occurred to me but of course it was true. "All these years," she said, carrying the bag to the kitchen table, and unpacking a plastic tub of soup and white Chinese-takeout boxes, "I've wondered what your grandparents' house was like."

"Come and see," I said. I showed her the dining room, the parlor, where she admired Mary's watercolors; my mothers' room, my grandparents' bedroom, the study. Somewhere on the second floor Yesim stopped talking, and she didn't speak again until we were back in the kitchen.

"Excuse me for asking," she said, finding bowls, plates, forks and spoons, carrying everything to the old scarred kitchen table, "but I thought you were supposed to be packing up?"

"I should be. But look at this place. I have no idea where to start."

"It's not hard. You just make two piles, one for things to give away and one for things to keep. Anything that's too big to go on one of the piles, you tag with a sticker. Color coded, red for keep, green for sell or give away." Kerem was right: Yesim was a born manager.

We opened the takeout boxes to reveal chicken and peanuts, broccoli, some kind of eggplant, this last, I thought, an almost Turkish touch. There was a little silence: so much not to talk about.

"So," I asked, "how was your day?"

"Not bad," Yesim said around a mouthful of chicken. The terrain park was almost finished but the contractor had gone AWOL. He didn't have a regular phone; Yesim imagined that he was some kind of elf, hiding in an enchanted forest of concrete. "What about you?"

"Oh," I said, "things with me are pretty quiet."

We finished dinner in comfortable silence. It was as if we'd always been there, the two of us, as if all the contradictions of our history were dissolving in cheap broth and brown sauce, and what remained was just this image, the Rowland child and the Regenzeit child at the ancestral Rowland table, eating soup from my grandparents' chipped white bowls.

"Don't worry, I'll get it," I said, as Yesim stood, plate in her hands, headed for the sink, but she was already washing the dishes.

"I like your kitchen more than mine," she said. "It's cozy. I never understood why my parents made ours so shiny and, you know, chrome-y. On the other hand"—she nodded at the clock in the shape of a cat, with a wagging tail and eyes set with rhinestones—"that's a weird clock."

"My grandfather bought it after my grandmother died. I don't know why."

"Oh. I didn't mean to imply that he had bad taste. I've just never seen a clock like that before."

"Get rid of it, you think?"

"I would," Yesim said.

So it began. It seems ironic that the one thing Yesim and I could talk about was my grandparents' possessions, the stuff that had brought me to Thebes in the first place, but it makes sense: everything else was too dangerous. When I had unplugged the clock and taken it down from the wall, it made sense to both of us that she would point at a ceramic beer stein, which had been full of pennies and nickels for as long as I could remember, and ask, "Are you going to keep that?" I asked if she thought I should.

"It looks kind of dirty."

"OK, stein, *Achtung!*" I said. "To ze garage mit you!"

When I came back she was looking at the coat tree. "I know," I said. "I'll take it out later."

It made sense that I would call Yesim at work the next

day, to ask if she could spare an hour or two, because I was cleaning out the library, and I could use her advice. Yesim came over and we spent the evening picking things up, showing them to each other, asking, Yes or no? Her advice was good, even if it tended to the nonaccumulative. That boat-shaped ashtray? Forget it. The box of matchbooks? The china shepherd? The green-shaded lamp? The lamp, maybe. It was a nice lamp. After a couple of hours, Yesim looked at her watch and said she had to go. Maybe she suspected that something else was happening, less innocent than the division of my grandparents' things into two heaps, because she drove the fifty feet that separated her house from mine, as if she wanted to emphasize that we were not together. But she came back the next night. We worked in the dining room, then in the living room, with increasing sureness and speed. The great mass of Rowland stuff gave way before us, like ice breaking and spinning away into a warming river, and what was, from my point of view, even better, Yesim and I learned things about each other. I discovered that she had no use for the kitsch that people in San Francisco liked ("Please tell me," she said indignantly, "what you are going to do with *Cooking with Pineapples*?"), but she showed a strange reverence for old-fashioned things ("You've got to hold on to these letter openers"), which I would have been happy ("*Five* letter openers? Yesim, I don't get any mail!") not to keep. We agreed about paperweights, planters, anything crocheted. These weren't the things we would have chosen to reveal about ourselves, but somehow that made them even more intimate, more revealing. They were the secrets we didn't know we had. How else, short of living together, would I have learned that Yesim didn't like pillows or mirrors, that she hated curtains and only grudgingly tolerated blinds? How would she have discovered my strange fascination with the electric toothbrush?

With the things came stories. Yesim wanted to know about the Catskill landscapes in the dining room; I told her about my grandmother's expeditions into the mountains, in all seasons, all weathers, expeditions that caused my grandfather furies of worry that didn't end until she came home, sometimes in the middle of the night, the back of her station wagon full of diminutive canvases.

"She was really talented," Yesim said.

"It's true," I said.

But my grandmother's interest in painting ended when my mothers went to New York to become artists: as if she couldn't stand the competition, or maybe it was just that, with her daughters gone and her son on his way to Vietnam, she didn't have anyone to run away from anymore. After that, my grandmother put her energy into her garden, almost as if she'd become the one who was rooted to the spot.

"She sounds interesting," Yesim said. "Not like my grandmother, ugh." But Yesim didn't talk about her grandmother: my house, she said, my stories.

On Saturday afternoon I found a box of my grandparents' records. Here was Gil Gideon and the Two-Time Tunesters with a double album of *Moonlite Melodies*, here were Benny Goodman, Harry James, Jimmie Lunceford, Chick Webb and all their orchestras. Some of the records were thick, ten-inch 78s; others were regular 33s, in bright, busy album covers that belonged to a world untouched or unretouched by the airbrush. I put on Gil Gideon and turned the volume up, and his songs became the soundtrack for our work in the parlor, which went faster now that there was music playing. "Give me a sign," Gil sang. "A spoon. The month of June. A reason to be fallin' in love."

"How did they meet?" Yesim asked.

"Gil and the Tunesters?"

"No, your grandparents."

The way my grandmother told the story, I said, Oliver had fallen in love with her at a college dance contest. He was no kind of dancer; his first words to her were apparently, "Is that your foot?" Mary was disposed to tell him off. She already had a beau, a Baltimorean named Brett, also an undergraduate at Bleak, who possessed a widow's peak, jet-black hair, commanding eyes, a sterling white waistcoat and one of each kind of foot. But something about Oliver stopped her. That was the word she used, *stopped*, as if it meant more than it did, as if Oliver stopped not only her lips but some crazy clockwork that had carried her from boarding school to boarding school, from state to state, from boyfriend to boyfriend, because young Mary was wild, or restless at least, very much like her daughters in that regard. If Oliver hadn't come along, she didn't know where she would have ended up. A lost woman, she said. Probably. Oliver stopped her. He was a talker; before the song was over he had told her how he came from a long line of tree exploiters: his great-great-grandfather had run a sawmill, and his grandfather had run a furniture company and his father made walking sticks and other wooden souvenirs for tourists in the Catskills. First trees, then chairs, then walking sticks: the only thing left for Oliver would be toothpicks, so he'd left home before the family business whittled him down to nothing. He got Mary to tell him her story. He listened, as though to him the music were no music, as though everything in the world were still except her voice, which grew still in turn, and the band stopped playing, and they lost the contest, and went outside for a breath of air.

Then came the Second World War. Oliver enlisted in the Army, hoping to see some action, but he was clumsy, clumsy, and in the interest of everyone's safety he was posted to a base in Florida, where he excelled as assistant quartermaster, and then quartermaster, and probably he would have made it all the way to half-master and master entire if the war hadn't ended when it did. He went back to Bleak and married Mary, and for a few months they lived in New York City, while they decided what to do with the rest of their lives. Mary argued for London; Oliver wanted time to think. They were still and moving at the same time. It was a strange experience, like being on a ride at a fair; you sat there and the lights went past, then passed again. Where were they going? Thebes, as it turned out. Oliver's father had died and left behind him a fat dark skein of unresolved business, which looked from the outside as though there would be money in it, but unraveled, and unraveled, until Oliver was left holding nothing, only the thin end of a thread that led to someone else's pocket. The Rowland Mill was bankrupt; the mill closed down. All that was left were the houses in town, and some securities, enough to live on if they lived in Thebes. Oliver liked the idea of having some more time to think, and besides, Mary was already pregnant with Charles. They moved to Thebes.

Instead of English hills, Mary got the Catskills, and not the busy Catskills, where the Jewish resorts were, nor the majestic Catskills as painted by Thomas Cole and Frederic Church, but Thebes, a town in the northeastern corner of Espy County, which she'd never heard of, a place so remote that the inhabitants spoke a foreign language. How good Brett and his urbane charms must have looked as the car stopped and the cold air came in, and Oliver explained to her that the house had been built in stages, that the original house had been only the kitchen and what was now the dining room and one of the bedrooms upstairs, that the parlor and library and the big bedroom had been added by John Rowland I, and his son added the bow window, a mistake, in Oliver's opinion . . . A commentary that did not cease until she fell sick and Oliver took her to a teaching hospital in Syracuse, forty-five years later.

Mary was stopped, and good. Even so, she was smart enough to guess there was a reason why everything happened, smart enough to guess that she was, in fact, smart. If she'd been in love with Brett she would have let him make love to her; but she hadn't. She had married Oliver for a reason, even if she couldn't say exactly what the reason was, now, standing on the front steps of the Rowland house, looking out at a valley where few people lived, and all of them odd. So she made the best of it. She took up painting and drove off to turn the vast Hudson Valley into tiny watercolors; she made molehills of mountains, and spider lines of streams; forests turned to blotches under her brush, stippled with orange as the fall approached. And she had Saturday nights at Summerland, the old resort. Look: Oliver is in his shirtsleeves; Mary's in a flared skirt that swings nicely when she swings, and she swings all right. Her hair is mussed. Now it's Sunday morning, the kids are going to be up soon and Mary will have to cook, but until then she's free to remember the night she's had, and the band that was playing, let's say it was Gil Gideon and his orchestra, and how she got Oliver to dance; when he was tired she danced with his friend Pete Samson, a doctor, who wasn't bad, and when they were done Oliver took her out to the garden, which was lit up like a fairyland. She let him smoke a cigarette and kiss her; she grabbed his big behind and had the pleasure of watching his eyes get all round.

"Mary, please," he murmured to her neck, "someone will see us."

"Who's to see? Everyone else is doing the same thing."

It was true; the bushes rustled with amorous activity. Now and then someone hooted like an owl carrying something soft away in its talons. She pressed his hips into her stomach, dug her fingers into the scratchy wool of the seat of his pants.

"Mary!"

She could feel his cock getting hard, though, and she wondered if she ought to drag him into the bushes. Instead they went indoors. Gil G. was pulling out all the stops. The drummer was soaking in his shirtsleeves and the trumpeter's eyes had gone red like sucking candies.

"Here's the champion!" Pete Samson seized Mary's waist and led her back to the dance floor, over Oliver's objections that a man ought to be able to enjoy a moment with his wife . . .

"Let's run away," Pete whispered in Mary's ear. He was ten years younger than she was, young enough to have strong blocky legs and a baby-boy face. His soft cheek pressed against hers. He was joking, but he wasn't joking.

"Where to?" Mary asked.

"Anywhere you want," said Pete.

"Not tonight," Mary said. "Call me in the morning."

"You always say that," Pete said.

"You never call."

Then she went back to Oliver, who was brooding. She squeezed his arm and told him to get her a drink. Mary knew that she was smart, smarter in fact than her husband, definitely smarter than Pete Samson, probably smarter than her children as well. She understood what none of them were even close to figuring out, that *this was all there was*. Wherever you went in the world, whatever you did, you would find more or less the same thing, people dancing in hot rooms, brooding husbands, gardens, lights, the sound of sex, children who wanted breakfast, and there was no point in wishing that life were otherwise, because if it was very much different from this, then it wouldn't be life at all. Give me a rock, she sings. A ring. The promise of spring. A season. A reason to be fallin' in love.

My uncle came over that night. "Hey," he said, "you're making progress!" He had been worried about me, but it looked like I was doing all right. "Maybe our talk did you some good," Charles said.

"Maybe it did," I said.

On Monday Yesim and I started on the parlor.

REGENZEIT

This is the good part: it's the story of Yesim calling me at midnight to say she'd changed her mind, I ought to keep Mary's sewing machine, and me saying, you're calling at midnight about the sewing machine? And Yesim saying, I couldn't sleep, I was worried that you would throw it out. It's an antique, you ought to hold on to it. And me saying, I promise, I won't make any rash decisions about the sewing machine until tomorrow morning at the earliest. And going back to bed, pretending to be annoyed that Yesim had woken me up for something so unimportant, but actually happy that she was thinking of me at midnight, that she was thinking of me and my grandmother's sewing machine. It's the story of Yesim calling me breathlessly in the middle of the afternoon to say she just saw a moose on the ski slope, a *moose*, can you believe it? And me saying, it couldn't have been a moose, and Yesim saying, you don't believe me? Come over and see for yourself. It's the story of the two of us walking all over Mount Espy looking for a hypothetical moose and coming back to the lodge almost doubled over with laughter and not being able to tell Kerem what was so funny. It's that story. You know how it goes.

But here are a few surprises: one afternoon when we were tired of packing, we sat on my grandfather's porch, watching yellow leaves skitter past on Route 56, and talked about things we'd done when we were kids. It was just like the fantasy I had right after that first dinner with Yesim and Kerem—months ago, it seemed, although it had actually been less than two weeks. I told Yesim the story of how I was expelled from Nederland, and Yesim laughed, and said, if *she* had been expelled from high school her father would have strangled her.

"He wouldn't let us do anything wrong," Yesim said. "If I got a B in school, he would shout, *Aren't you ashamed?*"

"That's pretty harsh," I agreed.

Yesim looked at me sidelong. "You have no idea."

Even before he came to Thebes, Joe Regenzeit had figured out that here, in America, there was no room for error, and no one to catch him if he fell, an impression that his experiences with the Thebans did nothing to dispel. If his shirt was wrinkled, it was because Turks were slovenly; if Snow-bird failed to file for a permit no one had ever mentioned until the deadline for it had passed, it was because Turks thought everything could be settled with baksheesh. What Joe Regenzeit received as prejudice, he transmitted to his children as obsession. He expected Yesim's and Kerem's lives to be as spotless as the glass-topped table in the dining room. His demands were all the harder to satisfy because he wanted his children to be perfect *and* Turkish, to show the town what educated Turks could accomplish in the New World. His idea of Turkishness came from Anatolia, where nothing was possible, Yesim said, and so it was only natural that it mostly took the form of restriction: no television, no parties, no short skirts, no jeans, no teen magazines. If Joe Regenzeit could have got into his children's sleeping heads he would probably have forbidden them to dream.

I had trouble understanding how this fit with what I remembered of the Regenzeit home. "There was Kerem's punk phase," I said, "and . . ."

"Yes," Yesim said, "that was when things got bad."

She and Kerem, as natives, had understood how the spirit of Thebes, and maybe of America in general, loves failure as much as or more than it does success. They started to make mistakes on purpose, to let their grades slip, to change the way they dressed. As they fell fluently into this new language of truancy and misdemeanor, Joe Regenzeit's anger grew. There was more shouting, more shaking, things Yesim didn't like to think about, even now.

"He must have hated me," I said.

"You? You were his great hope. The child of the oldest family in town, playing soldiers with Kerem! You were the promise that somehow things would work out, that we would be accepted here. Why do you think my parents let the two of us be friends?"

"I never thought about it."

"You had it easy," Yesim said. "You never had to think about anything."

Then came the night of the dress. We had finished the parlor and moved on to my grandparents' bedroom; I was taking bird books out of my grandfather's nightstand when Yesim held up a long blue dress with a low neckline and a fringed skirt, it must have been one of the dresses my grandmother wore to Summerland. "What do you think of this," she asked. "Isn't it elegant?" She held it to her shoulders. I don't know what I said, but Yesim carried the dress into the bathroom and closed the door. I asked what she was doing, and she said, "What do you think? I'm trying it on."

A couple of minutes later she came out wearing the dress, her breasts pushing their way out of its décolletage as though she were an allegory for something, Victory, or Liberty, or America. She spun around the bedroom in tiny steps, because the dress had been sewn for a woman half her size and fit her like a manacle. She stretched the seams and caused the tiny seed pearls sewn into the hem to tremble, shuffled back into the bathroom to look at herself and came out again, toward me, slowly, her lip curled in expectation of something terrible or wonderful, which, I realized, I was expecting too. Then Yesim slipped on the bare floor. The dress tore from knee to waist and she sat down heavily. "Whoops," she said. She retreated to the bathroom, tugging the ruined dress down over her white schoolgirl underpants. When she came out, she promised she would have the dress repaired, and asked, did I mind that she'd tried it on? I said honestly that I didn't mind, but maybe it would be a good idea if she didn't try on any more of my grandmother's clothes. Yesim said obviously she wasn't going to, she had just been curious.

That night, as if we'd crossed some frontier beyond which we no longer had anything to hide from each other, we stayed up late drinking tea and talking in my grandfather's kitchen. Yesim told me she'd often wondered what her life would have been like if she'd been born fifty or even a hundred years earlier. Would she have been more at home in Istanbul, where her mother's parents were from? She wouldn't have had as much freedom, but on the other hand she wondered whether freedom was really what she wanted. "There's something to be said for rules," she said. "Just look at poetry. Of course everyone writes free verse now but you can do some beautiful things with the old forms. *Desperate hearts: this ship is not the last to go, nor the last arrow of a life of sorrow. The lover and beloved wait in vain* . . . That's Beyatlı; do you know him?"

"Never heard of him."

"Actually, he's kind of corny. But it doesn't matter, all I mean is that form counts for something."

"Just as long as you don't choke on it," I said.

Yesim nodded. "I'm not going to let anything do that to me. Not again. What about you?"

"Me?"

"Would you have wanted to live a hundred years ago?"

"I used to be a historian. For me, the past is work."

"When were you a historian?"

"At Stanford," I said. "Before I became a programmer."

"Huh," Yesim said. "But studying the past isn't the same as living in it. You really wouldn't want to go back?"

"No."

"Not even to find out if you were right about whatever it was you studied?"

"It wouldn't be that easy. In some ways, it's easier to know *now* what was happening *then*. Anyway, my subject was a cult, I guess you'd say, who believed the world would end in 1844. I don't have to travel in time to know they were wrong."

"Why did you give it up?"

"I couldn't write my dissertation."

"I understand. It must be very hard."

I shrugged. "The problem was more that I lost interest."

"In the end of the world?" Yesim smiled.

"In the past generally."

After a moment, Yesim asked, "Did something happen? To you, I mean?"

"Yes and no. I mean, a lot of things happened. But nothing really happened to me."

"Do you want to talk about it?"

"I wouldn't know where to begin."

"I'm not in a hurry." Yesim smiled into her teacup. "Besides, I showed you mine."

"OK," I said. "I'll tell you."

SAN FRANCISCO, CITY OF GHOSTS

Victor and Alex and I moved to San Francisco together at the end of our first year at Stanford. We needed to be in the city, we decided, because living in Palo Alto was like being dead, it was like moving into your own tomb before your death, breathing in the eucalyptus-scented embalming oils, waking up every morning to the same light, encountering, every day, the same lifelike faces, which asked you the same question, "Isn't this heaven?" We looked at many unsuitable apartments, as well as a few that two of us liked but not the third. Alex wanted to live in the Castro, I wanted period charm, and Victor wanted a backyard where he could grill. Somewhere between Moscow and California he had picked up a love of barbecue; it had become indissociably linked to happiness in his mind, to the point where he would linger at even the most unbearable graduate-student parties as long as someone was cooking meat outdoors. We talked about splitting up, but none of us could afford to live alone, and finally we found the place on Sixteenth Street, which wasn't what we wanted— the apartment was dark, the street ugly and loud, there was no yard—but there was room for all of us to work, and a back porch where the landlady said it would be all right to put a grill. And there was something else, a Murphy bed that unfolded from the back of a cabinet door in the front parlor. I loved the old-fashionedness of it, and I joked that, like the Murphy bed, I wanted to live in the apartment until someone dismantled me and carried me off. A month later we packed up our incompatible belongings and drove them to San Francisco.

The city was even better than I had expected. It wasn't just like coming back to life, it was like coming *to* life, to a life I'd never lived before. Alex had friends in the city already, people he'd known in college, who had discovered a bar on Valencia Street, the Blue Study, which had a room in the back where no one went, with weather-beaten sofas, a patio table and a gray cat called Felix who glared at us from the corner. Alex invited me to drink with his group, and in this way I met Erin, who had been in a band in college and still dressed like a lounge singer, in low-cut dresses that set off her white skin, and a bobbed black wig, and sang, sometimes, when she was drunk, songs she had written, about people she'd loved so much she could kill them, and how she could kill them, exactly.

I fell in love with her. She didn't love me back, but that didn't stop us from spending hours sitting side by side on a sofa at the Blue Study, our arms around each other, talking about the countries we would like to visit, and when we would visit them together. Morocco, Argentina, Australia, Japan, the world, which had, until then, been made up of places that I would never see, became as close as a conversation, as close as the word *yes*, at least until Erin attracted Star, a short woman with a crew cut and red high-top Keds, and Star drew Erin into her orbit, never, alas, to return to my arms. It didn't matter. Love meant something different in the back room of the Blue Study than it did elsewhere; it was like a vibration in the air, which, although you directed it at one particular person, spread outward from you in an expanding bubble, until it was absorbed by the walls, the bar, the strangers at the bar who you would never meet, Valencia Street, the red light blinking at the top of Sutro Tower. My love for Erin flew out of me painlessly, and when it had gone as far as it could, it came back to me as taste. Suddenly I preferred the super vegetarian burrito at El Toro to its equivalent at the Taqueria Maya, I frequented the used-book store with the cat, and not the one run by the barely ambulatory depressive outpatient; I shopped at Rainbow Market and not Safeway, which Erin called *Slaveway*. I had been naturalized. My monochrome East Coast clothes made way for a rainbow of Thrift Town shirts and permanently creased polyester slacks. My hair became unruly; I grew a beard, which made me look like a rabbi, Victor said, not the effect I had been aiming at, but maybe not entirely wrong, my father had been a Jew, and now, who knew, in San Francisco I might become a Jew too. I started smoking and purchased a record player. I had no idea how close I was to him, my father, how much I had come to resemble him, but if Charles had seen me slouching from my house to Java Man, from Java Man to the Blue Study, in my green Arnel shirt and crackled leather three-quarters coat, the outfit in which, I thought, I was finally free from the past and all possible constraint, I think he would have told me, You look just like a young Richard Ente.

It was around this time that I met Swan. He spent his mornings at Java Man, writing his leaflets, and because I was also a regular there, we talked sometimes, mostly about his program to get himself elected mayor of San Francisco, or Swan Francisco, as he called it. He possessed a great deal of information, most of it fictitious, about Saint Francis of Assisi, who had been, he said, a huge pothead, which was the reason he could understand what the birds were saying. Saint Francis began as an ordinary monk, Swan said, then he discovered marijuana, which was brought to Italy by Marco Polo, along with silk and the numeral zero. Weed unlocked the door to the animal world, Swan said, and Saint Francis went right on through. He discovered that animals deserve our love every bit as much as human beings do, more, in fact, because the patience of animals is limitless, whereas human beings get sick of you, which is the cause of war. Saint Francis became a Buddhist and a vegetarian, he preached a gospel of unfettered desire and kindness to animals, and if elected mayor, Swan promised to bring these teachings back to this, his city. It would be the beginning of a world revolution: pot would be legal, and money abolished; animals would be cherished and might, once the mass of humanity had reached a sufficiently advanced state, consent to serve as our teachers. Swan always kept a bird near him, a pigeon, usually, often one with a broken wing. As he spoke, he stroked the bird's back; sometimes he raised the bird to his face and looked into its eye, and it seemed as though the two, Swan and bird, were really understanding each other, although no words passed between them. I liked listening to his unorthodox histories, and promised to vote for him as soon as he got himself on the ballot.

When my work was going badly, and the career I'd chosen seemed like a dull dream, as unfulfillable as it was unwanted, I wondered what decisions had made Swan Swan, whether they could be counted, how many they had been. How thick was the line that separated us, how easily could it be crossed, and, once you had gone over it one way, could you go back in the other? To this last question, at least, I got an answer, or deduced an answer, no, it was not possible. Swan refused to talk about his past; when I asked him even the least personal questions, where he had grown up, how long he had lived in San Francisco, he stopped speaking and turned his attention to his writing or his bird. Peter, the owner of the Latin Quarter Bookshop, told me that Swan had come from the Midwest, but where in the Midwest, and what he had done there, and whether he had been born there or had come from somewhere else, no one knew. Swan was Swan.

Once, on a rainy winter night, I felt a pang of concern for

him. I heated a can of soup and poured it into a big plastic mug and took it downstairs to the doorway where Swan sat on his bedroll.

"No, thanks," Swan said.

"Come on, it's just soup. It'll warm you up."

Swan didn't answer. I couldn't think of anything to say either, and after a minute my waiting there became absurd, as if I were in a Beckett play. Swan understood why I was there, though. He wanted me to know that he was all right. So he lit a cigarette and, blowing smoke through his clenched brown teeth, he said, "I think I'm going to run for president."

Gratefully I said it sounded like a good idea.

"If animals could vote it'd be a sure thing." He nodded impatiently. "You don't know what it was like when the door was open. It wasn't about drugs. Now people say, oh, you were a hippie, you took LSD, you're crazy. But it wasn't like that. We were getting hold of the truth. Why do you think they killed Dylan?"

"They killed Dylan?"

"They replaced him," Swan said, "with a robot from Disneyland. I knew the guy who made his face. He died of a heart attack in nineteen seventy-six. He was forty-one years old. A heart attack. Everyone who knows is in trouble. Are you a poet?"

"A historian," I said.

"Is that right? I'll tell you what you have to do. You have to write down what's happening in this place."

I tried to explain that the present wasn't my period, I was more of a nineteenth-century person. Swan didn't listen. "There are things happening right now that would blow your mind," he said.

"Like what?"

He gave me a leaflet.

Swan was right: things were happening that would blow my mind. Even as I was becoming a native of the Mission, in the winter of 1993–94, the Mission was changing, in part because so many people like me had moved there, but also because our presence in the neighborhood was a signal to other people, unlike me, I thought, back then, that it was safe to move in. They came from the Marina, from Pacific Heights, from Redwood City and Palo Alto and Menlo Park, from Burlingame, they came from El Cerrito and Chicago and Texas and New York. They drove up the rent and the price of shoes; they occupied all the tables at the junkie breakfast restaurant, which served eggs Benedict now, and not to junkies, the lights were turned up too bright for them, and the manager put a lock on the bathroom door and gave the key only to paying customers.

Money came to the Mission, leading women in high heels down Sixteenth Street on Saturday night. Money parked its car in the middle of Valencia Street and didn't care if it got a ticket, there was nowhere else to park, even the garages were full. You might as well live in New York, money grumbled. Money waited for a cab, but all the cabs were taken. Money went into the new Temple of Faith Bar on Mission Street, which had replaced the old Templo de la Fé church in the same location, but preserved the mural on the rear wall, of Jesus reaching down from the clouds as though to pluck a bottle of pepper-infused vodka from the top shelf of the bar. Money came out at two in the morning and eyed the donut restaurant across the street, with a big sign over the counter expressly prohibiting the sale of stolen goods on the premises. Money wanted a donut but was afraid to go in. Money had intense conversations just below my window. I don't want to go home with you, money said to money, I don't care about your business model, just get me a cab; but the cabs were still scarce, and in the end money said, OK, but please don't put the top down, it's cold.

Money was coming, like the wave in the postcard my grandfather sent me each year, threatening to drown us. Overnight my friends sloughed off their part-time jobs and like wastrel princes ascending to the monarchy they became professionals. Josh worked for a construction company, filing plans in AutoCAD; Erin got a job at a Web startup which proffered folk remedies to people who couldn't afford health insurance. In six months she went from half-time to full-time, from full-time to management, where she made a tacit policy of hiring only Wiccans. Even my housemate Victor, the medieval historian, started a company called MySky with some friends from Stanford. He wasn't allowed to tell us what MySky did, but it carried him off six days a week at seven a.m. and returned him late at night, looking furious and pinched. A couple of years later I'd see billboards for MySky on Highway 101; I'd read about it in the *Chronicle*, in the *Times*, and I'd realize, with a kind of shock, that *this was Victor's company*, that it belonged in part to the person who had lectured me about the hermeneutics of Saint Thomas Aquinas at our kitchen table. By then Victor was long gone from the apartment on Sixteenth Street. First he moved to Palo Alto; later, I heard, he bought a house in Sausalito, high on a bluff overlooking the bay.

By the middle of 1996 it seemed as if Alex and I were the last people in the Mission not employed by the New Economy, and Alex was increasingly caught up in the purposiveness of academia. He flew off to conferences, proposed panels, worked on *Stanford Historical Notes*. I had passed my oral exams, but still hadn't found a topic for my dissertation. In fact, I was coming to the depressing conclusion that nothing about nineteenth-century America excited me, apart from a few subjects which had been done to death. I told everyone I was working, but really I was drifting, and because I was drifting, I saw a lot of Swan.

Those were great days for him. Not only were the poor being forced out of their rental apartments to make way for airy live/work condominiums; not only was Clinton gutting the American welfare system and dropping bombs on Bosnia, but his car, a green VW Beetle that he had inhabited, literally, since the mid-eighties, had been towed, a consequence of too many unpaid parking tickets. Swan had never had so much to be angry about. When I saw him in the morning at Java Man, his fingers flew across the keyboard of the public computer, composing jeremiads in which he abandoned the doctrine of universal love and recruited the animals to go to war. He was so angry that he wouldn't give his leaflets to human beings unless they begged him, sometimes not even then. He stood on the corner of Sixteenth and Valencia with a stack of them in his crooked arm, like a statue erected to commemorate an old battle. Generalissimo Swan, who fought the world to a standstill in the Battle of the Mission.

All small cute women are agents, he wrote. *U can trust no one but creatures.*

Concerned, I tried to interest Swan in other subjects. "Hey, Swan, any luck with the car?" Or: "Did you see the crowd outside Blondie's last night? Man, they're bringing them in by the busload now." But he was completely caught up in his work, and I have to say I envied him for that.

Crews, take ur planes! Shoot the officers! Take ur tanks, men. Bomb all hi-rise+mansion areas! Get ready for the Coming of the Great Ghosts!

"What ghosts, Swan?" I asked.

He ignored me.

Bird Wars Rip City, Swan wrote. *Riots Blood Flames!*

"Hey, Swan," I said, "did you see, they're towing cars in the middle of Valencia Street!"

"Only allowed to park there on Sundays," Swan shot back. "Only for church."

Despite my clumsy efforts at friendship, we were never as close as we'd been the rainy night when I brought him soup. We would never be even that close again. Swan was becoming a prophet, a role that distanced him from the rest of the world—you couldn't get too close to a lighthouse. He typed furiously, monopolizing the computer in Java Man, and no one dared ask him to stop. *I will burn Spain with a ray from the ether*, he wrote, *I will crumple your planet like paper.* It was as if he were already living in a different world from the rest of us, a world where poets and animals had the power of gods. *I'LL show you what blood is, miles of iodine roses piled upon the ocean. O live in the thunder & lightning.* Then one day a man who'd been waiting to use Java Man's computer for half an hour finally shouted at Swan, "Dude, it's time for you to get up!"

Swan didn't answer.

"I'm telling you, dude!" the man said. "Don't you hear me?" He grabbed Swan's shoulder and some things happened very quickly: Swan stood up and reached out his hand, to steady himself, I thought. The man thought he was being attacked and shoved Swan, who fell to the ground and lay there motionless. "Damn," the man said. He turned to the barista and said, "You better call an ambulance."

I knelt by Swan's head. "Are you OK?"

"I'm fine," Swan said.

He lay there with his eyes closed for a minute, then got to his feet. He gave us all a magnificent look of contempt and walked out, his shoulders high with prophetical rage. A minute later the ambulance pulled up outside Java Man, its lights flashing, and an EMT came in with his gear.

"Where is he?"

The barista nodded at the street. "He's OK, I guess."

The EMT laughed. "OK for now."

The man who'd provoked the incident sat at the computer, not even typing. He didn't look at anyone. It was as if nothing had happened. I think that was when I first felt the desire to disappear.

In the bad winter of 1997, when the days lightened imperceptibly out of wet dark and ended in droplets of water sparkling on the windowpanes, at some point in that winter of colds and molds and beaches white with storm-brought foam, I dreamed of sneaking out of my own life and leaving only an empty place behind. Victor and Alex would still fight about whose turn it was to buy toilet paper, buses would still pull up outside Blondie's, the rain would still rattle the windows, everything would go on, but I would be elsewhere, becoming I knew not what. I daydreamed about renting a room in a single-room-occupancy hotel in the Tenderloin, or staking a claim to one of the Mission's many doorways. I thought about getting on an eastbound bus and seeing, for the last time, the white mound of San Francisco sink below the horizon. I don't know why that tempted me so strongly. Maybe it was the weather, or maybe I was afraid to stop being a young man with the potential to become anything, and to be something in particular, an academic historian. Maybe everyone wants to disappear at some point in their lives, and maybe all of us do. Some drop out of sight; others stay in the same place but vanish from each other; still others, most of us, maybe, vanish slowly from ourselves. I don't know. In the end, I went nowhere, and it was Swan who disappeared.

Ironically, it happened while I was working on my dissertation. After months of watching me mope around the Stanford library, Alex mentioned a grant, a Michigan historical society that invited scholars to peruse their collection of nineteenth-century newspapers. "What do I want with Michigan newspapers?" I asked, and Alex said, "A grant looks good on your C.V. Come on, you've got to do something." I couldn't disagree with him and remain in academia, so I applied, and to my mild surprise was accepted. My C.V. got to call me a Visiting Fellow, Wagner Center for Nineteenth-Century Periodicals, and I spent a month in East Lansing, a rolling terrain of frozen mud that made me think of the First World War. Against all expectation, I found what I was looking for: *The Michigan Midnight Cry*, a newspaper published by a society of

Millerites—or Adventists, as they called themselves—in Detroit. I had heard of the Millerites before, but I'd never thought of them as a subject worth knowing in detail. They were too religious and too marginal. But everything else in the Wagner Center was worse, and so, diffidently at first, then with curiosity and even something like excitement, I read the complete run of *The Michigan Midnight Cry.*

While East Lansing froze and crackled in one of the coldest Februaries in memory, I learned about an apocalypse long past. *The Michigan Midnight Cry* was part tract, part newsletter; articles explicating the prophecies in Daniel and Revelation alternated with stories about people in Detroit who needed a few dollars to get through the winter, recipes for "Jubilee Pie" and other such treats, poems, announcements of weddings, meetings, auctions. If it weren't for the weird phrase *if time continues*, which was appended at the foot of every published schedule, the Millerites could have been stamp collectors, pony breeders, almost any special-interest group in America with a developed body of knowledge. And yet I found myself getting strangely engrossed in their obscure debates about the fall of the Ottoman Empire—had it happened yet? was it a sign of the end times?—and the return of the Jews to Israel. I shared their enthusiasm as the summer of 1844 brought all-night bouts of singing and prayer, and their anxiety as the final days drew near. When was it too soon to give away everything you owned, and when would it be too late? No one wanted to be homeless in Detroit in October, but no one wanted to be burned up for covetousness either.

The popular press called the Millerites "raving maniacs" whose imagination had run away with them, but as I read *The Michigan Midnight Cry* another picture emerged: of people who continued to build houses and fences, to buy and sell livestock, to attend concerts and lectures, to read poems, to marry and give birth to children. Some of them spoke out against slavery; they argued for temperance and woman suffrage. They believed in reform, albeit the way you might believe in cleaning your house before you left for a trip. I didn't understand why these ordinary, good-hearted people had believed the world was about to end. And why *then*? The first half of the nineteenth century in America was a time of progress and rapid expansion: the number of states in the union doubled and the population grew by a factor of five; canals were dug all across New York and Pennsylvania and even in Ohio and Illinois, where, because of drought, they were useful only half the year. Steamboats plied the Hudson and the Mississippi and crossed the Great Lakes. The railroad was invented, and the industrial printing press, and the telegraph. Why, in such a giddy and optimistic time, had the Millerites dreamed of apocalypse? I thought of San Francisco, of money and the Mission, and I wondered if rapid change made some people *want* the world to end. I heard my dissertation ringing like a church bell, clear and close at hand.

I came back from Michigan in March and lost myself in research. I needed to know more about technology in early-nineteenth-century America, about Michigan and also upstate New York, where William Miller had lived: the region was a hotbed of religious enthusiasm in the 1830s. So my project returned me indirectly to Thebes, to my own history, which increased my sense of its rightness. *This* was what I was meant to be doing, and *I* was the one who was meant to be doing it, I thought, and if I didn't ever put the thought into words, it was always there, a living shape frozen beneath the ice of my unbelief in destiny. Enthusiastically, I spent weeks assembling a delicious absence, a palpably hollow space in the tangle of recorded knowledge, which my dissertation would fill.

When I looked around again, Swan was gone. He wasn't at Java Man in the morning; he wasn't asleep in an armchair at the back of the Latin Quarter Bookshop. At night Swan was not to be found on any of the doorsteps where he usually slept. I asked Peter when he had last seen Swan, but Peter couldn't remember. It must have been a busy time for all of us. I asked Josh, who lived on Twenty-fourth Street, if Swan had migrated to another part of the Mission, but Josh hadn't seen him either. In fact, he was going to ask me, had I seen Mr. Babylob? The one who stood on the corner of Twenty-fourth and Mission with a sign, WHORES OF BABYLOB, REPENT, FORNICATION IS DEATH. Whether *Babylob* was a deliberate misspelling or not, no one could say. Had something happened to them both? Josh said he would ask his friend who worked at the needle exchange, and was in touch with a lot of the street people. Weeks passed; I saw Josh but he didn't mention Swan. When I remembered to ask, he admitted that he had been too busy: this full-time thing, you know, there was more truth in those words, *full* and *time*, than he had ever imagined. He was on it now. The rainy season dragged on, cutting the short days even shorter, leaving the sky, in the rainless intervals, a washed-out blue that was the closest thing to winter you could find on the California coast. I wondered if Swan had died, he was older than most street people, and he smoked foul brown cigarettes, and his skin was yellow like an old tooth. It wouldn't have taken much for him to get pneumonia.

The thought that Swan might be dead would not leave me. It was a hollow feeling, as if I had skipped an important step in a complicated procedure and gone on to the next step, unaware that what I did now no longer mattered because the procedure was doomed to fail. It occurred to me that I could find out one way or the other, that people did not die without leaving a record, if there was one thing I knew from the study of history, it was that people left a record of their death, even when nothing else in their life was recorded. But I didn't do anything. Then one day I had a fight with Alex about whether or not to buy a car that Peter was trying to get rid of, an ancient Volvo that had once belonged to Norman Mailer, at least that was what Peter said. Mailer had once come to the Bay Area to teach a class at Mills College, this was the story; he bought the Volvo, then he became smitten with one of his students, a nymphet who happened to be the heiress to a canned-pasta empire; and this girl, who, for the purposes of the story, is called Noodle Girl, insisted that he get rid of the Volvo, because it reminded her of her parents, the canned-pasta couple, who were about the same age as Norman Mailer. So Mailer sold the car almost new to Peter, who was in those days a local literary impresario. He, Mailer, bought an MG coupe, and drove to L.A. with Noodle Girl, who left him there, or was left by him, and later became a member of one of the new religions that believed the cosmos was friendly, at least in comparison with the earth. That was the story. And the car was majestic, it had a big, confident body painted the deep blue of the sky in a Northern Renaissance painting, the blue of an illumination in an illuminated manuscript. I had to buy it. Alex said I was an idiot, the story was obviously false, and even tweediness had its limit, which was the cause of our fight, the word *tweediness*, because I had to point out that I did not own a single tweed garment, or even a pair of flannel pants or a blazer or anything with elbow patches. Alex said it didn't matter, I was a tweedy person, which cut me to the quick. I thought I dressed like an outlaw, and here my housemate was telling me that I was donnish.

"Don't worry," he said, "tweedy is good. This is just a case of taking it too far."

I bought Norman Mailer's car that afternoon for five hundred dollars and took it to a mechanic, who told me it would cost another twenty-five hundred to get it to the point where it would pass inspection. Fine, I said. And with the energy I'd got from winning that conflict, because it did seem to me that I'd won, with that rage, I looked up the City Records Office in the phone book and called them to see if they had a death certificate? "In what name?" the clerk asked. And of course I didn't know. I went back through my file of leaflets. Swan, he called himself, or Saint Swan, or Swami, or Swhandi, or Sewanee, or Swan the Swain, or Mayor Swan. I asked Peter, who said, yes, Swan had told him his name, but it was a long time ago, and he didn't remember it. David something? He thought it was a Jewish name, which surprised him, because he didn't think of the Jews as homeless, an irony that he had savored from time to time, over the years.

I should have gone around to all the places where Swan had been and renewed my inquiries; I should have put up a sign, stapled it to the utility poles and hung it in the windows of the hipster shops, to let everyone know that Swan was missing. But I was ashamed to do these things. I didn't want the neighborhood to know me as the person who was looking for Swan; and if there was some explanation, obvious to everyone but me, for Swan's disappearance, then I didn't want to be the asshole who didn't know what it was. And it was still winter, and the rain still hadn't stopped, and there was *The Michigan Midnight Cry* begging to be understood, and perhaps it was a kindness to let Swan alone. If he was not on the street in that ugly weather, maybe it was for the good; if he was unfindable in that dark season, maybe it was because he did not care to be found.

THE DAY OF OUTRAGE

That was what I thought, but I wasn't the only one who cared about Swan. Josh had reported his disappearance to a friend who worked for a nonprofit housing-rights organization, and they decided to use the disappearance of Swan and Mr. Babylob and other homeless residents of the Mission as an occasion to protest the city's policy of harassing homeless people and driving them out of gentrifying neighborhoods. They were going to have a rally and a march. The Day of Outrage, his friends called it. Josh asked if it was something I wanted to get involved in and I said yes, even though I was skeptical about the power of any protest to accomplish what I wanted, which was not the modification of city policy, but Swan's return. More generally, I was skeptical about protests as such, in particular about the ones Josh and his activist friends staged. I'd been to a couple of them right when I moved to San Francisco and they struck me as being almost completely self-enclosed, as though the world they were changing was uniquely that of the people who took part in them. Still, I felt like I owed it to Swan to do something. And in the back of my mind there was, if not the hope that the protest would bring Swan back, at least the superstitious belief that doing something was better than doing nothing at all.

Josh's friend had printed a stack of posters, and I volunteered to hang them. I mixed up wheat paste in one of Alex's Tupperware bowls and went out at night, slathering sticky white stuff on the sides of newspaper vending machines, construction hoardings and utility poles, and pressing posters into the paste to let people know the Day of Outrage was coming. My pasting technique was not good and often as not the posters went on crooked, part of their message swallowed by creases or torn off in my clumsy efforts to get them to stick. It didn't matter, I hoped. I was spreading the word. The strange, or not so strange, thing was that, as I worked, I came more and more to believe that the Day of Outrage would not be in vain. How could people see the posters I had spent hours putting up and not take action? I imagined a crowd of thousands, a march on City Hall. The mayor would speak to us from a window. We have a sane and reasonable policy, he'd begin, and we'd drown him out with our simple, irrefutable chant. Swan! Swan! Aides would be dispatched to find out what it meant. Records would be searched. Swan! Swan! Sooner or later a clerk would find the file of David Somebody, a.k.a. Swan, transferred from the Mission District to who knew where, on such and such a date. Advisers would tell the mayor to leave him where he was. An old man, in poor health . . . But by then the chant, Swan! would have become perpetual. SWAN would be spray-painted on the columns of City Hall; banners reading SWAN would hang from windows all over the Mission; airplanes would write SWAN over the city in ice crystal letters half a mile high. The only thing to do, the advisers would finally admit, was to send him back. One day without ceremony an unmarked white van would stop outside Java Man and Swan would get out, unbowed, making "V for Victory" signs with his nicotine-stained fingers.

If this sounds delusional, you have to understand, first of all, how badly I wanted Swan back, and second, that I was now not alone. Everyone I knew was doing something to get ready for the Day of Outrage, except of course Victor, who had vanished into MySky. We met at the Blue Study with our notebooks, and Josh gave us assignments; we e-mailed one another frantically, asking where the microphone stand was, who had the poster paint, who was going to choose the route our procession would take once it left the park. Erin's friend Neil volunteered to make puppets that would represent the people who had vanished, and suddenly puppet-related tasks sprang up. A week before the Day of Outrage I was drafted to drive to Hunter's Point to buy plaster of Paris from a wholesaler. He didn't want to let me go with less than five hundred pounds; I convinced him to sell me two hundred, and got halfway back to the freeway when I drove over a bump and heard something in the engine go *snap*. I was staring into the tangle of hoses under the hood of Norman Mailer's car when two men came up and asked if I needed help. Hunter's Point was a rough neighborhood and these guys looked rough, but in this case need trumped prejudice and miseducation. I said yes, please, help if you can, and the three of us pushed the burdened car a block and a half to an auto-body shop, where a Mexican mechanic diagnosed the problem as a broken fan belt and sent his friend to get a replacement from another garage. The two of them installed it in my car, asked me for twenty bucks and went back into the shop. I looked around for someone else to pay, but no one wanted my money; even the guys who had helped me push the car were gone. The whole process had taken an hour and a half and no one even wanted to be thanked. I drove back to the freeway, full of courage and hope: it was as if I'd just moved to San Francisco all over again, as if I had stepped over a wall that kept me from experiencing the mercy of the world. I delivered the sacks of plaster to Neil's house in Bernal Heights, we grunted as we carried them up the driveway to the garage where the puppets were being made, already some of them had giant heads and recognizable if unpainted faces, they looked up at us benevolently from the floor. I rubbed my eyes as though to wipe away sweat, in fact tears, small tears.

The Day of Outrage began as every day in San Francisco did that season, wrapped in a dense white fog that smelled of the ocean. By the time I finished breakfast, though, the air was warm and still. It was spring, but it felt like summer, real summer, as though we'd stolen a day from the world of seasons. I thought it was a good omen, and Alex agreed. We took the bags Josh had told us to pack, with water and chocolate bars and a list of phrases we were supposed to say if we were arrested, a highly improbable contingency. Dolores Park was full of people sunbathing; the tennis courts were full, the soccer field already churned to mud. Two kids were throwing a Frisbee back and forth, leaping in the air, running, catching it between their legs. After all the rain we'd had that winter, the grass shone emerald like a patch of wet Scotland hung out to dry here on the coast. Josh and his friend Todd, the organizer, were in the park already, talking on handheld radios to their distant minions, who, to judge from their voices, were not doing as they should. When Josh ended his conversation, I asked if I could do anything to help. Josh looked at my folded banner and emergency bag with distaste. "Not unless you have a sound system and a truck." This was at eleven o'clock. The rally began at noon. As the remaining hour passed, the story of what had happened to the truck and the sound system came to light, phrase by angry, garbled phrase. Erin's bassist Tristan had set off in the wrong direction, toward Berkeley; he got stuck in traffic at the entrance to the Bay Bridge, then the van overheated; it was an old van, it didn't like to idle. A tow truck was summoned; the van was dragged across the bridge and fixed, provisionally. Now the traffic was on the Berkeley side of the bridge and Tristan was afraid of another breakdown.

Erin and Star arrived with the literature table, and arranged the pamphlets and flyers published by the various organizations that were sponsoring the rally. We sat on the grass and waited for the crowd to arrive, while Josh and Tristan shouted at each other on their radios, and Todd called people who might own microphones and speakers. I lay back and closed my eyes. No speakers had arrived by noon, but on the other hand no spectators had arrived either. The sound system was back on the Bay Bridge, but now there was an accident on the bridge and nothing was moving. Alex and I drank beer and talked about Stanford.

"Did you know that Schönhoff used to be a Jesuit?"

"Sure."

"Did you know he was defrocked?"

"No."

"Absolutely. He slept with a seminarian."

"Is that a defrockable offense?" And so on.

One o'clock, one-thirty. Todd and Josh conferred on the

stage. A small crowd had gathered, drawn by the illusion that something was about to happen.

"OK," Josh announced, "we're going to go ahead without the sound system."

"How is anyone going to hear us?" Erin asked. She had agreed to sing, and Tristan would in theory accompany her on the guitar.

Todd took one of the posters and rolled it into a tube. "Hello," he said into the tube. "Can you hear me?"

Three or four people sitting in front of the stage nodded yes.

"Welcome to the Day of Outrage," Todd said. "I'm glad you could join us. Now let's talk about what this is all about."

No one was listening. This is a fiasco, I thought, and worse, it was just like every other protest I had ever been to. How could I have believed that it would be otherwise? I opened another beer.

"OK," Todd shouted, "we're going to have some music now. Sing us something, Erin!"

"No way!" Erin shouted from the literature table.

"You promised!"

"I promised when there was a microphone."

"Whose fault is it there's no microphone?" Todd yelled through the rolled-up poster.

"What do you mean, whose fault?"

"Why did your bassist go to fucking Berkeley?"

"I don't know, Todd. Why don't you ask him?"

"Because he's apparently switched off his fucking radio!"

Josh and I went to buy more beer, and came back with a fifth of Jameson, which induced a slight wobble in the rotation of the earth, a periodic dip, like cardiac arrhythmia. At some point Todd called to me to talk about Swan. I stood on the stage, overlooking the crowd, which, at this point, consisted of Erin, Star and Star's knitting friends. The makeshift megaphone was wet with spit, but I didn't mind, I pressed it to my mouth and spoke about Swan's plan to bring vegetarianism and the love of animals to San Francisco. I spoke about Saint Francis of Assisi and some aspects of his biography known only to a few enlightened souls, and how important it was to know these stories, the stories that only a saint could tell you. Then I said, "Holy shit, there he is." There he was, all right, twelve feet tall, colorful and impassive as a god, wobbling down the hill toward me at the head of a line of like-sized deities, coming down the hill in silence. "Motherfucking puppets," I called into the megaphone. "You're just a bunch of motherfucking puppets!"

There would be no procession. We finished the whiskey and used the banners to sit on. The puppets lay on the grass like passed-out revelers, their arms splayed and their faces turned to the sky. Now and then people who had heard about the Day of Outrage showed up, and we yelled at them to sit and drink with us. Some of them did, and as the sun went down our numbers grew, until there were thirty or forty people gathered in front of the empty stage. We had failed utterly to organize a protest, but something else was happening, something remarkable. Strangers were speaking to one another. Alex knelt by Erin, picking blades of grass and tossing them over his shoulder. Star was talking to Neil. I lay on the ground, my ear to the earth. This was good, this was very good. People were joining with one another. Even more than a protest, this was what we needed, for everyone to be joined together by many threads, we needed each person to be entirely surrounded by people, because we had seen what happened when you were at the edge of the crowd, like Swan and Mr. Babylob, you could be plucked from the world at any moment, you could vanish. By this measure the day was a success. We were bound to one another now; we could not disappear. We would remain in this place forever.

The sun went down; the dog people called their dogs

homeward. Tristan appeared just after sunset, his hands and face streaked black with motor oil. He looked at our little drunk crowd and howled, Bastards, you bastards, but it was no use, Todd tackled him and forced him to roll through the grass until he was happy. "We've at least got to set the fucking thing up," Tristan said, so we ran to the truck, which was parked illegally between palm islands on Dolores Street, and hauled speakers and cables from the back. Tristan and Todd carried a generator between them, and Erin danced around them, plugging things together while there was still light to see by. The generator roared like a failing car; we had power. Erin sang a song about being so much in love that she wanted to kill us all, then someone hooked up a portable CD player and put on one of Pearl Fabula's mixes. I pulled Star to her feet and we staggered toward the speakers. You could hardly call what we did then dancing. It was pure autonomous motion. I held on to Star's hand, because I was afraid if we were separated in that darkness we would never find each other again. If no one held my hand I might become one of the unattached people, one of the people who could be made to die. We staggered back and forth; someone elbowed me in the stomach; I tried to kiss Erin but bit her eyebrow instead. The music got louder, its beats and bleeps building toward something utterly magnificent, a universal binding together of all of us, and as it reached the peak of its intensity blue and white lights came on, flashing, making a real club of the stage. Our hands rose joyously into the air. For a moment it seemed as though we had succeeded in doing that impossible thing, we had made a complete, real, other world, then someone shouted, "Police!" and people were running, falling, getting up and running again. The music stopped. Tristan and Erin and Josh grabbed parts of the sound system, which were, un-fortunately, still cabled together. The wires got caught on a tree and they dropped the speakers and ran. I looked for the bag that contained my instructions in case I was arrested, but it was too dark to find an object that size in the disorder of empty bottles and banners, leaflets and posters. Neil was shouting, "Save the puppets! Save the puppets!" so I picked up a puppet, it was massive and difficult to maneuver, and stumbled down the hill, across the soccer field, toward the tennis courts. I was a giant, my shadow enormous in the tennis-court lights. I ran into the street, around the corner, this giant head waving above me like a flag, a totem, a burden. When I had gone far enough and no one was following me, I stopped. Only then did I look up to see whose head I was carrying: Swan's. Thus the Day of Outrage ended.

SAN FRANCISCO, CITY OF GHOSTS

Three months later, I dropped out of Stanford. There was no obvious reason why I left: my dissertation topic had been approved; all I had to do was write it. But after the Day of Outrage my heart no longer pointed in that direction. I struggled all summer long with the first chapter of *The Great Disappointment: Progress and Apocalypse in a Michigan Millerite Community*, and in September I sent a letter to my department chair, informing him that I would not be returning to the program.

"You moron!" Alex cried, when I told him what I'd done. "Go down to school right now and take that letter back."

"I can't."

"Why not?"

"I don't believe in history anymore." I hadn't realized that it was true until I said it. But actually I was angry at history, I hated history. It was good for nothing. Could history make Swan come back? Could it change anything about the city where I lived?

"So?" Alex said. "What does that even mean, you don't believe in history? How is that not a historical statement?"

"I think it's useless," I said.

Alex sniffed. "Baby, if you were looking for useful, you should have become a doctor."

"Well, I don't want to do it. If I'm going to do something I don't care about, I want to get paid for it."

We kept arguing, but Alex didn't change my mind. Finally he said, "Do what you want, but don't come crying to me when you're peddling your ass on Polk Street."

In another city, or another decade, he might have been right to worry, but this was San Francisco in 1997 and the Internet caught my fall. I mailed my letter to Stanford on a Wednesday, and the next Monday I was temping for Cetacean Solutions, LLC, and laughing at their motto, "We Go Deep." A few weeks later I let slip that I'd once written a BASIC implementation of Adventure, and my boss, Mac, urged me to get back into programming. I learned Java and C++ easily, and at that point Cetacean hired me and I was issued a key to the Fun Room.

If I had been thinking about it, I would have realized that my facility for programming was proof that the past mattered. In some significant if cryptic way I was picking up where I had left off when I was expelled from Nederland, as if everything I'd done since then was merely a detour or, as Swan might have called it, a *long strange trip*. But I wasn't thinking about it; I didn't want to think about it. I was happy to work long hours at Cetacean, managing other people's content, about which I knew nothing and cared not at all. On weekends I went dancing with Erin and Star and Josh. We took Ecstasy and promised to love one another forever, then, at a party in Oakland, I met a woman in a white fur coat. "What's your name?" she asked. I told her I wasn't sure, I had names for various occasions, names that revealed my essential self to greater or lesser degrees, this was, for me, the problem with Ecstasy, I was filled with love for those around me, but love, in my case, took the form of complex sentences, each of which had to be uttered with great care, because I loved the concepts they articulated almost as much as I loved the people I was saying them to, or maybe just as much, I had to think about it, and so, when I was rolling, I did nothing but talk, talk, talk. The woman in the white fur coat accepted my explanation. "I'm Alice," she said. It was deliciously simple. By the end of the night, my head was in her lap, and I had told her no fewer than three times that I loved her. Oddly, she seemed to believe me. And more oddly still, after the drugs had worn off, after the sun had come up and it turned out that we had been in a courtyard all night, and not, as I had supposed, a vessel hurtling through interstellar space, I believed it myself. I was happy, although in retrospect it seems to me that I was already becoming a ghost.

REGENZEIT

By the time I finished my story—obviously I didn't say everything I've written here, only the gist of it, and I left Alice out completely—it was after midnight and the tea had grown cold in our cups. Yesim was looking at me with affection and sadness.

"Swan never came back?" she asked.

"No."

"You should look again," she said firmly. "You never know, he might turn up."

It hadn't occurred to me that Yesim might take the story practically: not as an account of delusion or moral weakness or spiritual collapse, but as a problem that could be solved. But of course she was right, I had barely looked for Swan. It was possible that he was alive somewhere, and that he could be found.

"Where would you look?" I asked.

Yesim smiled. "One thing at a time. First let's finish with your grandparents' things, then we'll find your friend." She stood up. "Now it's late."

For a moment Yesim's face hovered happily beneath mine. I leaned down to kiss her and she stepped away. "I can't do that," she said.

"Because you might lose Mark?"

"Because I might lose everything." Yesim hesitated. Then she said, "Good night!" and went out to her car, to drive the fifty feet to her house.

It was only a matter of time before she changed her mind, I thought. I didn't believe sex was really her problem; what was so terrible about sex? I knew people in San Francisco who'd slept with far more people than Yesim had, and they were fine. They were sex-positive, they went to sex clubs, it was no big deal. By day they sat in cubicles like everyone else. If I could just convince her that I wasn't going to hurt her, that I wanted her to be happy and free, like, as my yoga teacher said, all beings everywhere, if I could only convince Yesim that I loved her, sooner or later she'd fall into my harmless arms.

But I was wrong, possibly in my diagnosis, certainly about what would happen next. Two days after she'd tried it on, Yesim brought back my grandmother's dress, its seam invisibly fixed, in a dry cleaner's bag. I asked if she wanted to come in, and she said, "I can't see you now."

"Why not?" I asked.

"Please, don't ask any questions," she said.

"Is it something I did?"

"Just be patient. I'll tell you when I can. OK?"

"OK," I said.

The next night her car didn't come home. Surprise! The good part is over. That's why they call it a *part*.

I didn't have the courage to pursue Yesim, but I couldn't let her go either. I drove to Snowbird, pulled into the parking lot, then turned around and drove away. I dialed her number but hung up before it rang. I stopped by the organic grocery in the morning, and ended up becoming friends with the girl who worked there, Carrie. She'd grown up in the valley; her parents had a farm out past Maplecrest. Her uncle owned the grocery. Yesim didn't appear. And she kept not appearing, through a week of blue fall days, as the leaves in the valley lit up, and the ones on the mountaintops fell, and lines of smoke rose up from the hillside like strings connecting the earth to the sky.

I sat in my grandparents' kitchen, looking across at the Regenzeits' house. Kerem came and went uselessly, but not his sister. Where was she? I imagined Yesim in Mark's strong former-construction-worker arms. I imagined her with Dr. Y, with Professor X, and at this point I began what I can only describe as an advanced degree in masturbation. Alone in my grandparents' house, I wrote a thesis in the bowl of the downstairs toilet, and my subject was Yesim. If it was a little theoretical—well, so are many dissertations. Its footnotes said everything there was to say about her feet, and its endnotes got to the bottom of her rear; the curls of her hair tangled in the index, on the title page I put her eyes and her mouth took the place of my name. I submitted my Yesim to the committee on Yesim in partial fulfillment of my need for Yesim; I submitted and submitted.

Then one night she came home and that was even worse. To watch her walk across the kitchen, take pins from her hair and make tea, to watch her pick up the phone and not to hear my phone ring; to watch her speak and hear nothing. Given that I'd never had Yesim, it shouldn't have been so bad to lose her, but in fact it was worse to lose her that way. I kept wanting to call her, to run across to the Regenzeits' house and pound on the front door, to throw myself at Yesim's feet and ask her to take me back, but I was keenly aware that she couldn't take me back, she had never taken me in the first place, unless you counted the things we did when we were ten years old, or that night in Kerem's study. I had no *standing*, as a lawyer might say, to plead before her. I was just a childhood friend with a house full of junk and a collection of unbearably vivid images of what might have been.

Finally, in desperation, I went back to cleaning out the house. I finished my grandparents' bedroom and started on the attic. I hoped there would be some treasure hidden there—a painting by Thomas Cole, a secret diary kept by one of my ancestors—but finding treasure in your grandparents' attic turns out to be something that happens only in novels and on TV. What I found were cardboard boxes of sweaters, a trunk with a missing hinge, extra leaves for tables that had long since vanished, mattress frames, box springs, empty dressers and cracked leather shoes. I slept; I woke; I packed; I slept again. I carried skis and tennis rackets down to the garage, and a box of dolls that must have belonged to the Celestes, curiously unlifelike in their stiff smocks, with their big, blinking eyes. When did dolls first have movable eyelids, I wondered, it must have been in the nineteenth century, when realism was in vogue and the simulation of domestic life was the business of novelists and playwrights and even husbands and wives, all of them concerned with getting the details right, from wedding banns to mourning crepe, and what game would have been more in keeping with the Victorian spirit than to make dolls sleep? But what about peeing dolls? Not a nineteenth-century invention, I thought. For realism that extended below the waist you had to wait for Freud. And then also plastic. Sometime after the Second World War, probably, you got peeing dolls, doll diapers, doll messes, Henry Miller, the apogee of scientific psychoanalysis, Nabokov. I put the dolls with the things to sell or give away, guessing that some child might be interested in them, if the fashion in dolls hadn't moved on to catch a new facet of the human experience: dolls who threw up, mentally ill dolls, dolls who grew old and hung on.

For the first time, I wondered who would receive what we were giving. A family of refugees, washed up on the American shore with nothing, maybe, or else a family whose belongings had been lost in a fire, although in either case, I reflected, looking over the great heap of Rowland junk, it would have to be a family with some unusual hobbies, or one that wasn't particular about what it owned. I called Goodwill and the Salvation Army, and left them messages describing the situation. I watched game shows on television, then dramas, then the news, which told us that a group of African-Americans in Minneapolis were building a space ark. They showed pictures of the ark; it looked like a big silver egg studded with colored lights, a Fabergé egg that could seat up to a hundred people. The TV reporter asked how it was going to fly, and the spokesperson for the ark project, a light-skinned black woman, said it wasn't going to fly, it would be picked up. "By whom?" the TV reporter asked, and the spokesperson said, "You will know them by their craft," a phrase that's stayed with me ever since. Still no word from Yesim.

I finished the attic and started on the study. The small room, with its single window that faced our other neighbors, the Karmans, was the place where my grandfather's presence could still be felt the most strongly, and for this reason I had avoided disturbing it. It was as though Oliver continued to exist as long as his clutter occupied the space he had given it. When all the signs of his life were packed away, then he would truly be dead. Now I wanted that moment to come quickly. I threw away catalogs from building-supply companies, letters telling my grandfather that the Republican Party needed his help because the Democrats were up to unspeakable mischief, letters from a foundation that worked to reunite missing children with their parents, the kind of mail that old people get from organizations that prey on their absentmindedness and goodwill, each letter annotated by my grandfather, *Can this be true?* and *Free calendar!* I threw away the book of word-search puzzles in which he had marked unfinished puzzles with Post-it notes. All At Sea, Creatures of the Night, Roman Holiday.

By morning the drawers of my grandfather's desk were empty. The closet was robbed of its wealth of original packaging, hard styrofoam pillows that fit the contours of long-gone machines. The bookshelf had surrendered its helpful volumes, *Bargain Your Way to a Better Life, How to Be a Nice Guy . . . and Still Win, How to Make Time for Everything,* to boxes with DONATE written on their sides, and now the bookshelf itself was labeled for donation. Maybe someone would take boxes and bookshelf alike, set them up in another study, and learn from them what they had been unable to teach my grandfather. More likely the books would be pulped. They would dissolve in a slurry of acids, fall fiber from fiber, until not a word of their advice remained, then they would be put together again in a new shape, cradling white, unbroken eggs. The floor lamp was gone, the set of five-pound weights was gone, the boxes of Christmas cards, which contained far more envelopes than cards, suggesting that my grandfather had written several drafts of each card he sent, were gone, although one box had a few cards in it, with pictures of a Japanese fishing boat and a fisherman waiting before a wave that was about to break.

All that remained were the dozens of thick folders related to *Rowland v. Snowbird*. They contained articles from law reviews and scientific journals, newspaper stories about snow-related accidents, photographs of cars and houses half-buried in snow. I felt a little thrill when I found the original complaint, with Richard Ente, Esq., listed as counsel for the plaintiffs. The facts were more or less as I remembered them from the research I'd done years ago: in October 1966 there was a big snowstorm in the valley. Sixty-two inches of snow fell in a forty-hour period, a white deluge that left Thebes submerged for days. Trees and power lines came down; cars went off the road. There were slips and falls, accidents of all kinds. And this was just after Joe Regenzeit had begun seeding the clouds—he'd even boasted about Snowbird's "scientifically augmented snow" in an ad. It looked awfully like his cloud seeding had worked, and Oliver, along with a dozen other Thebans, set out to make him pay for it.

Seen close-up, some of Richard Ente's arguments were far-fetched: could you sue someone for trespass because his snow fell on your land? If a storm knocked down power lines, was that theft of electricity? But there were masses of documents to support these claims. The files held analyses of the wind patterns in the valley, charts showing the seasonal fluctuation of temperature and precipitation in the area, affidavits from people who had seen the clouds change as the cloud-seeding plane flew through them, medical records of people who had slipped and hurt themselves. Then there were the counterassertions, doctors who admitted in deposition that their patients had been off-balance for years, meteorologists who pointed out that winter weather in the mountains was wildly variable. Had Regenzeit really made it snow? Had the snow hurt anyone? Behind or beyond these questions of fact were the questions of law. Did Joe Regenzeit have the right to seed the clouds that passed over Snowbird, and, if so, was he responsible for them when they passed over someone else's land? Where did Regenzeit's interest end, where did the public interest begin? Who owned the clouds?

I thought of Victor and MySky, which was making head-lines with its *weather mill*, its promise of renewable energy from medium-altitude wind layers. When Victor told me what MySky did, I'd laughed at him; it wasn't until I began to read about his company in the papers that I wondered if his engi-neer friends could really do what he said they could. Now they had *weather farms* in the Sierras where they were testing their technology, and protesters were gathering at their gates. What a strange world it was, I thought, where these dreams kept coming back. Human beings had been trying to harness the clouds forever, and no one had really managed to do it, but we didn't stop trying. It was just like with the airplane, thou-sands of years of total failure didn't deter us. And maybe MySky would get it right. Would the human race be better off if its weather mill worked? By any reasonable standard the answer was yes, clean low-cost renewable energy would make the world a better place to live, but a perverse part of me re-sisted this answer. For reasons I couldn't articulate—maybe I was just jealous of Victor, who used to be a graduate student like me, and was now so rich—I wanted MySky to lose. I wanted humans not to control everything. I felt a wave of un-expected sympathy for my father, who had fought Joe Regen-zeit with every legal argument he could think of. Why did he run away, I wondered, not for the first time, and just then, as if in answer to my question, I came to a thin folder labeled *Rich-ard Ente, Esq.*

I pressed my forehead to the cardboard in the hope that its contents might pass directly into my mind. But no, I had to open the file, to leaf through onionskin invoices for $100, $200, $500. Richard might have been cheaper than other law-yers, but he wasn't cheap. There were bills from the months before the trial: $400 for an unspecified meeting, $212 for "initiation fees," $675 for research. Where was Richard going, what was he doing? The last bill was for $3,000, trial prep, but it wasn't the last document in the folder. That was in an envelope, addressed to my grandfather in a big, spiky hand I'd never seen before. My father's hand. The letter was postmarked Denver, and it had been mailed in May 1970, about three months before my father died.

Dear Oliver,

You opened the letter. That's a good start. Now be brave and don't chuck it until you've read everything I have to say. First of all, forget about the lawsuit. You must know by now it couldn't have gone any other way. Little money loses to big money every time in America, and even with a lot more money you wouldn't have got what you wanted. The only way to beat the Regenzeits is to kick em in the nuts, I told you that. Now you know. And if you've really been thinking, you know the Turks are the ones who will lose in the end. You can twist Mother Nature but She springs back every time and woe to the one who bent her then. If it hasn't happened yet it will soon, and you'll be there to say you told them so. OK, now the tough part. Are you ready? Oliver, you may choose to be my enemy, and if you do, God knows you won't be the first. Plenty of people have hated me for my faults—and believe me, I know what they are, I know them like a high-diver knows his pool—as if they had never in their own lives made a mistake. I don't know if you can be bigger than that, I don't even know if I have the right to ask you to be bigger, seeing how small I can be myself. But if you can, Ollie, if you see what I see, that we're all creatures of more or less the same species dancing around on this planet for only an eyeblink and then forever gone, sans money, sans folks, sans everything, then maybe you'll be able to do what I'm going to ask you to do now. I'm enclosing a letter for Marie. I want you to pass it on to her—give it to her if she's at home, or else send it to her wherever she lives. For god's sake don't read it. I can't explain all the reasons why it's important for you to do this, but I'll tell you that in the last three months I have walked through hell on foot—literally, Ol, you should see my feet, what calluses, what cracks—and if she doesn't get the letter I will have made the trip for nothing. And I don't have the strength to walk back home.

I wonder if you'd know me if you saw me now? I've gone so far into my head these last few months, I'm as faint as a memory. I haven't cast out my demon but I've got the bastard's throat between my hands. And I'm squeezing. I'm asking you for help, Oliver, not just for my sake or even for the sake of Marie and her sister, but for your own sake. I know you won't want to hear this, but you've got to see what big plants your daughters are, and how you've tried to choke them, to keep them from the light—it's not just you, of course, but the whole system of socialization that came over in the Puritan ships—we've got to disentangle ourselves from it if we're ever to be happy. Happiness is love. Love is freedom. OK, but enough Richard Ente–izing. I trust you to do the right thing. I can't tell you how much depends on it.

    Peace,
        Dick

I wanted badly to know what Richard had written to my mother, but the second letter wasn't in the envelope. My grandfather must have done as my father asked. Which was big of him, under the circumstances: his lawyer run off, his case lost. I credited Oliver's gentle heart, but actually I didn't see how he could have refused Richard. Even I was moved by the letter, and I'd never known Richard Ente. More than ever it felt like a shame that I hadn't met my father: compared with Oliver, Richard was completely unreserved; compared with my mothers he was scintillatingly honest. He alone among everyone I was related to had an idea of what life was actually about, what it was *for*. But even as I missed this dead father whom I would never know, I mistrusted myself. Was Richard's letter one of the ploys Charles had told me about? Was *in the last three months I have walked through hell on foot* real contrition, or just my father telling Oliver what he wanted to hear?

I read the letter again and again, as if by memorizing it I could learn Richard Ente's heart. But his heart was not there to be found; all that happened was that my new affection for him was joined, more and more, by doubt. Who was Richard Ente, what had he meant, what had he wanted? The pain and guilt and *life* I'd felt when I read the letter for the first time gave way to a scholarly distance, as though Richard were becoming, before my eyes, a historical character. Soon, I thought, sadly, I'd be tracking down his references, *people have hated me*, even *the whole system of socialization that came over in the Puritan ships*. I called my mothers but no one was home. I phoned Charles at the shop and asked him about the letter. "I never saw it," he said, "and I have no idea what Richard was thinking, but I'll tell you, it doesn't surprise me. He liked to keep us guessing, and you know what? We're still guessing. God damn Richard Ente."

After a brilliant cold night when the stars seemed to part as I looked at them, as if the planet were moving deeper into space, a fog settled in the valley. The mornings were white and the days ragged and soft. I spent a lot of time watching TV, and trying not to look over at the Regenzeits' house to see if Yesim was there or not. It must have been around this time that I got an e-mail from Dave, the owner of Cetacean, informing me that my two weeks' leave, which had by now stretched to four and a half weeks, was never officially approved, and that I was fired. I didn't care. Honestly, it was hard for me to believe I had worked there at all.

Now I am coming to the hard part my story, but I don't want to tell it, not today. Let's talk about something else: history, for example. If I *were* to travel back in time, to check the accuracy of my guesses about the Millerites, one question I'd surely want to settle concerns their *ascension robes*, the white gowns they supposedly put on in order to go up to Heaven. Did the Millerites really wear them, or not? On the one hand you have a host of eyewitnesses who say yes, the Millerites wore white robes: a New Hampshire seamstress who made robes for her neighbors; a cloth merchant who ran out of white fabric as the final day approached; and so on. On the other hand you have the historians who say the Millerites never wore robes of any kind; they planned to go up to Heaven in whatever they happened to be wearing.

Just about everyone who writes about the Millerites weighs in on the ascension-robe question. You have to wonder, why was it such a big deal? When I was working on my dissertation, I thought about this a fair amount. The conclusion I reached was that the ascension robes, if they were real, were a sign that the Millerites' fundamentalism—their belief that the world would *really* end after however many years and days it said in the Bible—was just as petty and materialistic as the world to which it was opposed. If you believed in Jesus, what did it matter if you wore a robe or not? The robes made the Millerites ridiculous in the public imagination, but I couldn't help thinking that they also united the Millerites to a noble tradition of people whose actions respond, in the end, not to the real world but to some kind of dream. From the so-called pioneers of flight to the explorers who set off in search of a Northwest Passage to the Pacific, or even the timid people who sit down at their desks to write books, how much of what human beings undertake is based, not on a calculation of possibilities, but on the blind belief that if we just *act* on our desires, the world will somehow make them possible? Everyone believes what they want to believe, everyone sees what they want to see, if they want it badly enough, and all I can say is, the Millerites must have wanted the world to end very badly if they did dress up in white robes, but on the other hand I can understand them, I can understand wanting something badly enough that you are willing to make yourself ridiculous. If there's anything I can understand now, it's that.

I don't think you are reading these pages, Yesim, I don't see how you could be reading them, but if you are: I'm sorry!

REGENZEIT

One morning in early October I was in the grocery, telling Carrie about the summers I'd spent in Thebes, and I was just coming to the story of Kerem and Shelley and Shelley's brother's party when Yesim came in, dressed not in her secret-agent outfit but in a long blue coat that I had never seen before. Her hair was all askew, her blouse wrinkled and untucked.

"Oh, it's you," she said.

"Where have you been?" I asked.

Yesim looked surprised by my question. "If you have a minute, I'll show you."

In the parking lot she took my hand. "I've been up all night," she said, "so don't hold me responsible for what I do or say, OK?" She squeezed my fingers. It was as though a Morse message passed through her arm to mine, a secret pulse to let me know we were on again.

Yesim drove us out Route 56, past Snowbird, where mowers were clearing the slopes of the summer's grass in preparation for the first snowfall. She took the road up which I'd followed her a couple of weeks earlier, and where she had turned left before, this time she took the right fork. The road became a path, the path became a track. Branches scratched the sides of the Outback. Then we were in a clearing; before us stood a wooden ruin, painted white and green but nearly worn of its colors by weather and neglect. The siding sagged, the windows were blinded by boards, the porch had collapsed and only joists remained, the space between them full of earth and dead leaves, a red-and-yellow carpet that led to the front door. We got out of the car.

"Do you know what this is?" Yesim asked. "It's

the old hotel, or what's left of it. I wanted you to see it before it changed."

"Changed?"

"Can't you guess?" Yesim said. "We're going to fix it up. You can't tell Kerem I told you, or he'll never forgive either of us."

She pushed the door open and we looked together into the dim rotten house. Here and there a gap in the boards over the windows let in a slice of gray light, showing us a section of floor, a bit of mantel, a door. Yesim took a flashlight from her pocket and swept the beam over an old parquet floor twisted by damp. "As you can see," she said, "it's going to take a lot of fixing."

The hotel smelled like wet towels gone bad a very long time ago, a breath-stopping mildew smell that had itself decayed almost to nothing. The room we were in had been a lounge, from the look of it: a big fieldstone fireplace yawned across the room at what had been a bar. There was an indistinct area to the right that might have been a restaurant. Yesim said they were going to restore all the original details: the bar, the stage, the fireplace, the leather armchairs, even the deer heads on the walls. They were going to renovate the swimming pool, and reopen the gardens, and maybe put in some cottages in the woods. Oh, yes, and they were going to have music, just like in the old days. "What was the name of the band you played for me?"

"Gil Gideon and the Two-Time Tunesters."

"We're going to have music like that. We're going to advertise on billboards all the way down the Thruway. Summerland, the good old days are back, something like that. My brother wants me to write the ads because I'm a poet." Yesim laughed. "Do you want to see the upstairs?"

The air on the second floor was closer, harder to breathe. I covered my mouth with my hand. We walked down a long hallway, Yesim opened a door and there was light. We were in a bedroom that faced the upslope of the hill; beyond the window was a big tangle that might once have been Summerland's famous garden. The room had never given up its old furniture, an iron-framed double bed, a sink, a rocking chair with a collapsed cane seat. A writing table, a chair. On the table, a stack of paper, and beside it a loose sheet that Yesim quickly turned over.

"This is my secret," she said. "I'm writing again."

"That's wonderful," I said.

"I don't know if it's wonderful, but it feels right, so for the time being I'm going to keep doing it." Yesim looked bemused, as though she'd forgotten it was her birthday, and here were these presents to remind her.

"It looks like you have a lot of pages there," I said. "Is it poems?"

"Not really."

"A story?"

"Kind of."

"Can I read it?"

"Maybe later," Yesim said. After a while she went on, "It's because of you that I'm writing. I've been thinking a lot about you, these last few days."

"Me? Why?"

"Actually," Yesim said, blushing, "I was thinking about your shirt. The one with the monkey on it? I was really surprised when I saw you in the Kountry Kitchen, wearing that shirt. It was so ugly and so cheerful at the same time. I didn't think you would ever wear a shirt like that. If you had asked me, when we were kids, what you would turn out like, I would have said you were going to be kind of a nerd. You aren't offended, are you? I don't mean it in a bad way. I even think nerds are a little sexy. Anyway, when I saw you wearing that shirt, I thought, we don't *have* to become anything. We can choose. Although now that I think about it, the shirt is a little nerdy, isn't it?"

She looked so happy, it was impossible for me to be offended. "I'll loan it to you, if you want."

"I'm not sure it will fit me."

She sat on the bed and I sat down beside her. If I had known what would happen because of what I did next, all the terrible consequences that would follow, I want to say that I wouldn't have done it, but actually, when I think about that morning at Summerland, the dusty smell, the sunlight descending yellowly through a crack in the clouds, all I remember is how beautiful Yesim looked, even with dark circles under her eyes, and something in me was saying, *now, now, now!*

I don't remember what I said. Something about the cosmological constant—can that be right? And how the expansion of the universe is accelerating, how the stars we see in the sky are the only stars we will ever see, how the stars are retreating from us, in millions of years they'll be out of sight, and cool, and turn to iron, and the sky will be entirely black, I don't know, my mind, to change metaphors, was like a forest on fire, and thoughts were leaving it like animals, running away in packs toward a faraway river, but I remember how Yesim looked at me, perplexed, and moved to the far end of the bed. I swung my legs onto the bed and crawled toward her, because it wasn't fair that I should be such a poor persuader; it wasn't fair that Richard Ente had done so much harm without passing on to me the power to get what I wanted most in the world.

"No," Yesim said. "What did I tell you, I can't do this."

I kissed the hollow of her collarbone.

"Stop," she said, but I didn't stop, and a moment later she encircled my head with her arm, drawing me closer. I worked my fingers through the gap between the buttons of her blouse, and circled her navel with my finger.

"Fuck," Yesim said.

I took it as an imperative. We sank together; a puff of dust rose from the bed, composed of spores of mold, insect feces, particles of skin left behind by guests who were now in their graves, powdered wallpaper glue, all the dusts that fill a house when it has begun to die. I pulled Yesim's blouse up and kissed the stiff cup of her bra. "So good," Yesim said. I sprang her from her hooks and snaps, she slipped my buttons through their slits, our clothes came off, we lay together on the old poisonous mattress, pushing out clouds of dust. The bed's frame groaned happily, the springs yawned, it was as though the room were waking up, with each thrust a little life came back to the building. Soon hot water would be running in the pipes, maids would do their dusting, bellhops would buff their shoes and set their caps on straight, then come to attention as the grumble of the first car echoed up the road, the fire would be lit, the registry clerk would uncap his pen and prepare himself to write on the first page of his new book, the first new name.

"Yes," Yesim said, "yes yes yes!"

We lay there, just breathing, then Yesim felt the wet spot on the mattress and cried out, "What did you do?" She jumped up and gathered her clothes in her arms.

"I'm sorry," I said, but Yesim was already running. I ran after her, barefoot, naked, down the stairs, but she wouldn't stop; then I heard another voice say, "Yesh?" Kerem and a man who was probably his architect stood in the lobby, and now Yesim was in Kerem's arms.

"Yesh, what happened?" Kerem asked, then he saw me. His face changed, and a look appeared on it that I had never seen before, but that I understood at once. Fury. I'd seen the black eye he got in Philadelphia; I'd seen him at fifteen, kicking rocks and throwing beer cans, but I never figured out, never bothered to figure out, what he was feeling. Fury. I think he must have had it all along: fury at his parents drove him from Thebes and fury at the world brought him back, fury at the world that had fucked his sister up. Maybe that was the reason for the restoration, the secret project, maybe it was intended to keep Yesim interested, to keep her in Thebes. I was intended to help her too; it was as if Kerem had brought me in to help her, and now look what I'd done. Fury! Kerem lunged at me and I ran. I don't know how I got past him; I guess my desire to disappear was greater than his desire to catch me. I ran through the grass to Yesim's car and got in the car and locked the door. Kerem was shouting. He banged on the windshield with his fists. I noticed that I was sitting on something sharp, I reached under my buttock and felt the plastic haft of an automobile key.

"Sorry," I mouthed to Kerem, and I started the car.

He followed me, still shouting, as I backed up until the road was wide enough to turn around, beating the roof, the side windows, the hatchback, shouting words at me that I couldn't make out through the solid car. I drove back down the rutted road and after maybe a quarter of a mile the black Explorer appeared in the rearview mirror. I drove faster; the Outback bounced down the hill and skidded onto Route 23. I drove west, away from Thebes, too fast in the middle of the road. My teeth were chattering. Maybe I can go now, I thought. Maybe I can just keep going, take 23 to 88, 88 to 86, 86 to 90, and cross the country that way. I wasn't wearing any clothes, I didn't have any money, but maybe that was the only way I would ever leave Thebes. I fumbled on the unfamiliar dashboard for the heat and the radio came on. Gautier del Hum was bringing us the greatest hits of the 1980s and today. I wanted to turn the radio off but I couldn't find the control again, or the switch for the heat, and it was too much, I had to get my bearings, to figure out how the car worked. I stopped in the middle of the road and I'd just found the button for the radio when there was a sound.

The Explorer ran into the Outback; the Outback gave way before the Explorer. In another century, in another country, it might have been a tragedy, but these cars weren't built for tragedy. These were family cars; they crumpled where they could; beyond that they stood firm. There was a crunch, a curse, a hiss as the air bag let out its air. Then Kerem was standing beside the Outback, looking in through the window. He asked if I was all right.

"I think so," I said.

Kerem tugged at the driver's door but it wouldn't open. He walked around the wreck and tried the passenger door. "I think we're going to have to cut you out," he said. He went to the Explorer for his phone, then came back. "Why did you stop, anyway?"

"I couldn't find the heat."

"You what?"

"I'm sorry."

"You're sorry," Kerem said, "*you're* sorry? You asshole, these aren't even your cars."

In a quarter of an hour the tow truck came, its yellow lights flashing. Charles climbed down with his cane and limped over to us. He saw me naked and looked away, embarrassed. "Man," he said, "this brings back memories," and it was only then that I realized my father had done much the same thing thirty-one years earlier.

I spent the day in a hospital in Albany. There was almost certainly nothing wrong with me, a cut on my forehead, some bruising on my chest, but even so, said Dr. Weiss, the attending physician in the emergency room, there might be a tiny hemorrhage, something the machine couldn't detect, but which, if it went untreated, could give us problems. I think the fact that I was admitted to the hospital wearing nothing but a Mylar blanket had aroused his concern. And sure enough, when Dr. Weiss was gone, a nurse came in and told me that she was going to ask a few questions. What was my name? Where was I? What year was it? Who was the president of the United States? I answered the first three correctly and objected that the fourth wasn't a good test of mental acuity. Imagine a hermit, I said, who's been living without television in a hut in the woods, he's still clear in his mind, but . . . The nurse made a note in my chart and that afternoon I was visited twice by other nurses who took my temperature and blood pressure and asked me the same questions. Finally I told them who the president was and they had no choice but to let me go.

Charles was waiting for me with some of my clothes. "How would you feel about a beer?" he asked.

"I shouldn't drink. I might have a concussion."

"Just one beer."

He drove us to Maplecrest: a gas station, the cracked plaza of a supermarket that hadn't been able to stay in business, then my uncle's garage, dark for the night, a couple of houses decorated with jack-o'-lanterns and skeletons and American flags, a bar that took up the ground floor of a white, two-story house. The Crossroads, it was called, although there wasn't actually a crossroads there. Possibly it had moved from another location. Charles got us a couple of beers and we found a table at the back of the room.

"Listen," my uncle said, "there's something I didn't tell you the other day. When I was seventeen, eighteen, I was what you'd call a stoner."

"So?" I said. "It was the sixties, everyone smoked pot."

"That's true. But the thing is, when Rich, your father, came to Thebes, he didn't have a connection. I happened to be fairly well connected in those days, so I hooked him up."

"You sold my father dope?"

"I'm not proud of it," my uncle said.

"I'm sure if you hadn't done it, he would have got his pot from someone else."

"Very likely," said my uncle, laughing.

We sat for a while, watching bubbles rise up through the jukebox's glowing tubes.

"That's what you wanted to tell me?" I asked.

"I feel responsible for what happened," Charles said. "I didn't contribute to your father's mental stability."

I thought about this. "How much pot did you sell him?"

"The thing is," my uncle said, "it wasn't just pot. My friend Douglas Turpin had a brother who was a Hell's Angel in Albany, he could get us coke, speed, acid, PCP, and sometimes we sold a little, just between friends. Then Richard Ente comes to town, and he was so cool, I won't say I didn't feel the tug of the desire to do mischief. Not to hurt him, just to show him that we were all players in the same game. You know what I mean?"

What Charles did was, he found out that Richard had never dropped acid, and invited him to climb a mountain and watch the full moon rise. "When we were at the top of Espy Peak," he went on, "I took out my tabs, and Richard said, What's that? and I said, Acid, it's part of the ritual. He couldn't back out. I gave Richard a big dose, probably bigger than I should have given him, and he and Doug and I all sat there waiting for the moon to rise. Then it came on. I was, like, Richard, tell us about the moon! But Richard had turned very,

very white, and whatever he knew then, he wasn't telling. I guess he experienced some heavy things, like, afterward he told me he had died about halfway through the trip. He said death was gentle, like potting a plant in a bigger pot, you moved the consciousness into the earth, where it had room to grow, and if you left it long enough, you'd find you had a planet-sized mind. Fucking Richard Ente! I thought I was showing him, and there he was, showing me.

"Then Richard went away for a few months. When he came back that summer, he was, like, Charles, my man, I'm counting on you, you've got to fix me up with that good stuff that you were kind enough to procure once, in what seems to have been another life. Richard was always strange, but now he was *really* strange. He talked a lot about balance, about how evil was necessary in order to make good. Even the greatest evil, World War Two, and everything that happened to the Jews, was necessary. We paid in blood, Rich said, and now we will collect in light. I ought to have said something to Oliver, but how could I tell him that I'd given his attorney LSD?

"Meanwhile, Richard made me come with him to meet these old mountain freaks who lived on state land. They baked their own bread, and we brought some back to my folks. *Hoc est enim corpus meum*, Rich told them, holding out this little crusty loaf. I thought that was pretty funny. The truth is, I was in awe of him! The more drugs we took, the more it seemed like we were walking down a path together, a spiral path that led right to the center of a garden. The garden was all of human thought, and when we climbed the hill in the center of it, we would understand everything anyone had ever said or done.

"Also," my uncle continued after a moment, "there was a social benefit to be reaped from supplying Rich with drugs. For a while, I was the second-coolest person in Thebes. You should have seen, I had this black leather cowboy hat with a green feather in it, like Robin Hood had stuck in his hat, or hood, whatever. I'm only telling you so you understand, I wasn't trying to harm Richard in any way. I only wanted to be someone different, not just a Thebes kid anymore; and I was, I *was* different. I drove Richard down to Albany to hear Janis Joplin at the Civic Center, we got good tickets from Doug Turpin's brother, in the front row, and a drop of water landed on my cheek, I thought from nowhere, and Richard said, Holy shit, you know what that is? That's Janis Joplin's sweat, don't touch it, that's some precious sweat you've got there, mister. I wiped it off. It's sweat, I said. Don't sweat it. Like it was nothing to me then."

My uncle stopped talking, and I didn't know what to say either. I didn't understand how Charles could have sat by and watched as Richard Ente lost his mind, and at the same time I appreciated how completely he must have been under Richard's spell. What a number Richard had done on him, I thought. What a number he'd done on all of us. Finally I asked, "What did he promise you?"

"What?"

"You said he promised everyone something. What did he promise you?"

"You really want to know? You and me, he said, you and me, Charles, we're kindred spirits. We both want to know the truth of things. I want you to go to college and read everything. You have a first-rate intelligence; get it in order. Because one day, you and I are going to meet again. We're going to talk this life business through, and we're going to blow it open. Richard suggested that I move to California. San Francisco or Big Sur, some place by the ocean. I'll find you there, he said. I'll always know where to find you." My uncle coughed. There was a deep knocking in his chest, like a vending machine delivering a can of soda.

I went to the bar and ordered us two more beers. I put a dollar in the jukebox, because I thought we needed music to take us away from ourselves. Soon Robert Plant was singing, Good times, bad times, you know I've had my share, which fit the moment, even though I hadn't chosen it for that reason, I didn't know Led Zeppelin at all, I had chosen these songs because they were the only recognizable noncountry tunes on the jukebox, with the exception of a *Best of Frank Sinatra* album that I knew we needed to avoid. Charles's big gray head rose and fell to the music. In the orange light of the jukebox he looked at once older and younger: younger, because I could see how he had looked when he was twenty. His hair was restored to shoulder-length luxury; his mustache grew black and sleek; in his eyes the certainty that he was at the center of the room, wherever he happened to be sitting, that he, Charles Rowland, was an event, a sensation, shone like a stage light. Older because I knew how many years had passed since that moment, and because I could see how badly those years had used him. He had been fixed too many times already, and when the next thing broke, whatever it was, his hip, his lungs, he would be beyond repair. Richard might have broken him first, or it might have been Oliver, who had ruined even his girls. With his only son he must have been a terror. Always tinkering with the last male Rowland in history, always making improvements. Now look. Charles doesn't see that I'm looking at him. His thick gray fingers drum on the table and his lips move to the song. Good times, bad times. His eyes are lost in a past he will not share with me. Maybe he's back in Vietnam. Maybe he has gone to California at last. I bring the beers back to our table and he grins at me.

"Fucking music," he says.

He salutes me with his mug and I salute him back. Charles sets the mug down and belches. End of story. Or not quite the end. When he's finished with his beer, Charles looks up at me with a sly, almost evil happiness that makes him look like the uncle I remember from childhood. "You know what we ought to do right now?" he says. "We ought to go see some girls."

This is going to be a mistake, I thought, as I got into Charles's truck. We drove north on Route 296, away from Maplecrest. Charles had the radio on, and we listened to Talking Heads' "Burning Down the House," and Bon Jovi's "Living on a Prayer," a strange combination, as though, as these songs grow older, all their actual, musical qualities are forgotten and the only thing that anyone remembers about them is that they're from the past.

"You like this stuff?" I asked.

"Not really," Charles said, "but there's no radio for men like me."

He stopped the truck in an unpaved parking lot outside a concrete pillbox with a yellow sign atop it that read SPHINX CLUB.

"I used to go to a place like this in San Francisco," I said.

"No shit?" Charles said. "I bet that was sweet."

It wasn't. In the gloomy winter of 1997, I'd gone a few times to a club where you got to sit in a dark cubicle and look at naked women through an almost soundproof sheet of glass. I went in the afternoon, mostly, though the word *mostly* makes it sound like more of a habit than it was. At first I was charmed by the collegial atmosphere that existed on the other side of the window; the women were all in one big, bright room and as they gyrated they talked to one another. It was impossible to eavesdrop on them through the glass, but it looked like they were having pleasant conversations. As I watched them dance I found myself wondering what they were talking about. I imagined that they were acquaintances who used their time together to catch up on one another's lives, the way women in other casual settings might do the same thing. Johnny's fine, I imagined one of them saying to another as she twirled lazily around the silver pole in the middle of the room, he's going out for the soccer team, and he's decided this year, no more Spanish. —Is that so? the woman who was leaning against the window right over my head replied. Marcia didn't take Spanish either after the seventh grade. I wonder what it is, do they have a bad teacher? —They think it isn't cool, said the pole girl. Oops! Looks like you dropped something! —Thanks! said the other woman, and she got down on all fours to look for it. I found this fantasy strangely erotic. I wanted to be idle with the women in the big bright room, where sex was as simple and harmless as a conversation in a supermarket.

I stopped going to the club when I found out, by looking in the mirror at the back of their room, that the women could see me almost as well as I could see them. They knew my face; they might remember me from previous visits; they might, and this was the clincher, they might make me a topic of conversation. The guy in booth three is a serious masturbator, I imagined the pole girl saying to her friend. You can tell by the way he holds his dick. Her friend looked down at me. He's not touching himself! —Make him start, said the pole girl. Her friend made a face at me as though we were having sex. I see what you mean, she called over her shoulder. What is it, something in the wrist? —It's his concentration, said the pole girl. Do you see how he's frowning? —Oh, my god, you're right, said her friend. That's so intense! Hey, have you ever been to the Zen Center?

I sat in the darkness, holding my penis as though to protect it from the cold, and I thought I saw the women look at me, and there was no companionship in their eyes, nor any compassion. That was unpleasant, but it was clear as soon as we stepped inside the Sphinx Club that this was a much worse place. The loudspeakers played Nirvana for a skinny girl on a stage that stuck into the room like a wooden tongue. The girl looked too young to be there, and really was too thin; her torso rested on her hips like a puzzle piece that didn't fit the piece below. There was a red spotlight on her, but even so you could see the blue tracery of her veins.

Charles was saying something, but the music echoed so loudly off the concrete walls that I couldn't understand him. He motioned for me to stoop so he could shout in my ear. "You know what I call this place? The Kountry Kunt. With two *K*s, like the Kountry Kitchen and the . . ."

"I get it," I shouted.

We sat next to an old Latino in a blue-checked shirt and a younger man who could have been his son. As we watched, the girl took off her top, exposing small white breasts which she took by the nipples and tugged in one direction then another, as if to show off their mobility. She looked like a salesclerk showing us how to use a new household object. The old man seated next to us put a five-dollar bill on the stage and the girl knelt and did the breast demonstration again. Up close, she looked older, twenty-five or even thirty, in the red light it was difficult to tell. The song ended and the woman paused, then the Guess Who's "American Woman" came on, and she stood up, turned her back to us and dropped her underwear. Next to me, Charles was rocking back and forth to the beat of the song.

"You like this?" I shouted in his ear.

"It's better in the wintertime," he shouted back. "This is the off season."

His breath steamed and I realized that it was cold in the Sphinx Club, not as cold as it was outside but much colder than you'd expect a man-made structure to be at the end of the twentieth century. I didn't like to think how it felt to the woman onstage, although maybe she was used to it. Or maybe the Sphinx Club was having trouble getting heating oil, maybe their tanker was delayed because of the hurricane also.

"Wait till you see Barb, though," Charles said. "She comes on later."

The woman spun around a metal pole that pierced the tongue stage at its widest point. She climbed the pole, embraced it with her legs and let her torso fall backward so her hair brushed the floor. I shivered. How could anyone want this, I wondered, but I couldn't look away. I was ashamed of what I'd done at Summerland. How could I have forgotten everything Yesim had told me? Why hadn't I been able to stop myself? The woman doubled over and looked at us from between her legs. Yes, she seemed to say, that's the riddle. —Do you know the answer? I asked. Do I know, she said, do I know? I'm the country cunt, I know everything. —OK, I said, what is it? —Guess, said the country cunt. Love? I said. Love, she repeated, don't make me laugh. You want love, take a look at this. She reached back and grabbed her goosefleshed thighs and pulled the lips of her vulva apart for the benefit of the man beside us, whose hand lay paralyzed on top of the five-dollar bill he'd set on the stage. You feel that? the country cunt said. Brr. —Give me a hint, I said. It starts with the letter *h*, said the country cunt. Hope? I said. Not even close, said the country cunt. Guess again. But I didn't want to play her game anymore.

"I don't feel well," I shouted at Charles.

"You want to leave now?" Charles asked, surprised. "But we only just got here."

"Yes, now."

I left the Sphinx Club. A moment later Charles came out and we stood beside his truck.

"It's too bad," he said, "I would have liked for you to meet Barb."

Just then a blue Toyota raced into the parking lot and stopped, and a chubby black woman climbed out, wearing black leggings and a fur-collared bomber jacket.

"And here she is," Charles said. "Barb, hey! Come over here and meet my nephew."

Barb shook my hand. "He's a lot bigger than you."

"Aah," said Charles, "I just shrunk."

Barb asked if we were on our way in, and Charles said no, in fact he was taking me home. "He was in a car accident this morning."

"Well, then," Barb said, "you get him home, all right? You got to take care of him." She jogged around to the back of the Sphinx Club and vanished.

"She's a nice girl," Charles said as we climbed into his truck. "I don't know where she comes from, but I told her I'd take care of her, if she wanted. You know what she said? She told me she was waiting for a rich man to come along. A rich man! God bless her, but I don't think she's going to meet one in that place."

"It doesn't look promising."

"On the other hand, maybe I'll get rich," my uncle said.

It occurred to me that you could never know other people, and that no matter how much you learned about them, they would always have another side that was hidden from your view, a dark bulk that made them complete but that you would never understand. By then we were back in Thebes.

"Where's your car?" Charles asked.

"At the grocery store, but I don't think I can drive. I'll get it tomorrow."

"You forget that we have a tow truck."

"No," I said, but it was too late, he was already pulling into the parking lot. He climbed down and hooked tow chains to the front fender of Norman Mailer's car, which was strangely unscathed by everything that had happened. With a grinding sound, the car rose to its rear wheels, like a begging animal. We drove back to Thebes with it rolling behind us, and when we got to my grandparents' house Charles backed the truck deftly into the driveway and lowered Norman Mailer's car to the ground. Then: "Hey," I said, pointing. The lights in the kitchen and one of the upstairs bedrooms were on.

"Uh-oh," said Charles.

I knew without being told that Kerem was inside, waiting for me. Or else he was vandalizing the house, ruining it, as I had—so I thought—ruined his sister. As if to confirm my fears, Charles opened the glove compartment and took out a .45 automatic. Holding it with its muzzle pointed at the sky, he slipped from the cab of the tow truck and motioned for me to wait. I sat helplessly in the passenger seat, sick with guilt and fear, imagining my uncle surprising Kerem in the living room. Kerem had a short temper; my uncle hated the Regenzeits. I was sure one of them was about to kill the other, or that they would both be killed, and that it was going to be my fault, and when, a moment later, a woman screamed, I thought, Yesim! and came running out of the truck to see what terrible thing had happened.

Charles stood on the porch, the pistol dangling at the end of his limp arm. He turned to me, his face pale, and grinned irritably. "It's your mothers," he said.

LOW-FLYING STARS

When I left Stanford, with only the most confused of explanations, four years into my doctorate, the Celestes said they loved me as much as ever, and wanted me to be happy as much as they always had, but they became noticeably remote, as though my decision had revealed something about me that they did not understand and could not embrace. We talked every week, but their questions about my job at Cetacean were pro forma; the days of Celeste's puzzled interest in computer programming were long gone. I tried to understand their disapproval. They wanted me to be poor but noble, like them, I thought. They didn't like the idea that I was making money in the *business world* or, worse, that I might, by some ordinary standard, be more successful than they were. My

Christmastime visits to New York became strained, then stopped completely.

But when I saw the Celestes sitting side by side on my grandparents' sofa, their lower bodies covered by an afghan, their faces still animated by the shock of nearly being shot by their own brother, I realized that this had all been illusion. My mothers weren't poor. Marie wore a deep-gray cashmere turtleneck set off with a wide gold necklace; austere Celeste wore a blue denim shirt and fleece vest specked with white paint. Four brand-new hiking boots stood in a line by the kitchen door. My mothers must have bought them for this trip, as though they were going into the wilderness, and not back to their childhood home.

"We took a cab from the train station," Marie was saying. "We thought you'd gone out to dinner, so we let ourselves in. I didn't know Thebes was so dangerous!"

"We thought you were burglars," I said.

Celeste looked at me sternly and asked, "What happened to your head?"

"Car accident," I said. "I got rear-ended."

Charles said nothing.

"Oh, dear," said Marie. "Were you wearing your seat belt?"

"Yes. I'm fine. It was a low-speed collision."

My mothers felt bad about having sent me off to Thebes to pack up the house on my own. For several weeks they'd wanted to come up, but New York was so busy in the early fall, they'd had to wait for the Columbus Day weekend. They'd called me to say they were coming, but got no answer. "We thought you might be camping," Celeste said, a little maliciously.

"We were just having a beer," I said.

"Before the accident, or after?" Celeste asked.

"After."

"Just a nightcap," my uncle said, as if this were the normal course of things: accident, drink.

"Well, we're glad you didn't shoot us," Marie said.

Sure, now, that they would be staying, Celeste carried their bags upstairs. Marie made tea. Changing the subject, she told us she'd been promoted. Now she was the style editor at *S*. "It's an almost meaningless distinction," she said, "but I do get to travel. Milan in October, Paris in January. Celeste is jealous."

"She's not coming with you?" I couldn't imagine one of them going anywhere without the other.

"She has a show. You should ask her about it, she's been making the most incredible . . ." Then her phone rang. "Hello? Just a sec." Marie went into the parlor.

"Thanks," I said to Charles.

"Thanks for what?" asked Celeste, coming downstairs again. She poured herself a mug of tea, and when neither of us answered her question, she went on, her voice expressing surprise and possibly disapproval, "How nice of you to leave our room the way it was."

My mothers stayed for two days. It was the first time since I was in high school that we'd spent so many hours together, and I found them different than I remembered: gentler, less insistent on their own apartness.

"It's too bad you didn't come to the funeral," Celeste said, on Saturday afternoon. We were sitting in the parlor while Marie circled the house, her telephone pressed to her ear. "You would have heard some stories about your grandfather. Did you know, he went to visit Gabby Thule when she was in the hospital, and he brought her wildflowers? He was a generous spirit, that was the phrase one of his friends used."

I didn't point out that *generuz de son esprit* meant something different. "It sounds like you miss him."

"Miss him?" Celeste said. "I don't know. Sometimes I feel like he's still here, and sometimes it's like he was never here at all. Although I had a dream about him the other night.

He had sent me a pair of wool socks, and I called to say thank you. Wool socks!" she repeated, smiling. "It's very strange."

Celeste fell silent. I asked her about her show, and she said it wasn't her show, it was a group show, organized by an arts council in Lower Manhattan. "You know who had a big show, though? Guy Anstine."

"The white box guy?"

"That's him. Only now he's tied his boxes together with string, and people are saying they represent some kind of network, *a hermetic system of historical reference*, what bullshit. Of course, Guy is a man." Celeste tapped her finger on her knee. Cautiously, as though she didn't know how her words would be received, she began to indict the system that elevated guys like Guy to the heavens while she was left somewhere in between, not obscure but not brilliant, ascending with infinite slowness. As she spoke I understood that Celeste didn't care whether I was an artist or an intellectual or a computer programmer: all she wanted from me was to know that I wasn't part of the system she was constantly fighting against, the one that wanted her to be unfamous, unknown. If Celeste had seemed to withdraw from me, it was because she worried that I wouldn't care so much about *her*.

That evening at dinner I mentioned that Yesim and Kerem were back in Thebes. I didn't say anything about having seen them, but Marie saw through my feigned casualness. "What a coincidence," she said, "that you should all come back here at the same time! It must be nice for you not to be alone."

"Didn't you used to like the Regenzeit girl?" Celeste asked.

I had no idea that she'd known. "Sure," I said. "I liked both of them."

"What's she like now?" asked Celeste.

"Older," I said, and the conversation went tactfully on to other subjects.

The next morning Marie went for a run and I had coffee with Celeste. We talked about New York and San Francisco, then suddenly Celeste turned to me and with a sweet, sad smile, said, "I remember the first time I fell in love. It was with a Thebes boy, Vaughan Oton, Mo's son. I don't think you ever knew him. He was your uncle's age, and very good-looking. He and Charles used to ride their bicycles all over town. Vaughan! Vaughan! I'd chase after them, but they never stopped. So one day I waited right outside the house, here, and when I saw them coming up the hill, I lay down in the middle of the street. Like I was one of the perils of Pauline. Help me! I might even have shouted. Help me!"

"What happened?" I asked.

"Vaughan ran me over," Celeste said. "I'd like to think that he didn't see me, but I'm not sure. I was in the middle of the road."

"Were you hurt?"

"Not physically. I did become more cautious, though."

This was the first time Celeste ever voluntarily spoke to me about her life in Thebes. At first I didn't understand why she had told me about Vaughan, then I realized she had some-how intuited the connection between my mentioning Yesim and the cut on my forehead. The story was her response. A lesson, maybe. Be careful who you fall in love with. I felt that Celeste and I were in rare sympathy. It was like we were re-ally what we seemed to be, more and more, as we got older, not mother and son, not aunt and nephew, but people of the same generation. Two old friends talking in the kitchen on a gray Sunday morning. "Why did Marie fall in love with my father?" I asked.

Celeste hesitated. "Freedom is very attractive," she said at last. "To us, as girls in Thebes, in the sixties, Richard was freedom. He was the first person who told us it was all right to do what we wanted."

I couldn't help noting that she'd said *us*. "Were you in love with him, too?"

Celeste made a face. "I never trusted Richard."

"Why not?"

"It's hard to put into words. It wasn't how he dressed or what he said, or even what he did. But there was always this feeling of there being something else that we should have known about but didn't. As if he had cancer, or a family somewhere."

"Did you find out what it was?"

"I'm not sure there was anything to find out, really. It was just my feeling about him."

"You didn't ask him?"

"You may not believe it," Celeste said, "but I was too shy to interrogate grown-ups back then. Why all these questions?"

Impulsively, I got my father's letter from the pile of things to keep. Celeste read it and put it down. "I always thought there must have been something like this," she said. "Where did you find it?"

"In Oliver's files."

"How sad," Celeste said. "None of us could bring ourselves to throw his letters away."

We went up to her old bedroom. Celeste took *Being and Nothingness* off the shelf, opened it to the last page, and removed the letter that had been folded there for thirty years. "Kind of a morbid hiding place, don't you think?" she said. "I had a strange sense of humor when I was seventeen." She glanced at the letter, then passed it to me. "You know, when I called you, to ask if you wanted to come here, I think I was hoping you'd find this."

"I would never have found it. This room freaks me out."

"Yes," Celeste said, "it is a little weird."

Happenstance Institute
Denver, Colo.
May–June, 1970

My star,

beyond dearness. You must be wondering why I ran away. I have been wondering the same thing myself. Me, wretched Dick, lame Duck (that's what Ente means *auf Deutsch*—some crazy Jew chose it for the family a couple of centuries ago, a man who loved ducks, I guess), not a day passes that I don't ask myself that question. For a long time I couldn't answer. Just a voice in my head shouting, Go. Lately my ideas have been getting clearer, maybe on account of the mountain air. Also, I have fallen in with some fellows here who have an institute. They've latched on to the old Indian idea that we choose a life because there's something we want to figure out. Each of our lives, and we have many, is like a book you pick up because there's something in it you want to learn. I did some sessions with them early on and they told me what my problem is. It's pride. I want to take all the world's sorrow on myself. I look back at my life and everything fits into that pattern. Top of my class at Bleak, but a lousy law school. Top of my law school class, but a lousy job. And even that was too good for me; I had to quit S & M (I mean Silberman & Mischeaux), and do two-bit private law and live among bums. I had to find the greatest love I'll ever know in my life, the only real love I've ever known, and run away from it. I look for the darkest spot in the woods and I run right in, hoping to make it less dark. That's pride. I'm ready to let it go, and right now. Not in the next life, when I'll probably be a rat or an ant given how I've screwed this one up. Getting to this knowledge has been hell, and a long trip, too. You wouldn't believe some of the places I've been in the last four months, the dark spots I got into before I saw which way the light was. I slept in the woods with the Indians back of Jewett and got them so drunk, they agreed to do one of their most powerful curses for me. Together we blasted the whole USA, this sick land, and we begged the sky to take revenge on the bastards who shoot their chemicals into it, beginning with Joe Regenzeit and then all the way out from him. We stuck knives in our arms and bled for it to happen. Then I was on the South Side of Chicago, sleeping at the Y, talking to a disc jockey named A-10, who plays outer-space music from 2 to 4 a.m. because he wants the aliens to feel at home. I told him I was from Mars and he believed me. Apparently a lot of Martians go to Chicago, and all over the Midwest. He was going to take me to a nightclub for Martians but I got pneumonia and checked myself into the hospital and when I got out I left Chicago and drove all night to Santa Fe, where the air is pretty good. Spent some time there with a rabbi named Yoel Hernandez who tells me that half the population of New Mexico are Jews only they don't know it. I was looking for a way back to the God of my fathers, then I saw it was all wrong, you don't go backward to find God. God is in front of you if It is anywhere. So I went to Denver, met the institute folks, and here I am. I'm up at 5 a.m. every day to stare at my bellybutton; after three weeks I've come to think there might be something in it. I've given up pot and everything, even coffee; now I drink tea made from sage twigs and eat rice we get surplus from the US government, with weevils in it. I don't eat the weevils. With the help of the good people here, I'm moving out of the darkness. I'm unjewing, laying down the ancestral guilt—I could write a book just about that. I sleep four, five hours a night. I don't talk to my mother in my head. I teach english composition in a school that's mostly Pueblo kids with bare feet and fantastic hippie hair. If they let me, I'm going to organize a debate team. I'm telling you this so that you'll know it's real, what I'm telling you. I hope you can see that. You always saw through me, you see into people as clearly as any swami, you have the magic eyes of serious purpose. I hope you can see me writing this in my little room, outside nothing but bushes and some uncollected litter and the big big night. I won't promise you anything because promises are for liars, but if you come out here, I know you can trust me not to run. I love you with the real love. Nothing that happens will change that. But hope with me that it isn't too late to make the wrong things right; hope with me that we can all still be fixed. I ran from you and it was the worst mistake of my life. But you can fix it, if only you'll f

and then a square cut from the corner of the page where Richard Ente's last words would have been. *Ollow me.*

"Marie gave it to me," Celeste said. "After Richard died, she didn't want to keep it. I doubt she even knows it's here."

I'd like to say that when I read my father's last letter everything became clear, and that I knew for certain who Richard Ente had been, but actually what I thought was, Holy shit, he sounds just like Swan! And for a moment, just for a moment, I allowed myself to imagine something so sweet I could barely hold it in my mind, like an atom of an element not meant to exist in this world. What if Richard had lived? What if he hadn't died in Denver, but had merely stolen away, in the darkness, on foot, and made for the narrow end of America's funnel? What if after untold adventures he had settled in San Francisco and what if he found there the true visionary powers he had been looking for. What if he had become Swan. What if I had known him. U think? said the Swan in my head. U really think? Then the vision, or whatever it was, fell apart, and I began to think about the letter. "How come she didn't go?" I asked.

"She couldn't," Celeste said. "You weren't there, you don't understand. Richard turned her inside out. He was such a fucking liar! He made us all live in a world of lies. But you know, when he left, the rest of us came out of it, and Marie,

Marie *didn't*. She, you know, she was pregnant, and we knew that, and she was certain that Richard would come back. Then he wrote her that letter, and your grandfather gave it to her, which was not conscionable. Because she wanted to go. Marie wanted to live with Richard Ente in the world of lies! I was the one who persuaded her to go to New York instead. Can you imagine what would have happened if she'd gone to Colorado? Can you imagine what her life would have been like? Living out there, in *dirt* . . ."

"Hello?" Marie called. "Where are you people?"

"We'll be down in just a minute, Marie." A door closed and we heard water running in the sink. "In the end, I made her choose," Celeste said. "Richard or me. If you stay, I said, I'll stay with you always. If you go, you're on your own."

Celeste looked at me uncertainly. She wanted me to tell her she had made the right decision, but I wouldn't say it. Celeste had kept my mother from going to Richard. And then, heartbroken, presumably, Richard had killed himself. I couldn't forgive Celeste for that, even if, at the same time, I knew that the person I really could never forgive was Richard Ente, who had killed himself and left us all to think about him endlessly. I was angry, and my anger focused itself on the hole in the page. How could Celeste have cut up Richard's letter, as if it were just material? It didn't occur to me until much later that the collage might have been more than a simple act of destruction, that for Celeste cutting might have been a way of coping.

"You killed him," I said.

"No. You don't understand. You don't . . ."

"What are you two doing up there?" Marie called up the stairs.

"Coming, Marie!" Celeste shouted. "We're coming."

Weeks later, when I'd left Thebes and gone to stay with a friend in New York, Marie sent me a letter. It was three typed pages long, and I guessed that it had been through several drafts. She expressed her sorrow at what had happened to Richard Ente, and her guilt: if only she'd gone out to Colorado, Richard's life, and hers, and mine, and everyone's, might have turned out differently. But at the same time she felt that she had made the only choice she was capable of making. And although Richard's death was an irreparable tragedy, she believed that she'd made the right choice, and that the consequences, for her, and Celeste, and me, were mostly good ones. You have two loving parents, she wrote, and you had a stable environment as a child. But finally, she wrote, we can never know what would have happened if I had made the other decision. Our lives are what they are, and I hope you can forgive me for being young, and confused, and scared of the unknown. She loved me, and one decision she would never regret was the decision to have a child.

I cut the letter into hundreds of pieces, which I put in a paper bag. I planned to make a collage out of them and send it back to Marie by way of an answer. But unlike Celeste I wasn't really a maker of collages, and when I moved out of my friend's house I left the paper bag behind. I asked my friend about it months later, and he said he must have thrown it away.

THE RICHARD ENTE PERIOD

Was my father a lover or a liar? Was he sane or mad? I've asked those questions a lot in the last several months, but I still have no answer. My father is dead. What I have are stories. The real Richard Ente is a continent on the far side of an ocean I cannot cross. He is undiscoverable, and maybe he always was.

On Monday morning I drove my mothers to the train station in Hudson. Celeste went to get tickets, and Marie took my hand. "I feel like there's so much we have to talk about," she said, but then Celeste came back with the tickets. My mothers boarded the train, and I saw them walking down the aisle, looking for seats. I thought of something that had happened a long time ago, when Marie started work at *S*. A host of names had joined us at the dinner table: Marcia the intern, Frank the managing editor, Nancy, Marie's boss, the despot of Quick Styles and Personal Health, Mitch in the mail room. As Marie became familiar with these people, they acquired attributes that were as immutable as the epithets in Homer. Sing, Muse, of Marcia of the striped stockings, who was into Japanese men; and of Frank, whose lover was sick, very sick, Frank, whose lover was dying, Frank, who lost his lover to a long illness; sing of AIDS, or don't sing, Marie didn't, and I didn't figure out what she meant by *a long illness* until later, much as it didn't occur to me until I was an adult, looking at the Pacific Ocean on an overcast afternoon, what Homer had meant by *the wine-dark sea*. Sing of Nancy, that bitch, and sing of Mitch, a nice guy. Later, when Marie had been at the magazine for about a year, one name started to appear with more frequency than the others. Jean-Luc, the photographer, whose attribute was that Marie couldn't see what all those women saw in him, was working with her on a story about dietary fiber. They went to the supermarket together and shopped for cereal, wasn't it ridiculous? Jean-Luc was at the launch party for a line of clothing made from actual rags, wasn't it funny? Marie spent the whole evening talking to Jean-Luc. He wasn't so bad, she said, and that became his new epithet. Jean-Luc, who, it was true, had dated a lot of women, but was a good storyteller. Jean-Luc, who had been a photojournalist, and had a scar where a bullet had passed through his upper arm on its way from one part of

Cambodia to another. Wily Jean-Luc, he had made himself a main character, and from that point on the story went in a new direction.

"I don't like where this is going," Celeste said. "It sounds to me like he's just using you."

"For what?"

"Don't be naïve."

"Have you considered the possibility that *I'm* using *him*?"

Celeste snorted. "Don't let the women's-magazine rhetoric go to your head, Marie."

"It's not rhetoric."

"Please. The only thing worse than telling lies is believing them yourself."

New crises arose at the magazine: there had been a small but significant misprint in the fiber story, women in Ohio were giving themselves colitis by eating hundreds of servings of Chex, and Jean-Luc vanished from our conversation for a while. Then he was back, he was flying to Los Angeles and he wanted Marie to come with him, it was a business trip, sort of, they were going to scout designers.

"Actually," said Celeste, "what surprises me is that you seem to be asking for my permission."

"That's not it," Marie said. "I just want to make sure you're comfortable with the idea that I'll be gone for a few days. And to make sure there aren't any, you know, conflicts."

"Why, are you afraid of conflict?"

"You know what I'm talking about."

"I'm not going to reassure you. In fact, if you were asking my permission, I would say no, because I don't like the way you're trying to disguise a romantic getaway as a business trip. If you had said, Celeste, I'm going to California to fuck . . ."

"Celeste . . ."

"If you had told me you wanted to fuck this guy's brains out on the beach in California, at least that would have been honest, and I would have said, go, have fun, just make sure this

French creep doesn't get his hooks in you too deep, because you know where he's been. But that's not the situation."

"No, it's not."

"As it is I have nothing to say. You don't need my permission. Do what you want."

"Jesus, Celeste," said Marie. "Why do we have to fight about this?"

"I'm not fighting."

"We're separate people. I wouldn't do this to you if you were going away."

"That's because I'm not going away," Celeste said.

"Well, I am," said Marie.

But she didn't mention the trip to Los Angeles again. She did mention Jean-Luc, but only once, to say that he had turned in some photographs late. It was as though he were one of those Homeric sailors whose names are mentioned only as they die in a shipwreck. We talked about ordinary things again, about those morons at the *Times*, about whose play was opening at La MaMa, about the terrible people on the subway and in the supermarket. Then Marie vanished. The phone rang while Celeste and I were eating dinner, Celeste answered, she said, "I see," and hung up. "My sister isn't coming home," she said.

"Where is she?" I asked.

"Downtown."

"When will she be back?"

"I don't know."

"Tonight?"

"No more questions," said Celeste.

Days passed. We didn't talk about Marie at dinner. Instead Celeste talked about her work: she was thinking of writing a book, she said, but not a regular book, it would just be quotations from other books that she fit together so it looked like they all belonged. It would have a story, only she didn't know what the story would be yet; that was the thing about this book, it was the kind of story you wouldn't understand until it was finished, which was, she said, true of all stories, only people kept getting themselves into trouble because they thought they knew what they were doing in advance. And indeed the story of my mothers was already turning in an unexpected direction. Celeste was happier than I'd ever seen her. Her voice was louder, her gestures larger, as though she were gaining volume to compensate for the twin who had left. One night the famous art critic came to dinner. She sat in Marie's chair and smiled indulgently at Celeste's *poulet basquaise*. Celeste explained that the recipe was a relic of an old plan to move to Paris, and the famous critic did not disapprove, either of the plan or of Celeste's failure to carry it out. She chuckled and lit a cigarillo off the candle flame. "Paris, Paris. It's not what it used to be. Do you know the poem by du Bellay? *Nouveau venu, qui cherches Rome en Rome, et rien de Rome en Rome n'aperçois* . . . Nowadays it's all Russians with too much money, Russians and Japanese. Do you know why the Japanese photograph everything? They're documenting, so that when they get home, they can reproduce it all in miniature." Another dark chuckle. "No, that's unkind. Celeste, my darling, do you know that I once had a penis?" I stifled laughter. "Yes, it's true, I wore a penis to a Surrealist dinner. A lovely pink plastic penis. In more or less the appropriate location. Were the Surrealists amused? My dear, they were not. There was quite a scandal. *Mon chéri*, said our hostess, the wife of some painter or other, *cette personne a oublié de fermer sa braguette!* She forgot to button her fly! Oh, oh, Paris, really, it hasn't been Paris since Gertrude Stein passed on to whatever was left for her to discover . . ." A long thin sigh of smoke. Another story. How she had hitchhiked all the way from Paris to Geneva with a fork in her purse, with which she planned to stab any man who dared to touch her. How she still had the fork. Though nowadays, she said, she preferred to be touched. "Which reminds me, my dear, what happened to your sister?"

"She fell in love," Celeste said.

"*Enfin!*" said the critic. "I was afraid it might never happen. And now, how magnificent, you're free."

"I suppose so."

"What are you going to do?"

"I don't know."

"May I give you a word of advice?" asked the critic. "Live. The road to art passes through extravagant life."

Celeste smiled. "That's easy to say."

"Everything is easy to say," said the critic. "Also, I would suggest you cut your hair short. As it is, you look like someone's grandmother." She shot up from her chair and kissed the top of my aunt's head. "I must go."

Celeste did not cut her hair, but she spent more hours working on her project. I missed Marie, but as the weeks passed the way I missed her changed. I didn't imagine her coming home to live with us; instead, I pictured myself going to visit Marie and Jean-Luc downtown, shaking hands with old J-L, walking with them along the South Ferry piers. The sunlight was clear and strong. I balanced on a bollard and spread my arms like wings. You've grown, said Marie. Have I? I asked, archly.

My understanding of how that scene would go was so complete that when Marie actually came home, and told me it had all been a terrible mistake but she was back now, she was back, and she would never leave again, I was confused. This was no longer the dream I wanted to come true. Surely there had been a mistake, a moment misfiled in the big cabinet of time. We didn't talk about what had happened downtown, and I never knew whether she was, as she said, overcome with remorse at how she'd left her sister and her son alone, or whether Jean-Luc got tired of her, as Celeste had predicted he would. My discretion was less perfect than Marie's, though. I mentioned that the art critic had come over to dinner, and we'd all had a good time. I asked Celeste if she might come again, and if she had any more stories about forks.

"Forks?" Marie said. "What about forks?" Her voice was bright, but it was clear to us that she was searching for an explanation.

Celeste only nodded and went on eating, and it fell to me to say, portentously, as my sole and ample revenge for what she had done, "There's a lot you don't know." That was what I thought of as I watched my mothers walk through the train, looking for two seats together; and it occurred to me that they had paid for the decisions they'd made thirty years ago. They had chosen each other. They were together still.

REGENZEIT

On the way home from Hudson, I stopped for lunch at a diner. I was still angry at my mothers, but as I replayed our conversations in my memory, and came up with even more devastating things that I might have said, I found myself thinking of the story Celeste had told me on Saturday, and its conclusion: *I became more cautious.* And soon I found myself thinking about Yesim. *We're all creatures of more or less the same species dancing around on this planet for only an eyeblink and then forever gone,* Richard Ente had written. What was the point of being cautious? I borrowed a phone book from the cashier and called Snowbird. The secretary said Yesim was out of the office for a few days, and I said, OK, I'll try her at home. The secretary must have recognized my voice, because she said, "Actually, she's gone away for a rest, but I'm not supposed to say that. Do you want to leave a message?"

"No message," I said. I guessed where Yesim was.

The Pines sat on a hill about fifteen minutes northwest of Albany, in a place where the suburbs began to give way to forest. A double row of pine trees stood alongside the driveway, as if to demonstrate that this at least was a place where words and things corresponded. I parked by what looked like the gatehouse, a pink cottage with lace curtains in the windows. It was unseasonably warm, and the last cicadas of the second millennium C.E. were clicking away in the tall grass. The feeling of the place was secluded but not confined: there was no fence, no gate, no signs warning unauthorized persons to keep out. In fact, I thought, the Pines didn't look all that different from Summerland. Put in a big swimming pool and an ornamental garden and the two places could have been siblings. I talked to an attendant in the pink cottage, who made a phone call and directed me onward to the main house. "Wait on the patio," he said, "she'll meet you there." I walked up a crunching gravel path and found myself facing a big gabled Victorian which could have belonged to an Albany industrialist a century ago. Some outbuildings stood farther away, former sheds and stables, probably. I sat at a white metal table strewn with pine needles and closed my eyes. The low sun sent light slantwise through the trees; a bird called out softly and got no answer. This was the kind of place you'd want to go after you died, I thought: not heaven with its harps and clouds and cherubic whatnot, but a quiet hill in the middle of nowhere, with some cabins, some grass, a fireplace to keep you warm in the winter. Then I opened my eyes; Yesim was coming out of the main house, dressed in a long gray sweater and jeans and a baseball cap. She looked gaunt and tired.

I remembered where I was, and what Yesim was doing here, and I opened my arms and mouth to express my dismay, but before I could speak there was a terrible howling overhead. A passenger jet was falling out of the sky; as I watched, it dropped rapidly toward us and disappeared behind the trees at the top of the hill. I must have looked terrified; Yesim laughed and, when the howl faded to a rumble, said, "The airport's just over there."

"This is a hell of a place for a sanatorium," I said.

"It takes getting used to," Yesim agreed, "but one of the things about being crazy is, you have to put up with a lot of interruption." She told me that the Pines once belonged to an Albany banker—so my guess was more or less right—but when the airport was built his grandchildren had donated the house and land to a hospital. The property had lost so much value, there was no point trying to sell it. "Anyway," she said, "it's not a very busy airport."

"How are you feeling?" I asked after a moment.

"I don't entirely know," Yesim said. "I've only been here a couple of days."

"Yesim," I began, but she interrupted: "If you've come to tell me that you're sorry about what happened, forget it. I should come with a warning label."

"You did come with a warning label," I said.

"But I didn't push you away, did I?"

"You didn't push me away."

"That's my problem," Yesim said.

She told me that after Summerland, it was as if she'd slipped backward in time, toward some earlier and more dangerous self. She'd tried to hold on to the Yesim who ran Snowbird and generally kept things going, but it was no use; that Yesim now seemed to her like a character in a play, a role she'd studied without ever really understanding its motivations. Why shouldn't she fuck whoever she liked? What was the use of restraint? She came up to Albany and slept with a friend of Mark's. "Then Mark left me and I realized I was in serious trouble again. So here I am," Yesim said, spreading her palms upward on the white table. "Did you just come to say hello, or is there something you want?"

That was when I realized something that has probably been obvious for a long time: the Yesim I'd wanted to fall in love with ever since I saw her at the Kountry Kitchen was the one who was ten years old and still playing at *Man and Woman*. But that Yesim was no longer anywhere to be found—if she had ever been anything other than a creation of my memory.

The Yesim who was waiting for me to speak was the only Yesim in existence, and, for the first time, I saw her. Before my eyes the duck changed back into a rabbit. It was a very strange moment.

"I don't know," I said.

Another airplane roared by, coming in for a landing.

"Forget it," Yesim said. "Do you want the tour?"

She led me across the lawn to the mansion, and into a marble-floored hall, where a stone cherub perched on the edge of a stone bowl, his mouth open, as though to vomit. "This is the dining hall," she said, opening a door and showing me in to a big room with a polished wooden floor, long tables, heavy-looking chairs. "The food is better than you'd think. The other night we had lobster rolls! Really, I don't know why anyone lives out there." Yesim gestured toward a mullioned window through which we could see only grass and trees. "Except, I guess, that no one can afford to stay here forever. Come on, I'll show you the library."

She showed it to me—it wasn't so much a library as a comfortable room in which to read, or sleep, or write letters, which, she told me, people here still did. The Pines was probably one of the last places in America to make use of the U.S. Mail for personal correspondence. "In twenty years the only people who write letters at all will probably be in mental institutions," she said. "Just imagine, the postal system will exist only to carry letters from one nuthouse to another." I asked where the other people were, and she said, "Mostly in their rooms. In the morning we all get up early for Group, and after that there are classes and individual therapy, so by lunch we're pretty worn out." Yesim led me out the back door and down a gentle grass slope to the vegetable garden, where some yellow-orange pumpkins were pushing their way out of a tangle of vines, like moons emerging from behind stringy clouds.

"There's a pond, do you want to see it?" Yesim asked.

"Is it OK if I pass?"

"It's better. Let's sit down and have a cigarette." I took one from her and we sat on a bench by the garden, our feet pushing against the plastic fence that kept the deer away. "How's the packing?" Yesim asked.

I told her what had happened with my mothers, and about Richard Ente's letter. "I guess he was crazy," I said, "but at the same time, I can't help wondering whether my mothers could have saved him. Even if Marie didn't run away to Denver she might have been able to do something."

"It sounds like a terrible situation for everyone," Yesim said. "Your mother was so young, and Richard was sort of taking advantage of her. And maybe your grandparents didn't know what was going on. Kids that age don't usually confide in their parents, at least not about sex. I certainly didn't."

"But they could have saved him! If Marie had just gone there, he might still be alive." But it occurred to me that Richard Ente had been the same age as my grandfather. Even if Marie had saved him, by now he would probably be dead. I began to cry. I was crying for Richard Ente, who died alone in Colorado, but also for Swan, wherever he was, if he was still alive at all; I was crying for my grandfather, who'd died alone in his cluttered study. I was crying for all the people it was too late to help, even if there had never been a way to help them, even if they had died before I was born. I was crying because there was nothing else I could do.

Yesim touched my arm. "One thing they tell us here is that the only person you can ever really save is yourself."

"Thanks."

"Although maybe you don't want to take advice from a person in a mental institution?"

"At this point," I said, "I'll take any advice I can get."

How many times did I visit Yesim? It can't have been more than four but it seems in retrospect like hundreds. Therapy must have put her in the habit of confessing; she told me about sexual fantasies she'd had as a girl, involving classmates, teachers, friends of her brother, *sex movies*, she called them, which she watched with closed eyes as she waited to fall asleep. "Just fantasies, but fantasy has a way of becoming reality," she said, "or rather, it has a way of making life just part of fantasy." But turning life into a *sex movie* in a town as small as Thebes was dangerous, to say the least. By the time she was fifteen, Yesim was struggling to keep her sexual escapades secret. She found herself lying so much and about so many things, it was like she was a fictional character, or really like several fictional characters, none of whom could know anything about the others. It was a miracle that her parents didn't find out what, *who*, she was doing; sometimes Yesim suspected they were doing their utmost not to know. The end of that period of her life came when she drove to her math teacher's house to have the next installment of what was already a fairly useless and unpleasant sexual relationship, and found his seventy-year-old father waiting for her in his wheelchair. He threatened to expose her, so she fucked him in the wheelchair, which creaked back and forth, straining against its brakes. At that point Yesim realized she had to get out of Thebes. Mercifully, she had worked almost as hard in school as she had at covering her tracks; before she turned seventeen she was off to college, where she met a wise poet, W, who taught her to love her desire and forgive her past. All might have been well if she hadn't moved to Cambridge and fallen in love with Professor X, who took cold, jealous possession of her body, leaving her choked—literally—and starved—literally! Yesim slept with so many people, trying to get over what Professor X had done to her, you would need a whole different kind of alphabet just to keep track of them. That was when she realized there could be no peace between her and unappeasable want, this thing of darkness she'd acknowledged hers, but which refused to be owned, this desire that sucked the world into the vortex of its tight, hopeless little dream. Mark was a truce that Yesim had allowed herself to mistake for an armistice. Now he was gone, Yesim realized that making peace wasn't enough: she needed to change her life. Here she was, thirty years old, and she hadn't *done* anything but fuck. She wanted to make something she could be proud of. "The social worker who runs Group says I have all the insights," she said. "It's just a matter of putting them together. As if my life were a jigsaw puzzle. Which," Yesim added after a moment, "is how I've been treating it. Trying to stick all those little knobs into those little sockets." She grimaced. "I guess I'm not cured yet."

Maybe she was right, but every time I came to visit there was a little more of her: her eyes brighter, her voice fuller, her hair thicker. She talked about what she'd do when she left the Pines. Maybe she'd apply to graduate school in poetry, or maybe she'd work for a foundation and put her managerial skills to good use. One thing was for sure: she was leaving Thebes. "Too much history here," she said. "And to tell you the truth, I don't give a shit about winter sports."

"Not one sheet?" I asked.

Yesim laughed. "I want to live someplace *warm*."

Airplanes passed over us, carrying people to Albany from distant cities, or carrying them away to places neither of us had ever been, places we were unlikely ever to go, airplanes shining in the sunlight and moving darkly through the cloud. We were going to be all right, I thought. We had made mistakes, but we could still get off the ground.

The warm weather ended. The next time I went to the Pines Yesim met me in the library, and we weren't alone: two residents shot pool on a magnificent, uneven table, and others sat by the fire, reading newspapers from days and weeks before. Yesim and I shared a pink sofa, tucked away in a corner, but we had trouble finding things to talk about. I thought we might be inhibited by the other people in the room, or maybe we were tired. I didn't mind the awkwardness. It was as if, after everything that had happened, we were finally having our first date.

"So," I said, "read any good books lately?"

Yesim bit her lip. "I'm pregnant." She'd missed her period; she'd peed on the little stick. She was sure. After a while she asked, "What are we going to do?"

"I'll do whatever you want," I said.

Yesim burst into tears. She had been up all night thinking about it, she said, and on the one hand a child was the last thing she wanted, when her life was so uncertain. She was a resident at a *residential treatment facility*; she had to worry about her own future and not that of a hypothetical other person, a helpless innocent who had done nothing to deserve a mother like Yesim. "But on the other hand," she said, "I wonder if this isn't the change I was looking for?" A child might be what she needed to come out of her erotic tailspin, a creature whose need to be loved was even greater than her own. "Is that very selfish of me?" she asked.

"People have had children for worse reasons," I said.

We sat there, not talking, while, with terrible symbolic aptness, billiard balls shot by lunatics rolled over the hills and humps of the pool table and found their way softly to the pockets. The possibility of having a child, which hadn't existed just a few moments ago, now floated in the air between us. It was something we could look at. And like other sudden revelations, like the sudden ones more than the gradual ones, probably, it had a kind of rightness. If we were floating, as Alice had put it, drifting through a weird time between childhood and adulthood, a child would anchor us. If we were wondering what would happen next, a child would answer that question. If we were frightened, a child would make us brave. Almost immediately, the possibility began to assume a kind of magnificence: a child, offspring of the Rowlands and the Regenzeits! A union of the feuding families, an end to the old fight, in Hegelian terms an *Aufhebung*. I'm sorry: I was trained as a historian and the words still rattle around in my head. A transformation that preserved us even as it carried us forward, into the future.

"I could do it," I said.

Yesim looked at me, or seemed to be looking at me, sizing me up. In fact I think she was looking at the possibility of the child too. "You're not the one who would have to give birth."

"That's true. And maybe you wouldn't want to have me around."

"If that was how I felt," Yesim said, "I wouldn't have told you."

Time passed. We were still on the sofa. The sky had gone dark. Yesim and I were talking about the future, our words shining in the dimness of the room. Yesim wouldn't leave Thebes right away: for the time being she would stay in her house, and I'd go on living in my grandparents' house, at least until it was sold. I'd find someone to sublet my apartment in San Francisco but I wouldn't give up the lease: we might move there one day. Yesim would finish her treatment program, which had only two weeks to run, then go back to work at Snowbird. Neither of us would say anything to Kerem yet. We wouldn't talk to our parents, either, until we had made our plans. We would make plans. We wouldn't commit to anything, but we were both excited about this idea, the idea of the child, and at some point we must both have realized that the possibility had become a decision. Then they called Yesim for dinner. I promised to come back the next day: we had so much to talk about. I drove home in the dark, humming along with the radio, and began, like a Millerite, to prepare for an impending change, the real nature of which I could barely imagine.

Imagine what it felt like to *be* a Millerite in the early fall of 1844: to go about your business with the certainty that the world was about to end. You'd have to live a kind of double life, supporting, with a minimum of effort, the outward person who still ate and bathed and wrote in the ledger, the one who admired the first tinge of red in the maples and thought, on the first frosty morning, how autumn paradoxically felt like the time when the world came to life, whereas in fact in three months it would be winter. You'd have to shine your shoes and you'd still be put out when the mail was late. But most of your attention would be on the inner self who in three months' time would be in Heaven. You'd touch the white ascension robe (if such things ever existed) that hung by the bed, and look forward to the day when you would wear it: the dress in which regardless of your sex you'd wait for the Bridegroom to show up. You'd spend as much time as you could with the other people who were Going Up, because they were the ones to whom you could speak as your inner self, and be understood. You'd read every word of the *Midnight Cry,* even the birth and death announcements, the silly songs, the stories for children rewritten with the moral *And that's the way the world ends*, not because you cared especially for the stories but because they belonged to the world in which your inner self lived. You'd send dollar after dollar to the newspaper society because without them your inner self would wither like an unwatered plant. And when the Millerites' tent came to town you'd sing and shout and dance all night, your outer person utterly forgotten, and it would be as if you had already Gone Up, as if you were in Heaven already, except with bodies and grass and fog lying low in the valley at dawn. You would love it all. But, loving it, would you wonder, as you walked home, whether Heaven could be this good? Would you wonder whether you *wanted* this world to end?

As it turned out, I didn't visit Yesim the next day. That morning a woman from Goodwill called and said she had received my message about a house of stuff to be donated. "Unfortunately," she said, "the regional center is full." Property prices were up, and people all over the Northeast were looking for ways to share their good fortune, only the people in need of good fortune were either ignorant of Goodwill or unwilling to visit. If I could wait until after Christmas, the woman suggested, they might be able to squeeze me in. Or if I could transport the goods to the national center, they would be happy to accept my donation.

"All right," I said. "Where's the national center?"

"St. Louis, Missouri," she said.

I told her I'd try the Salvation Army, and she warned me that they hadn't been accepting donations since August. Forgetting, in the face of this setback, that just the day before I'd decided to stay in my grandparents' house indefinitely, I called Charles and told him that we would have to take everything to St. Louis. He laughed at me. There was no way he was going to drive a truck to St. Louis and back, he said, even if he had a truck the right size, which he didn't. If I wanted to pay for a truck and drive it to Missouri myself he might be able to get a couple of his boys to help with the loading. For the unloading I would be on my own.

"Well then," I said, "what do you suggest?"

"We could just leave it where it is. Let whoever buys the house deal with it."

"Then what have I been doing, sorting the good stuff from the junk? Was I just wasting my time?"

"Calm down," my uncle said. "We'll figure it out." He said something about taking it to Canada and dumping it there, just taking it over the border and leaving it in a field; after all, Canada was a big country, probably no one would notice if we left a little pile of things in a field where no one went.

"Absolutely not. This is American junk, it's going to stay in America."

"Then we'll sell it."

"To who?"

"Whoever wants it," Charles said.

So for the second time in my life I found myself making signs and taping them to lampposts, tacking them to bulletin boards in the laundromat and the public library, setting them by the door to the Kountry Kitchen and the Kozy Korner and the organic grocery, to say that the Rowlands were having a garage sale. Hundreds of antiques priced to move. Everything must go. I took a photograph of the house and used it to illustrate the sign in the hope that the historic exterior of the Rowland home would create the illusion that the items for sale were equally impressive. Now and then someone who saw me putting up a sign would nod and say, "The Rowlands? That must be quite a sale," and they would laugh.

"Yes," I said, "it's going to be quite a sale."

Like a Millerite, I knew that I was carrying out two incompatible plans: on the one hand I was going to live in my grandparents' house, and on the other I was selling their stuff. I was preparing for both cessation and survival, but somehow the incompatibility didn't bother me. The house wasn't livable as it was, with everthing in piles; maybe Yesim would move in with stuff of her own. Maybe it was important to create an empty place for the child. Anyway, having sorted my grandparents' things, it would have been a step backward to unsort them, and if I did I would never have the energy to sort them again.

"You might as well go ahead with it," Yesim said when I mentioned the sale to her. "Who knows, you might even make some money." She lay back on the sofa and groaned. As if deciding to keep the child had hastened her pregnancy into a new phase, she'd been having morning sickness. The smell of coffee made her want to throw up, but everyone at the Pines drank coffee. Everyone smoked, too: it was a pregnant woman's nightmare. She had told her nurses she had the flu; she was afraid that if she told them she was pregnant, they wouldn't let her leave. Or that they'd advise her to have an abortion.

"Only two more weeks," I said.

"Twelve days," Yesim sighed.

I asked if I could bring her anything: flowers? Something to read, to take her mind off of the Pines? I still had that copy of *Norwegian Wood*.

"I don't think I could read." Yesim made a face. "Am I going to have baby brain? What will I do about my work?"

"You'll manage. I'll help you."

"Be careful what you offer."

I squeezed her hand. Yesim squeezed back. "It's funny," she said. "My body feels more like it's mine now that something else is growing in it."

"It's paradoxical," I agreed.

"I'm not going to think about it now," Yesim said, and closed her eyes.

"Anyway," I said, "I'm not going to sell anything we might be able to use when our child comes." That was the first time I'd said *our child*. Yesim smiled, but didn't open her eyes.

We had the sale a couple of days later. With the help of an off-duty driver from Rowland Towing and Salvage, Charles and I carried everything out of the garage and set it on the lawn. My grandparents' things looked even less appealing by daylight than they had in the house; like an accusing finger the sun found the scratches, the stains, the chinks in the enamel, the hidden spots of rust. Charles asked if we should put prices on things, but I said no, it would take too long, we'd just let people pay what they wanted. For what we hoped would be the last time we arranged the shadeless lamps, the plastic ladle with the half-melted handle, the trunk missing a hinge, the fire tongs, the skis, the ancient after-dinner drinks, the calcified colander, the immersion coil, the trunk of curtains, the mound of towels, the gardening tools, the gardening gloves, the straw hat, the box of matchbooks, the boat-shaped ashtray, the pot holders, the wicker wastebasket, the vases, the planters, the paperbacks, the paperweights, the party napkins, the coatrack, the boot scraper, the sweaters, all five letter openers, the humidifier, the dehumidifier, the fans, the dolls, the plastic boxes that covered kleenex boxes, allowing my grandfather to buy cheap generic tissues, the bird books, the china shepherd and milkmaid, the playing cards, the road maps, the old magazines, the beer stein, the coasters, the cookbooks, the kitty-kat clock, the box springs, the napkin rings, all the lost things.

Soon the first people from Thebes arrived to see what we were selling. "Wow, look at all this stuff," said the owner of the Kountry Kitchen. I said she might be able to find some things to round out her collection.

"My collection!" She laughed, but when I came back a few minutes later she was kneeling by the mixing bowls. "How much do you want for these?"

"How much do you want to pay?"

"I'll give you five dollars for the set."

"Hey," said her husband, holding up my grandfather's binoculars, "are you letting these go?"

Already another car had pulled up to the curb. The driver introduced himself as Cal, the owner of Stuff n' Things Antiques in Saugerties, and he paced through the collection, touching one or another piece of furniture, saying to himself, "I remember this, I remember this." The neighbors who lived on the other side of my grandparents' house, the non-Regenzeit side, Dr. and Mrs. Karman, bought a drawer's worth of forks and spoons, which were almost the same design as their own depleted set, for three dollars. "Look around," Charles told a stranger. "You might find something to round out your collection."

All day, people came from Thebes, Maplecrest, Hunter, Catskill, Hudson and beyond. They took things, they gave me money, they left, and slowly, as the day passed, the driveway and the lawn uncluttered themselves. Just before dark, I saw Carrie with an older woman, looking through my grandfather's records.

"Oh, hi!" She beamed at me. "I want you to meet my mom."

"I know you," her mother said. It was Shelley, Kerem's old girlfriend. Her blond hair had streaks of gray at the roots and she'd put on weight, but even so she didn't look very different from when I'd last seen her, twenty years ago. "You're Kerem's friend."

"Oh, my god, Mom, you know him?"

"What are you doing back in Thebes?" Shelley asked.

I told her about my grandfather. "Well, that's too bad," she said. "And how do you know my daughter?"

"Mom," Carrie said, exasperated, "he's the one who comes into the *grocery*."

"Oh?" Shelley raised a pale eyebrow. "I thought you were talking about someone younger. Not someone who's basically my age."

"*Mom*," Carrie said.

"So, tell me," said Shelley, "what have you been up to?"

I gave her the shortest possible version of my life story while Carrie stood by sullenly, looking at me as though I had betrayed her. "How exciting," Shelley said. "You've really moved around." She told me that Mike, her brother, owned the grocery, and she had a farm in the mountains, which she was turning into a kind of artists' retreat.

"For all the truly great people," I said.

Shelley laughed. "That's right."

"You told me about it twenty years ago. It was your dream, you said."

"Did I? How long are you in town?"

"I don't know."

"Do you want to come up next weekend?"

"Dad has the farmhouse next weekend," Carrie said.

"Right," said Shelley. "Well, you could come up during the week, if you don't mind a simple dinner."

"Don't invite him for dinner," Carrie said.

"Shh, sweetie. Have you seen Kerem?" Shelley asked me.

"A couple of times."

"I think it's sad, what happened to him. All he does is drink and worry about his crazy sister."

"Yesim isn't crazy."

Shelley laughed. "You don't know her. Did you know she tried to set fire to the ski lodge? It's true, it happened last summer. The police caught her pouring gasoline all over a wall. They should have arrested her, but since it was her place, and her dad was already gone . . ."

"How do you know that?" I asked.

"Everyone knows. Ask Kerem if you don't believe me."

Whether it was true or not, this story left me with not much interest in talking to Shelley. I asked her some inane question about the farm, and she gave me an equally inane answer, and repeated her invitation to dinner.

"Mom, I'm freezing," Carrie said.

It had in fact become much colder, as if Thebes had gone from fall to winter in the course of the afternoon. Shelley gave me her number and Carrie hurried her back to their mini-van. I watched the two of them go, two backs, two heads of dirty-blond hair framed in the minivan's open door, then the door closed, they were gone. Everyone else had already left, and I helped Charles carry the things we hadn't sold back into the house. We'd done better than we expected: more than half of my grandparents' possessions were gone, off to begin new lives in the houses of people we didn't know. I thought about what Shelley had told me about Yesim. What was I getting myself into? Thebes was microscopic, a cuckoo clock where the same people came around and around again, none of them really changing, only getting older, and having children who you also ran into, over and over. How long would it be before we ran into the math teacher and his wheelchair-bound father? If there was this one story about Yesim setting fire to Snowbird, how many other stories were there that I didn't know yet? That was when I realized that, in my heart, cessation had won.

As soon as my uncle was gone, I went upstairs and packed my clothes. I carried my bag out to Norman Mailer's car, then went back into the house and took *Progress in Flying Machines*. I got into the car, then I realized that I'd forgotten the charger for my cell phone, and when I came out with it in my hand Kerem was standing on the porch.

"Are you going somewhere?" he asked.

"Just over to Maplecrest," I said. "I'm taking some stuff to my uncle."

"You going to be gone long?"

"Maybe half an hour."

"When you get back, will you come over to my place? I need you to sign some insurance forms."

"Sure," I said.

"I can't believe winter is here already," Kerem said.

"It's good for business, right?"

"So long as it snows, it's good for business."

I drove away. I was glad Charles wasn't there: I didn't need him to tell me that, thirty years ago, Richard Ente had done what I was now doing, running away from the mother of my unborn child. I drove slowly down the hill, then picked up speed as I got out of town. By the time I got to the place where Route 56 joins Route 23, hard little snowflakes were falling, and even as part of me wondered whether I was making a terrible mistake, another part decided that I was leaving just in time.

FOUR

THE RETURN OF RIP VAN WINKLE

I stayed that night in a Kingston motel, where I lay awake listening to the trucks pass on the Thruway, and the next morning I drove to New York City. I stayed with a friend named David Rice who I knew from college. He worked for a company that invented financial instruments of increasing complexity, not options, not derivatives, but derivatives of derivatives, products so complex that he and his colleagues referred to them simply as colors: Rose, or Lime, or Buff. David had done well with Peach, which went to telecommunications companies in the Southwest; now he owned a brownstone in Brooklyn, which had belonged a century before to one Elijah Scruggs, the captain of a whaling ship. Although neither David nor anyone else knew anything more about Elijah Scruggs, since he moved in David had created a kind of myth of Scruggs, and decorated the house with knickknacks from the sailor's supposed travels: coconut-husk masks from the South Pacific, whalebone toys, the shell of a Galápagos tortoise, and, above the fireplace, an oil portrait of a white-bearded man who David swore was Scruggs himself. Apart from the ghost of Scruggs, David lived alone; there was a guest room on the second floor that overlooked a weedy garden and the neighbors' better-kept yards. David was working late, so I ate leftover samosas from the fridge, showered and fell asleep at nine o'clock.

I slept until the middle of the next afternoon, an incredible sleep, which made me feel as if the last ten years had been a dream and I was twenty again, ready to begin my life. A voicemail from David told me to meet him in an East Village bar. It was only when I came out of the subway in Manhattan and saw people on the street with little I VOTED stickers on their lapels that I realized it was Election Day. I hadn't followed the campaign; no one in Thebes had talked about it. I had no idea whether Bush or Gore was favored to win. I was like Rip Van Winkle, coming down from the mountains after a long sleep to find his country changed; all I lacked was the long white beard.

"Are you shitting me?" David said when I told him about this. "What were you doing up there?"

"I told you, I was cleaning out my grandparents' house."

"Don't they have a TV?"

"They did, but . . ."

"Get this man a fucking drink," David said to the bartender. We watched the returns come in, the states turning red and blue. Each was a shock to me: an entire state full of people who had remembered to vote! It was the most ordinary thing, but it seemed incredible that all over the country people had gone to their polling places and voted for the candidate of their choice, who would in a few months' time be president. We had a president! We were a nation! The size of it, after the smallness of Thebes, was thrilling. All those blank states waiting to be filled in! Then it became clear that this was not an ordinary election. "What the fuck?" David howled as the newscasters called it for Gore, then for Bush, then for nobody. His thumbs composed urgent messages to politically connected friends, begging them to explain. We forgot to eat dinner and by the time the bar closed we were very drunk.

The East Village was full of people like us, drunk people staggering to the subway, asking each other silently, what was going on?

David took the next day off from work and we sat on his sofa, drinking coffee and shouting at his plasma-screen television. David's appreciation of the sporting-event side of American politics was contagious, and besides, I had to affirm my citizenship, to compensate with insults and groans and hurled popcorn for my weird absence from the world. We watched television until midnight, then David went to bed and I kept watching. I watched for days, following in numbing detail the recount of the Florida ballots. I meant to call Yesim. I knew she would be wondering where I was, but it had only been a couple of days, and she had her program at the Pines to get through. Maybe it was better that I didn't call. Anyway, I needed to think things over. Hadn't Yesim herself told me at one point that she couldn't see me because she needed time to think? I felt like I had the right to do the same thing, even if it wasn't exactly the same thing. So I waited, tortured by an inarticulate feeling that I was on the wrong track. Like the rest of America, I was in the middle of making a costly mistake that I could not stop myself from making. It was as if I were watching my own life on David's TV set: the person who shouted *No!* at the screen was hundreds of miles from the person doing the bad action, and although I could see that person, we were separated by a distance that my *No!* was powerless to cross.

Finally, I did call Yesim. Six days had passed since I came to New York, and the terror that had driven me out of Thebes, the need to disappear from my own life, was beginning to fade. I told myself that Yesim was a fallible, changeable person too, so there was reason to hope that she would forgive my error. Eventually we'd laugh about it: Remember that time you ran away? —Sure! I was scared shitless! But the duty nurse told me that Yesim was no longer at the Pines. She'd checked out early, was all she could, or would, say. I called the Regenzeits' house, and Kerem answered.

"Where are you?" he asked.

"New York."

"Have you been there all this time?" He sounded less angry than puzzled.

"Yes. Listen, is Yesim there?"

"My sister is in Turkey, with our parents."

"Oh?" I remember thinking, that was fast. "I thought she didn't want to go."

"What are you doing in New York?"

"I had some things to take care of."

Kerem was offended by the blandness of my lie. "Things?"

"Can you give me Yesim's number? I really want to talk to her."

"She doesn't want to talk to you," Kerem said. "I don't want her to talk to you. *I* don't want to talk to you. What the fuck is your problem, anyway?"

If I could have answered his question, maybe he would have helped me, and this story would have a different ending; but I couldn't answer him. My problem was Richard Ente; my problem was myself. "I'm trying to figure some things out," I said. There it was again, that terrible word *things*, which soared like an airplane over life's specificity, lumping together fields and trees, cities, lakes, rivers, mountains, places where people lived and places where they didn't. *Things* was what the world became when you didn't love it enough to pay attention. "Please," I said, "just tell me how to reach Yesim."

"Why should I?"

"Because we're going to have a child."

Kerem laughed unhappily. "If it were my decision, there wouldn't *be* a child. As it is, if I ever run into you again, you'd better fucking watch out." I could hear the bravado in his voice, the fifteen-year-old punk making a threat. It was almost as if he were giving me, as a parting gift, a memory of the friendship we'd once had.

Gore conceded to Bush, and I felt only the mildest indignation. Really, I was beyond caring. I spent most of my time playing Final Fantasy IX on David's PlayStation and accumulating empty beer bottles which I arranged in vaguely nautical clusters on his kitchen counters. Finally, at the end of December, David asked me to move out. He was worried about me, he said, but he couldn't have me around anymore. I was becoming a fucking downer. I understood. With the money I'd saved working at Cetacean, I rented a room on West Fifty-fourth Street, in the apartment of a Broadway costumer named Elena. The second millennium of the Common Era came to an anticlimactic end, and in January I looked fitfully for work as a content manager, but the slowdown that was now making my friends' lives difficult in San Francisco had flattened the new economy in New York, and no one was hiring. I remembered my old plan to move to Europe, or to Canada, maybe I could still go, maybe if I left America things would be different; but the idea of leaving was utterly abstract. More and more, my own mistakes were the only things that seemed real. It wasn't fair that Yesim had left so fast, one part of me raged, but another part, the part I was, increasingly, coming to hate, even as its voice grew louder in me, asserted that what had happened was merely just. As it had been with Richard Ente, so it was with me, and so it would be, unto the end.

After a few weeks I stopped going to the library. I spent a lot of time sleeping and playing with Elena's cat. I was allergic to the cat, but it didn't matter; my watering eyes were a small price to pay for the pleasure of being near a living creature and having it not recoil in horror. I went to bed every night with the idea that tomorrow I would get my life back on track, but I must have known the truth, that my life was *on* its track, which had been laid down for it thirty years earlier.

LOW-FLYING STARS

At some point during this period I got a letter from Marie, and cut it up.

THE RICHARD ENTE PERIOD

One morning in February I got up early and walked along the Hudson, past the great gray bulk of the *Intrepid* bristling with defunct warplanes, past weedy lots of suspicious parked trucks. The river was deep blue and calm, still benighted at six-thirty a.m. I picked up the path that rounds the tip of the island, past the World Trade Center and the Battery, park, cannons, plaques commemorating the days when lower Manhattan was the frontier between one world and another: the British and the rebels, the Indians and the Dutch. The sun rose and the Staten Island Ferry pulled into its terminal, huge and orange, honking. Soon people were coming out of the terminal, their faces sad, as if something terrible awaited them, and perhaps it did, perhaps it did, there in the Financial District, what did I know about the days that were waiting for all those people? They walked north, their heads tucked down against the cold wind. I slipped through them, blown along by my personal weather. Past South Street Seaport with its lovely reproductions of human transport from a century and a half ago. The wind slacked off. A few tourists in brightly colored anoraks gathered on the wooden planking of the pier, as though they were about to leave for an expedition to the North Pole. When I was in high school I used to cadge drinks from a Mexican restaurant in the seaport mall: I had no taste. And look what I became, a content manager, a pioneer of the new commerce, brighter and cleaner even than the mall. I walked north, past Fulton Fish Market, already closed for the day.

I'd never seen it open. Everything is like that, I thought, everything keeps its own hours. The only traces of the fish trade were some puddles of slick fishy water, three pallets stacked by the shuttered front of a market stall. A coil of green hose. What does a world leave behind when it goes? A question for archaeologists, historians. Of the three of us, Victor and Alex and me, it was Victor who believed most in the evidence of the past. Then he gave history up and founded MySky: maybe the evidence of the past wasn't so appealing. Maybe it was better to leave nothing behind, or as little as possible. I kept to what became a path beside parks. A track, a ball field. The middle-aged businessman's basketball league at morning practice, brokers in sweatsuits and headbands trying to grab hold of the sky's rim. A parka'd kid riding in circles on a trick bicycle. Nothing to stare at. What would any of us leave behind? E-mails, files on our laptops. As long as we didn't print out we'd disappear, or maybe even if we printed. A professor at Stanford once told me that toner isn't archival; the day will come when the letters literally fall from the pages and turn into a layer of black dust at the bottom of countless filing cabinets. Our legacy, our gift to the next civilization, will be blank pages and black dust. Scuff marks from our exercise shoes. Fouled weather. The Brooklyn Bridge soared over the waterside path; I turned inland. The old heart of the city in systole, workers gathered into the buildings, the streets nearly empty. Breakfast carts packing up, lunch trucks not yet arrived. I found the path onto the bridge, joined the crossers. There's an old joke: a man walks up to a bridge, gives the toll collector fifty cents. The toll collector says, hey, buddy, toll on this bridge is a dollar. That's OK, the man says, I'm only going halfway across. I went halfway across and stood at the bridge's highest point, looking out at the water. A friend of mine in high school knew someone who jumped from the Brooklyn Bridge and lived. A classmate's father: apparently he swam to Chinatown and got lunch there. Ginsberg wrote about him in *Howl*. How he jumped is a mystery to me; you'd have to climb over the traffic lanes; more likely you'd fall and get run over. But how had I, who grew up in New York, not known the layout of the Brooklyn Bridge? Embarrassed, I turned back, and walked up Centre Street to Canal, the Manhattan Bridge. The pedestrian walkway was closed for construction but it looked solid enough. I was just swinging my leg over the CLOSED sign when a red-cheeked Chinese woman looked at me, alarmed. I nodded to her. Yes, I'm going. Everyone makes their own accommodations to the city, the crowding, the noise. She passed me and didn't look back. I climbed over the sign and walked halfway across the bridge. I put my hands on the railing and looked south at the Brooklyn Bridge, and, past it, the widening of the river. Governors Island. The invisible place where the ocean begins. It wouldn't take much: one foot on the low bar, other leg over the fence. Leap or just let go. Then do what I'd always wanted to do: disappear. I thought about the so-called pioneers of flight. How many of them wanted to fly, really? And how many knew what they were doing. All those hours in the workshop, building their complicated machines, trying out steam engines, pulleys, gearing schemes, nights and weekends, while their wives complained, all that time they knew what the end would be. Not up, down. The guy who invented the ornithopter was surely a suicide at heart. A water taxi crossed from Manhattan to Queens, and I thought of my old neighbor Robert, waiting in an apartment in San Francisco. Waiting for what? The inspiration that would allow him to fix his life, to fix the world? Let someone else get it right, I thought. Someone always does. Someone will get it right and we'll go on. I put my foot on the rail. There wasn't anything more to think about. I grabbed the top of the fence and pulled myself up, a monkey hanging now from the monkey bars. Curious George. The shirt Yesim had liked so much. The air smelled of ice and ocean. *Even the ones who fail get us somewhere*, my grandfather had said. Maybe some future person would learn from my mistakes, invent a better version of me, a non-fucking-up human being, but I didn't want to know about it. The failures were the ones I had always loved. Let the explorers find their new world, let the believers go to Heaven, let the entrepreneurs get rich and take to the air in their private jets. I wanted to remain here, on the ground. Huh, I thought, then I let go of the fence. And landed on my feet, I mean, on the walkway. How would I be writing this, otherwise? A miraculous survival? Flight unassisted by any sort of machine? No. All I did was get down and walk away, back toward the Manhattan side of the bridge. I wasn't ready to die, and I had nothing to do in Brooklyn.

I walked into Chinatown and ate lunch, such an enormous lunch as I've never eaten before, dim sum from every cart. Beef noodles, taro cakes, spare ribs. As I ate, I felt a strange thing happening: Richard Ente was relaxing his grip on me, and almost physically leaving my body, as if he had been the ghost all along, not me. Not me. I ate until my stomach hurt and I kept eating, filling the void that Richard Ente had been. Shrimp in translucent shells, pork buns, rice in lotus leaves. Phoenix feet. After a while, even the cart ladies looked at me with wonder. What would happen? Would I burst? How much longer could I go on? Then I was full. I paid the check and headed north, back to Elena's apartment.

THE GREAT DISAPPOINTMENT

I think I understand now why some Millerites preferred to believe that the world did indeed end on October 22, 1844. There's something terrible about the fact that things go on. It's not just the embarrassment of having been wrong, of having not Gone Up in your ascension robe, like a little luminous airplane; it's the sheer overwhelmingness of the world, where the wind keeps blowing and the sky darkens with rain, where people sell bread and sharpen scissors and pack up their wagons, their cars, and go on trips and fall in love and none of it seems likely ever to stop. Here it all is and no one will tell you what to do about it, where to go, how even to begin to understand all the things that are taking place. Compared with the world's bigness, the apocalypse would be a relief.

After I decided not to leave the world, the world grew around me, grew immeasurably, and I blew through it like a leaf. Everywhere I looked people were doing things: ripping up the streets and paving them, waiting purposefully for subways, hailing cabs, striding in and out of buildings, their eyes turned a little upward, not to the sky, which they didn't care about, but to the invisible goals which floated above everybody else's heads. For lack of anything better to do, I returned to the public library on Forty-second Street, the same one I'd visited as a child, trying to prove that America was discovered by the Chinese, but even the people in the Reading Room, tourists and semi-homeless seekers of respite from the unwelcoming street, knew what they were doing more than I did. Like Mr. Casaubon in *Middlemarch*, they were looking for the key to all mythologies, or the lost continent of Atlantis, or, more mundanely, for a job, a lover, a place to spend the night. Whereas I had no goal; when I looked up, all I saw was the blank air. I envied the disappointed Millerites: at least they had one another. They could (and did!) hole up in abandoned houses, singing and praying and promiscuously washing one another's feet. I would have welcomed the chance to wash someone's feet, to wedge my soapy fingers between a set of warm human toes, never mind how gross, but by the winter's end I had no friends in the city.

The person who returned me to the world of time and purpose was, unexpectedly, my aunt Celeste. She came to see me on Fifty-fourth Street one day in March—there was some question of what to do about the things I'd left in Thebes, which had been annoying Charles for months, and which had finally reached a crisis because my grandparents' house was going to be sold. A lawyer named Rich was buying it, a coincidence of name and occupation that we all preferred not to think about. My left-behind things made their way into the mail; for weeks they remained in the hall of my mothers' apartment, and finally Celeste showed up in a taxi and told me to come downstairs and get my stuff already. She came upstairs with me, and when she saw the purple book on my nightstand, she flinched.

"God," she said, "you took *that*?"

Celeste told me that my grandfather had read *Progress in Flying Machines* to her and Marie as children, too. "You can imagine how interested I was," she said, "in the carrying loads of pigeons." Then to my surprise she imitated my grandfather's baritone: "But, Celeste, you must understand that these were *important experiments.*" We both laughed. "Come on," she said, "let's have lunch."

We went to a French restaurant on Ninth Avenue, one of the heralds of a new neighborhood which had not yet entirely realized itself. I asked Celeste about her work and she told me she was making stop-motion animations. "Of all the stupid things I could have done." She looked well, though: her hair had grown long and gray, distinguished. Her face was pink. I suspected that another reversal had taken place between my mothers, and Celeste was once again ascendant. "And you?" she asked. "You know, we've been a little worried. Do you have a job yet?"

"Not yet."

"You should think about teaching. Couldn't you teach computers?"

I said I'd think about it. I still had some money from Cetacean, so it wasn't urgent.

"But it's your life," Celeste said. "Isn't there something you want to do?"

"I don't know," I said. "How's Marie?"

"Fine," Celeste said, and she went back to talking about her animations. I wondered if she was avoiding the subject of Marie, whose letter I still hadn't answered. I wondered what part tact played in Celeste's life: for someone who was, often, unusually blunt in her speech, she seemed also to have a strange ability to know when *not* to speak, so that I couldn't tell, in the end, if her bluntness was really thoughtlessness or if it was the product of an incredibly delicate calculation, the navigation of an inner landscape mined with subjects which might cause her or her listener pain. What made Celeste Celeste? What made anyone anyone? My thoughts drifted into generality. In half an hour we'd finished lunch and headed in our separate directions, Celeste downtown and me up, well-meaning but still mysterious to each other.

The box Charles had sent from Thebes contained a coat I'd left in the downstairs closet, my copy of *Norwegian Wood*, and, wrapped in a towel, two of my grandmother's water-colors. One showed the woods and mountains that rolled westward from the peak of Mount Espy, and the other, snow falling in the Kaaterskill Clove. So this was what I was left with, I thought, barely enough stuff to fill a medium-sized box. After all the work I did! Suddenly I found myself laughing: at the box, the monstrous disproportion of effort to result, above all else at myself. I imagine that some of the Millerites must have felt the same way when they returned, finally, to their shuttered shops, and surveyed the bare shelves, from which they'd given everything away in anticipation of the end. What had they been thinking? What had *I* been thinking? The next morning I went back to the library and began to write about what had happened in Thebes.

This account has gone faster than *The Great Disappointment* ever did. In three months I wrote almost two hundred pages, rarely stopping to think, carried along by the momentum of the story I was telling. As spring gave way to summer, though, I found myself thinking more and more about Yesim. I tried to imagine what her life has become: Yesim in a room with white walls and an ocher tile floor, watching television while Mrs. Regenzeit cooked her something bland. Yesim dozing in a beach chair in a courtyard among fluttering lines of laundry. Yesim swimming in a lake—apparently Anatolia is full of saline lakes, it's one of the things I've learned from the *Britannica* in the reading room—her pregnant belly poking out of the water like the Loch Ness monster's head. Yesim rising out of the water, shaking out her hair, arguing with her father. Yesim about to call me, then deciding not to call. I began a letter to her, asking if she could forgive me, but stopped when I realized that I didn't know where to send it. I had no way of reaching Yesim: no phone number, no address, no e-mail, if they even had e-mail in Akbez. Kerem didn't return my calls. The only other person who might have known how to find Yesim was her ex-boyfriend, Mark, and I didn't know his last name. Not that he would have talked to me anyway.

There was nothing I could do but work, so I kept working, but by the hot gray middle of July my hope had given way to frustration and disgust. Was I accomplishing anything by revisiting the past? Wasn't my problem that I lived too much in the past already? As I got closer to the end of my story, my anxiety increased. What would I do when it was over? Was I ready to go back to San Francisco and pick up where I'd left off? I was thinking uneasily about this prospect in the first days of September, when someone whispered my name. An unfamiliar man in glasses, a V-neck sweater, a rumpled dress shirt, he could have been my double if he'd been thirty pounds lighter. "Matt Bark." He looked at me eagerly, as though he'd presented a winning lottery ticket for payment.

"From Nederland?"

"That's right. Man, it's been a while."

"Years," I said.

We sat on a stone bench in the rotunda of the library, and Matt told me in brief the story of the last seventeen years of his life, how he'd gone to Princeton, married a woman named Dana, gone back to school after a disillusioning year at Merrill Lynch, received a Ph.D. in history from Columbia, and how he was teaching at William and Mary and had two lovely, lovely children. "What about you?"

"I was in American history at Stanford."

"You, too? That's great! You teach?"

"I dropped out. Now I'm a content-management special-ist." Matt looked at me blankly. "A kind of programmer."

"Interesting. No question, academia's a tough proposition with the job market like this." He brightened as he told me about his dissertation, a history of corporations in early New England, which was going to come out as a book next year. Harvard was doing it, Harvard University Press. "It's a new field. There aren't a lot of us in corporate history. But I'll tell you, it's the next big thing." He was planning a book on Silicon Valley. "The first start-ups, you know?"

"I know. I lived in San Francisco for most of the nineties."

"Oh, hey, that's amazing. You were in the middle of his-tory being made, right there." Matt bobbed his head. "What are you doing on Friday? I'm having a beer with Andy Ames. We reconnected at the reunion, I guess it was a few years ago, wow. You should come out with us."

"I'll try to," I lied.

"You have to, dude," Matt Bark said. He was about to go, but turned back. "You were in Mr. Savage's class, right?"

"That's right."

"It figures you're in history, then. Or that you *were* in history, sorry. It's too bad, what happened to him, don't you think?"

"What happened?"

"You don't remember?"

"I don't know. I left Nederland in the middle of the year."

"Right, that's right. Savage was fired. He got into an argument with David Metzger's dad. Poor guy. He knew about history, but he didn't understand the first thing about money."

"That's too bad."

"Dude, that's an understatement!"

Matt left, and I went back to my seat in the reading room. Across the table from me, a man with a thick, undivided eyebrow was reading a book called *What Remains to Be Discovered?* I tried to turn my mind back to the question of what I was going to do, but Matt Bark had stirred something else up, not plans but memories. There was David Metzger, and there was Mr. Savage, and Ronald Kaplan and Gideon Peel shouting Flip him! Flip him! And there, slipping in among the people I'd already written about, was my friend Luis, moon-faced, smiling metallically: Luis who had taught me the little programming I learned at Nederland. How had I left him out of my story? But here he was, and he wasn't the only one, I had left out all sorts of people, Momus, for example, my friend at Bleak College who came very close to killing me because of something I told his girlfriend; and Deirdre, my girlfriend at Saint Hubert's Prep, sorry, Dee! I haven't said a word about you or the night we set the Dumpster on fire. And they were only two of the people who had mattered to me, and to whom I'd mattered, the lovers and not-quite lovers, the enemies and friends, the people I'd worked alongside, taken classes with, argued with about historiography and the precedence of object classes, the many people who'd been kind to me and asked for nothing in return and the few who'd been mean or mad, all of them were waiting for me in my memory, as though they had gathered to give me a surprise party, as though they had been waiting in a dark living room for years, and now I had finally opened the door they were all able at last to shout, Surprise! I closed my eyes and let them come. My god, I thought, I could be writing about these people for the rest of my life. In a strange way the thought was comforting.

I opened a blank document on my computer and began to type notes for what I was already beginning to think of as *the second part of my project*, but then, with the total inconsistency of which I have always been capable, the flight from one thing to another which has often been my downfall, but which was, in this case, my salvation, I got on the Web and, with the last of my Cetacean money, I bought a plane ticket to Ankara, which is the city closest to Akbez. As soon as I had paid for the ticket it was clear that this was the solution I had been looking for all along. This story is done. It may not be done well but it is done *enough*, which is the point of writing history: not to exhaust the past, but to know it well enough that you can move on. Don't tell anyone at Stanford I said so! Now I am leaving. I don't know if Yesim will see me; maybe her parents will chase me off. But as long as I am alive I want at least to try to meet my child.

CONTACT WITH OTHER WORLDS

Nothing is simple, though. If you learn only one thing from history, learn that nothing is simple. On Monday I worked in the library, writing about Matt Bark. I finished my story just as the library was closing, and went down to Bryant Park. The summer heat had finally broken; there was a marine smell in the air, like a new season coming on. The leaves of some oak trees were already trimmed with rust. Everything goes on, I thought, it goes on and on . . . Overwhelmed by the thought of seasons succeeding one another endlessly, summer then fall, winter then spring, again and again, without ever improving on the seasons that had come before, I sat on a bench. Pigeons gathered at my feet, but I had nothing to feed them. They pecked at white pebbles on the path, as if to save me from embarrassment. A lot of people were lingering in the park, released from work but not ready to go home. They sat at the metal tables and talked on their phones, or stood on the lawn in little groups, like guests at a party. They shifted their leather bags peacefully from shoulder to shoulder. The light was beautiful; even the shadows were good. Before long the people on the lawn would disperse: some would go home to their families and others would go home alone; some would take taxis and others would decide it was a fine evening for a walk. In an hour or two they would be working out, walking their dogs, cooking dinner, listening to music, shifting their bodies tactically on the banquette of a bar and wondering how to keep talking so the person sitting opposite would go on listening, and not just listening, but listening with precisely the look they had now, as if the past existed only in words and the future would never come. For the first time in a long time, I felt like one of them. I was no longer a ghost; I was just an ordinary person who was going somewhere. It was an extraordinary accomplishment, much harder than discovering a new continent or flying off into the sky. I'd found the place where people live.

The next morning I switched on the television and saw that planes had flown into the twin towers of the World Trade Center. This isn't happening, I thought. Then I thought, this is the end of the world. Ironically, the one thing I didn't think about was the Millerites: their apocalypse clearly had nothing to do with the pillar of black smoke I could see from my living-room window. But later that day, when I'd stopped weeping, it occurred to me, as it must have to many other people, that the planes hadn't come out of the blue, empty sky. All the time I had been working in the library, all the time I'd been in Thebes, and probably long before that, something had been going on. People had been preparing this event, and they had themselves been prepared by other events that I didn't know anything about. I realized then that my ignorance was vastly greater than I had supposed. Even if I had somehow managed to tell the story of every person I'd ever known, what I would have written would be, like Thebes, only a little world, which seemed complete while you were in it, but in fact was not complete. There was always another world waiting to make contact. There was always a wave waiting to break. Now it had broken. And I sat there, staring at the screen, trying to figure out what was going on.

POSTSCRIPT

TEN YEARS LATER

Entrance to Cave
You are standing outside a dark and gloomy cave:
www.luminousairplanes.com

>

ACKNOWLEDGMENTS

Thanks to Emily Barton, Amy Benfer, Wayne Chambliss, Rebecca Godfrey, Maureen Howard, Noah Millman, Ethan Nosowsky, Herb Wilson, and Jeff Zacks for reading some of the many non-flying versions of this book.

Thanks to the John Simon Guggenheim Memorial Foundation, Bard College, the New York Foundation for the Arts, the MacDowell Colony, the Corporation of Yaddo, the Rockefeller Foundation, Ledig House/Art Omi, and the Château de Lavigny for supporting my experiments.

Thanks to the incomparable Gloria Loomis and Julia Masnik at Watkins/Loomis, and to Jesse Coleman at Farrar, Straus and Giroux for getting the book off the ground.

Finally, thanks—more than thanks—to Sarah Stern, who never stopped believing that *Luminous Airplanes* could fly.